The Torment of Jamie Dower

A novel

by

M D Cartwright

The Torment of Jamie Dower

Michael Cartwright

Copyright © Michael Cartwright

All rights reserved. No part of this publication may be reproduced, stored in a retrieval system or transmitted in any form or by any means electronic, mechanical, audio, visual or otherwise, without prior permission of the copyright owner. Nor can it be circulated in any form of binding or cover other that that in which it is published and without similar conditions including this condition being imposed on the subsequent purchaser.

Published by M D Cartwright

This book is produced entirely in the UK, is available to order from most bookshops in the United Kingdom, and is globally available via UK based internet book retailers.

ISBN: 978-1-7398309-2-2

Dedication

To Anna and Bertie for their help

Thanks also to Brian Skinner for his invaluable guidance and Mathew Cooper for his help in getting this book into print

Michaels other books are:

The Yeomans Challenge, published by amazon.co.uk
ISBN: 979-8-5588133-8-8

Sleep Easy Brother, published by M D Cartwright in conjunction with WRITERSWORLD.

ISBN: 978-1-7398309-1-5

CHAPTER 1

Four children looked out of the main drawing room window, they watched as the frost glistened in the morning light. The family resemblance on their faces was plain to see, there were three boys and one girl, their ages ranged from the youngest, Robert at seven followed by John their cousin who had just had his eighth birthday, then the two eldest, Sarah at nine and lastly Peter at eleven. Peter turned to his siblings and spoke in what he thought was an adult voice,

'Grandfather should be with us shortly. He has promised that he will tell us the story of our family and how we came to be here.'

Robert asked if it was going to be about soldiers and fighting? Peter smiled and said, 'It may

be.'

They all heard the door handle turn and looked around expectantly, the door opened and their grandfather appeared. He was a man of some fifty-eight years, his figure was upright although a slight stoop could be detected as he walked into the room. His grey hair framed a lined face that had seen many a summers sun. He looked at his grandchildren and smiled. To him they were his life, what he had worked for and if necessary, what he would die for. The children stood and ran to him, Robert grabbed his knee and hugged it while the others took his hands and led him to his favourite chair. In the year of 1714

Thomas Dower had reached a point in his life when he felt he had completed all that he had worked for and could now relax. As he sat, he looked around the room. It had taken blood sweat and many tears to arrive at this position in his world. It was a fine house built of red brick in a symmetrical style that fitted with his view of the world, everything in its place, evenly spaced nothing out of position. A sense of pride and achievement washed over him as he sat and faced his audience.

'Will you make sure you are comfortable as the story I am about to tell you may take some time.'

The children shuffled around and sat together on two bench seats that had sheeps fleeces on them for a little more comfort.

'If you are ready, I shall begin.'

The children replied in unison,

'We are ready Grandfather.'

He took a sip of water and began.

'I will tell you the story that my mother told me, it begins a very long time ago.'

The young faces looked at their grandfather with expectation.

'My mother, who would be your Great Grandmother lived in this area which was very different in her day. She had married very young to her childhood friend with whom she had spent her early years. It was taken for granted that they would become man and wife. Their families had adjoining farms and could only survive if they helped one another.

They married when your great grandmother was only seventeen. Although young she was wise for her years. She had been brought up to work hard and worship god. When she was able to reach the cows udders she was set to milking. Her life was spent learning how to milk, make cheese and butter. The man she married was David Brooks who was five years her senior. He had been schooled in husbandry by his father and uncles so he was well equipped to take on the running of the farm when his father passed away shortly after his wedding. The couple lived the hard life that was farming in the Cambridgeshire fens. They had livestock consisting of sheep, pigs and cows and together with one hundred and fifty hectares of arable crops which made life bearable. His father's tenant farmers did not present a problem, anything but, they helped David to become established in his own right. It was after the first year of their marriage that Sarah gave birth to a baby boy. He was born strong and healthy and named William after the conqueror.

Hard work and the support of their families enabled them to improve their house and after building a sturdy barn they managed to store their precious crops and give shelter to livestock in the worse weather.

A strange thing happened when William had just passed his first birthday. Sarah left the house to fetch water, David was chopping wood, he had spent the early hours taking care of his animals. As Sarah made her way to the well, she heard a strange noise coming from the lane that ran passed their house, she stopped and listened but she could not see where it was coming from. Although she tried, she could not make out what was making the dull monotonous drone, it seemed to come out of the mist that had been laying on the ground that morning. She called to her husband who had also heard the noise and as he went to his wife's side, they both saw men appearing through the mist, a large number of men. They were walking four abreast and seemed to be from another world. Both Sarah and David drew breath, they looked at each other with puzzlement in their eyes. As they watched the column of men draw closer a figure appeared on horseback, he approached them slowly, they could hear the creaking of his saddle and the jangle of the horse's bridle. The rider was in the uniform of the parliamentary army, his red-coloured coat stretched down to his knees, it was gathered together at his waist by a brown sash. He wore no helmet but instead had a broad brimmed leather hat beneath which was a tired sweat-stained face. He looked down at the couple,

'Good morning to you, I am Sergeant Saunders of General Cromwell's dragoons and I am tasked with taking these men to the drainage works at Earith. Can you tell me how far I have to go?'

David knew of the work that was being carried out to drain the fens and increase the land for growing crops, he like many others was not wholly in favour of what was happening especially as it meant the loss of common land. David went towards the rider and stroked the side of the horse's neck,

'You have about another three miles to get to Earith but as far as I know the work is taking place nearer, about two miles from here.'

'Thank you, how is your well, is the water good?' David was curious.

'Why do you ask?'

'These men are thirsty, they have been marching since dawn, can they quench their thirst at your well?'

David looked down the lines of men, his well had always been a good source of water but this many men would take a lot and it would take time. David looked up again at the sergeant,

'I have some jugs and a few beakers that they can use but it will take time and I need to see about my farm.' The sergeant looked around and spotted the trough used to water cattle and horses. 'If you could fill those troughs the men can use their hands.' David shrugged his shoulders and looked at Sarah,

'We will try to keep the troughs filled as the men pass.'

The Sergeant seemed satisfied and called out to his four soldiers who stood watching the lines of dishevelled men. David noticed that they were all dressed in the same dirty white thick coarse Kersey cloth, their boots looked fairly new but some seemed to fit better than others. The order was given and the men started to move slowly passed the troughs cupping their hands to get as much water as possible. David and Sarah watched the men and could only feel sympathy towards them. Sarah approached the sergeant's horse and looking up asked,

'Where are these men from?' The sergeant looked along the lines of sorry looking humanity,

'They are prisoners from the battles fought against parliament. There have been two, one at a place called Dunbar in Scotland and the other in Worcester. General Cromwell was victorious in both and now we have the survivors to deal with.'

Sarah had no idea about the fighting that had taken place. The country seemed to have been divided and at each other's throats for so many years that she had forgotten the reason why. She looked again at the men and thought of their families that probably didn't know if their fathers, sons and brothers were alive or dead.

It took nearly an hour for the lines of men to pass. David estimated that there must be in excess of one hundred and fifty men and with only five soldiers to keep order David thought how the sergeant had his work cut out. The sergeant thanked David for his assistance and turned the head of his steed making his way to the front of the column of prisoners. Sarah stood by David's side as they watched the ghostly figures depart and taking hold of David's hand was thankful that he had not been embroiled in the conflict.

*

The children were listening intently especially when their grandfather told them of the strange men in the mist. He leaned forward in his chair as he looked at each of his grandchildren and thought how much their distant relations would have delighted in seeing them in their current surroundings.

'When can we hear what happened next grandfather.' It was the eldest who asked the question.

'Soon, it will be soon.' As he spoke the door opened and his daughter appeared.

'Come along children or you will tire your grandfather.' The children got to their feet and one by one went to their grandfather and planted a kiss on his cheek. 'Can I get you anything father?' His daughter asked. Thomas Dower made himself a little more comfortable in his chair,

'I would very much enjoy a glass of your good cider.'

'I will have one of the children bring it to you directly.' She ushered the children out of the room and turned to watch her father sit back with a faraway look in his eyes. His grandchild Peter returned with a large glass of cider,

'Here you are grandfather.' He placed the glass on the table at Thomas's side and quickly departed.

*

Thomas Dower closed his eyes and the memory of his mother telling him how his family came into being appeared before him. He took a sip from the glass and the taste of summer came back to him as the vision of what he had been told so many years ago entered his mind. She had told him that the lives of Sarah and David continued and as the weather started to change the fields became greener and the livestock fatter, the gods seemed to be smiling on them. In Thomas Dower's mind's eye, the vision of his forefathers began to appear as if his dream had taken on reality and he could see David and Sarah's son begin to move across the floor and try to take his first steps, all seemed well on Brooks Farm. It was three weeks after the prisoners had passed through the farm that unexpected visitors appeared at their door, it was the sergeant with another more official looking man also in uniform, the cut of his cloth was far superior to that of the sergeants. They dismounted and made their way to the farmhouse door where Sarah met and welcomed them. The sergeant spoke first,

'I am sorry I did not ask for your name when we last met?' Sarah looked at the man and for some unknown reason felt a little embarrassed,

'My name is Sarah Brook and my husband is David, what can I do for you?'

The sergeant looked at his companion and then turned to Sarah,

'This is Captain Emery.' The man then spoke with a slightly irritated voice,

'It's alright sergeant, I have a tongue in my head and know how to speak.'

The sergeant coughed and took a step back allowing the captain space to address Sarah.

'My name is Emery and I have the honour to serve the Lord Protector. My purpose today is to establish supply lines, together with the quartermaster, for the men working on the excavation of the new drainage ditches and I need to speak to your husband regarding how he can assist.'

Sarah was a little bemused, how could someone unknown to them appear and request them to supply produce to feed his prisoners.

'My husband is in the fields checking the crops and then he will be with his workers instructing them on the day's tasks and what is needed over the coming week.'

'And pray what time will he be back?'

It was the captain's turn to be annoyed. Sarah looked at the man in front of her, she could imagine him bullying his men into action rather than leading them.

'I expect him back at midday before he visits his tenant farmers.'

The captain looked around the farm yard he could see several women in what looked like the dairy and two men repairing a cart, 'Please tell your husband that I shall return at midday and need to speak to him urgently. Sarah nodded and watched the two men mount their horses and head out of the yard. As soon as they were out of sight Sarah called a young lad to her and instructed him to find her husband in the lower fields and tell him to return home. The lad nodded, turned and ran out of the yard disappearing into the fields. The lad was out of breath when he reached David who had to sit him down and give him a drink before he could give his message. Panting the lad told David that he was needed which alarmed him,

'Is there something amiss?' He knew his wife would not send for him unless there was something she couldn't handle and she could cope with almost anything that happened on the farm. He told the lad to help with the work in the field then leapt onto his horse and headed for the house.

Sarah saw David reigning his horse in and went to meet him as he dismounted. He had a worried look on his face,

'Is there anything wrong?'

She looked at his weather tanned features and sturdy figure, 'It's alright David, I had to get you back to the house.'

'Why?'

'We have had visitors, do you remember the sergeant who came through with the prisoners? Well, he arrived this morning with a Captain from the drainage works and wanted to see you to discuss the supply of food for the men. I told him you would not be back until midday and he said he would return to speak to you. David's brow creased as he tried to think of what the captain wanted.

'He didn't give you any other information?'

Sarah shook her head, 'No he just said he wanted to speak to you.'

'Ah well it's at least two hours until midday so we shall be ready for him when he returns.'

True to his word the captain returned as the sun reached its highest point of the day. He was accompanied by the sergeant who followed in silence.

'Good day to you Mr Brooks.' His voice was sharp without humour. 'I need to discuss the provision of supplies for the men digging the waterways.' He climbed down from his horse followed by his sergeant.

'Please come into the house I am sure you could use something to quench your thirst.'

The three men entered the house, David led them into the main room which had a substantial table and six chairs. They sat, the two soldiers removing their hats and relaxing into the chairs. David asked how he could assist and that his wife had mentioned something about supplies.'

Sarah walked into the room and asked if they would like something to drink, the captain said that a glass of ale would be most welcome. Sarah looked at her husband he nodded, she turned and left to get the drinks. The captain spoke first,

'As you may be aware, we have many hundreds of men working for us on the construction of the drains and new rivers in this area together with many more digging diversions to existing rivers. They are mainly prisoners captured following the battles of Dunbar and Worcester. They have been marched for many weeks and are not in the best of condition. We need to get the men working so that we can achieve our goals and to that end we need to feed them as best we can. They have accommodation of sorts, mainly huts that can be moved on as the work progresses however, we must ensure that supplies of food are maintained and to that end we are speaking to farmers, such as yourself, in the area and agreeing on what they can supply at a fair price. I understand that you have both arable crops and livestock on your farm and we need both. To give you some idea we have already gained the agreement of your neighbours to supply various amounts but we need more.' Emery looked at the farmers face trying to gauge what his response would be but David Brooks did not show any sign of enthusiasm. Emery then told David that at this time he did not have a Quartermaster and that any final quantities and timings would be his to negotiate and confirm.

At this point the discussion went into the amounts required and the price that could be paid. David did not hand his produce over lightly, he bargained hard and at one stage slammed his fist onto the table asking the captain if he was trying to rob him. It took several hours for a conclusion to be reached. Amounts of beef, mutton and pork were agreed along with beans, peas and barley. The foodstuffs would be collected by wagon each Tuesday and payment would be made the following day when the rations had reached the camp. Although David was unsure of how the payment would work, he had no option as there was a possibility that the army could just take what they needed and ruin him. The captain was pleased with his talk but stressed again that his quartermaster was the one who would make the final decision on amounts, delivery and price.

CHAPTER 2

The arrangement made between David and the new quartermaster started well, produce was collected not only from his farm but also from those of his tenants without problem. Payment was made efficiently without argument and it seemed that both parties were satisfied. It was during the third week that things started to go awry, payments were held up but the demands the army made grew evermore strong. The rains had arrived and the land became waterlogged with rivers and ditches overflowing. The work on the drainage system seemed to come to a halt but the men still needed feeding. David had no option but to go to get things sorted out with the military. He set out in the rain leaving Sarah to take care of the daily routine. When he arrived at the camp the rain had eased and there was a break in the clouds. David managed to tether his horse in the shelter of nearby trees and made his way to where he thought he would find Captain Emery. He saw the figure of the sergeant standing before several troopers giving orders in a sharp uncompromising voice. The sergeant turned and could see David struggling through the sodden, slippery mud,

  'Mister Brooks, what brings you here on such a miserable day?'

David pushed the brim of his hat up so that he could see the sergeant more clearly,

'I need to discuss payment, or should I say lack of it, is the quartermaster available to answer some of my questions?'

'I'm afraid he has been called to Cambridge, a question of money, it always seems to be a question of money. It is possible that the captain may be able to help you, he is aware of any payments made.' David was not sure whether the captain could help him but he had travelled through the downpour and he would be grateful to get out of the miserable weather. 'If you wish to speak to the captain he is at the far end of the embankment.' David did not want to have to visit the camp again.

'How do I reach him?' The sergeant pointed along the bottom of the trench that had recently been cut.

'The quickest way is along the bottom of the trench but it may not be safe, the rain has made things unstable.' David just wanted to get his visit over as quickly as possible and return home, so he thanked the sergeant and headed along the bottom of the excavation.

David could feel his boots sinking into the mud and began to change his position to what he hoped was firmer ground. He was close to the latest workings and the bank that rose next to him looked threatening. It was totally unexpected, the huge bank of mud suddenly moved, there were shouts from the men working nearby and David only had time to look up as the freshly dug soil cascaded in his direction. He tried to get out of the way but his feet were so deep into the mud that he could not move. The men closest to him tried to make their way through the thick slime but failed to reach him. They could only watch as David struggled for his life. Two men made another attempt to reach him one of whom struggled to stay upright but was dragged under the torrent of mud, the second man was pulled back by his fellow workers. They could do no more but watch as David became engulfed by the rapidly moving mud slide.

The two men tried again and together with another made a desperate attempt to drag David out of the quagmire, the first of the men called out. 'Tom,' who was trying with all his strength to pull David clear, 'Take care.'

It was a hopeless cause, the bodies of David and Tom sank out of sight. The first man, Jamie, felt arms around him pulling him back, he struggled, he did not want Tom to die, he was all that was left keeping him sane, he stood helplessly and watch the mud cover the place where Tom and David were last seen.

The captain watched as the tragedy unfolded and could do nothing. He shouted instructions to his men but they were unable to carry out his orders. Most of the men managed to retreat to firmer ground and wait for the rains to pass. It was not until several hours later that Captain Emery could retrieve David's body together with that of the man who had tried to rescue him. His thoughts were of David's family and those who worked on his farm, how would he tell David's wife that he died in a mud slide while he was waiting to speak to him. Emery looked down at David's body, the men had tried to clean away most of the mud and his features were now clear to see,

'Bring up the wagon and the farmer's horse.'

Emery's voice was loud and clear and the men tried their best to get the wagon closer to the body. Eventually they managed to haul David's lifeless form onto the bed of the wagon. Slowly the soldiers got the wagon onto some firmer ground, Emery could now see David's face clearly, it was pale beneath streaks of mud, his eyes were closed and his hair plastered against his head. Emery knew it was up to him to return the body to the farm and explain to David's wife what had happened. His first move was to report the incident to his superiors, the best way to achieve this was to send a rider to Cambridge with a message explaining what had happened then it would be up to them to take any action. It would take several hours for the message to reach Cambridge and a reply brought back. Emery had to make a decision whether to take the body back to the farm or wait for a reply. His decision was to return David's body to his wife but before doing so he would make sure the body was cleaned and presented in a better state.

    He looked around at the men trying to remove the mud from their clothes and boots. He could see one man who appeared to be taking a great deal of care with the body,

    'You, you with the body, come here.' The man looked up it was difficult to judge his age as his face like all the rest of his fellow workers was covered in a beard and together with grime and mud covered his features. As he approached Emery the man wiped his hands on the filthy, coarse shirt he was wearing. 'What's your name?'

    'I am called Jamie Dower, sir.'

    'Well Mr Dower I want you to stay with the body until I give you further orders, is that understood?'

    'Understood, sir.' The voice had a thick accent which made it difficult for Emery to understand. Jamie did not want to leave Tom's body to be handled by strangers. He looked up at Emery.

'Can I bury my friend?' Emery was a little surprised at the man asking such a question,

'I don't think he will be buried today, but rest assured I will make sure you will be able to see he is treated well.' Jamie looked again at Tom's body, he was the last of the friends he had made on the long and gruelling march and he felt totally deflated. He would not let the officer forget his promise and he would make sure that Tom was buried with prayers said at his graveside.

Emery made his way through the slime and mud to assess the damage done to the bank that had collapsed. He met the engineer who was overseeing that part of the works,

'What do you think, will this delay us for very long?' The engineer looked around he took mental note of the size of the collapsed bank.

'We should be able to repair any damage within two days so our schedule should not be affected.'

'Thank God for that.' Emery was not a religious fanatic like some of his fellow officers but at times he knew that thanking the almighty might help him. 'I am going to take the body back to his wife so I may be gone some time, do you need me to give any further instructions to the men?' The engineer was aware that the army felt that they were in control of this part of the workings but in reality, it was the engineers who called the shots.

'No, I shall be able to begin the repairs as soon as we get a reasonable break in the weather.'

Emery turned back to the wagon and made his way through the mud to where David's body lay. He had to think of how and what he was going to say to the farmer's wife. Emery did not like admitting responsibility for the accident, and that was what it was, an accident. He had an idea that may only be a gesture but hopefully would appear that he was trying to help. He turned to the man standing by the wagon,

'What was your name again?'

The man looked around at Emery,

'Jamie, Jamie Dower.'

'Well Mr Dower I might have a job for you, do you know anything about farming?'

Jamie Dower had been brought up on a small farm and was aware of what was needed in running cattle but did not have much of an idea about crops, if that might jeopardise his chances of getting away from the purgatory that was the never-ending digging of heavy peat soil he would not tell.

'Yes, I know about farms and livestock, why do you ask?'

'Just come with me and all will be revealed.'

Emery went to get his horse while Jamie stood and wondered what the future might have for him. The captain returned astride his horse and ordered the wagon to be made ready to move. It took some time to get the horse in position and the wagon released from its muddy surrounds. Eventually the horse was steered onto the track that led off of the workings.

As they approached the farm Jamie thought of the ways he would be put to work, anything would be better than the daily drudge of digging trench after trench. Perhaps he would be able to meet other people with interests other than where their next meal was coming from. His mind focussed on food, it had been a long time since he had had a meal that could be called 'enough'. A farm would have milk and fresh eggs, perhaps chicken or pork, he dreamt of beef and the smell of it roasting. Suddenly the wagon jolted and Jamie came back to reality. The captain signalled for Jamie to stop the wagon,

'I want you to do just as I say when we reach the farm, is that understood?'

Jamie had no idea what was in the captain's mind but he was willing to go along with whatever it was as long as it was to his benefit. They moved off, it was another half mile to the Brooks farm and they could see the farmhouse before them. As they neared the farmhouse Emery tried to clear his mind and focus on what and how he was going to break the terrible news to the farmer's wife.

They pulled up outside the house and Emery called to a boy who had emerged from the stable,

'You boy, tell your mistress that Captain Emery is here to see her.' The boy ran to the back of the house and disappeared. Emery dismounted and stood by his horse's head looking up at Jamie he said,

'Remember do as I say and no more.'

'Yes sir'. Jamie's response was one of subservience, he knew that he had no option but to do as he was told.

Sarah Brook came from the rear of the house, wiping her hands on her apron, she had been working in the dairy as she did most days. As she turned into the front of the house, she could see a man standing with his horse, he looked at her as she came closer, his face was stern without emotion. She then looked at the wagon, it was the one used to collect the produce, the only reason she could think of why it had been brought was to pick up more supplies, but that was odd because collection had been made the day before. The driver of the wagon watched her as she talked to the captain.

'Why are you here, the rations were collected yesterday, is there something wrong with them?'

Emery walked towards her,

'I am afraid I have some very bad tidings to give you.'

Now Sarah began to get concerned. She tried to see what was in the wagon but could not see over the side.

'What is it, what is so bad that you had to make a special trip to deliver whatever news you have?'

Emery gripped his belt as he moved a step towards Sarah.

'I have grave news regarding your husband,'

'What.' Sarah's voice was full of disbelief, her husband had not ventured anywhere dangerous, he had just gone to the diggings to discuss payment.

'There was a terrible accident, the heavy rains caused a landslide and I am afraid your husband was caught in the disaster that followed.' Sarah swallowed hard and looked from the captain to the driver of the wagon.

'Where is he, is he injured, what's happening?' Her voice was faltering as she looked from Emery to the wagon.

'I am so sorry.' Emery did not quite know how to phrase the news. 'It is with deep regret that I have to tell you that your husband died beneath the collapsed bank along with the man who tried to save him.' Sarah's head dropped as her hands gripped her apron.

'Where is he?' Emery turned and looked at the wagon.

'Oh my God, he is in there.' She ran to the back of the wagon and looked over the tailboard. She could see a figure wrapped in a blanket, its body and face were covered so she could not see any sign that it was her husband. Jamie jumped from his seat and ran to the back of the wagon, he unhitched the tailboard so that Sarah could reach her husband's body. The blanket was slowly drawn down revealing the farmers head, his face was without blood his lips blue and thankfully his eyes remained closed.

People started to venture into the yard to see what was happening. The two women who worked in the dairy ran to Sarah's side, they could see the body lying on the bed of the wagon and that it was that of their master. One woman called for help, the farrier stopped shoeing the dray he was working on and with his apprentice ran to see what they could do.

Sarah found difficulty in speaking, the elder of the two dairymaids told the men to take the body into the house, Sarah nodded in agreement. The two men assisted by Jamie managed to get the farmers body into the house. Sarah followed them in and told them in a faltering voice that her husband was to be placed in the parlour on the large table. Captain Emery followed the men carrying the body, he looked at Sarah and could feel nothing but pity and sorrow for her. She turned to him,

'Thank you for bringing him home, you can leave him with me now and I will take care of him.' As Emery turned to leave, he said to Sarah that he would leave the driver with her and if she needed anything that she should send word with him back to the workings. Emery took Jamie to one side,

'You will stay here until nightfall then return to the camp, you will report to me and let me know exactly what happens, is that understood?'

'What about the wagon, it might be needed?'

'I will take care of any needs that might arise you just concentrate on what happens here.'

'As you wish sir.'

Emery then turned back to Sarah, he could see that she was washing her husband's face with such gentleness that he did not wish to disturb her but he had to tell her he was departing.

'I am going now but if we can do anything please send the wagon driver to the camp and I will do all I can to help.' Sarah did not look up she continued to gently wipe her husband's face and as she did her tears fell onto his blue lips, Emery's words fell on to deaf ears, Sarah was trying to take in the fact that her husband would no longer be able to share her life. The captain left the house and walked towards his horse, he looked around searching for the wagon driver. Jamie had helped lay the farmers body onto the table in the main room of the house and made his way to the door, his eyes met those of Emery's.

'I want you to report to me when you return, help as much as you can then bring the wagon back.' With a last look around the farm yard Emery swung up into his saddle, it had not been the best of days, he left the farm not really knowing what to do next.

Jamie was at a loss, after he had helped bring the farmers body into the house he felt as if he was in the way. Men and women were moving in and out of the house mainly to see what had been the cause of the commotion. He looked at Sarah who was still by her husband's side, she looked up and saw this strange shadow of a man in the door way,

'Who are you and what are you doing in my house?'
Jamie was lost for words, he gulped in some air,

'I am Jamie Dower and I have been ordered by Captain Emery to stay and give any assistance I can.' Sarah shook her head.

'Please keep everyone away from me, nobody else to enter.' Jamie turned and stood in the doorway, the many people who worked for the farmer had no idea who he was and his appearance did not project an air of authority. As two more of the farm workers tried to get passed him into the room, he said that the mistress did not want to see anybody else.' One of the men tried to push past but Jamie's slight figure belied his strength. Although his food was poor, he had gained strength by digging for the last months all it took was his hand on the man's chest to stop him. The worker came to a halt and could sense that the unwashed bearded fellow standing guard was not in the mood for talking so he stopped trying to pass Jamie and with a grunt of foul language turned and left. Others who tried to gain entry were dissuaded.

After an hour had passed Sarah pulled herself away from the body of her husband and looked again at the stranger standing in the doorway.

'I need to contact my brothers, please go and get one of the stable lads and bring him to me.' Jamie nodded and left the house heading towards what he presumed were the stables. As he walked across the farmyard faces turned towards him and he could hear low voices mumbling their curiosity, who was this filthy, poorly dressed individual? He didn't care he had grown a very thick skin over the past years and just got on with his task. He found two young men just inside the stables,

'Your mistress wants one of you to go to her brothers farm and tell him of the death of your master.' His voice had a Scottish bur and he had to repeat himself before he got the message through. The tallest of the lads stepped forward,

'I'll go, I know the way and I have worked on the mistress's brother's farm.' Jamie did something that the lad had not experienced very often, he thanked him. As soon as the young man had mounted a horse and left the yard Jamie returned to the house. He found Sarah still with the body but now she seemed to be more composed. There were three women with her and all four were arranging the farmer's body. They had stripped it and were washing it thoroughly. Jamie had not experienced the laying out of a corpse and did not want to become involved. The farmer's wife looked up,

'Have you sent word to my brother?'

'Yes, a stable lad who has worked on your brothers farm has gone with the message.'

Sarah looked up from what she was doing and noticed for the first time what a pathetic sight the man in front of her was. He was about as tall as her husband but that's where any similarity ended. His matted hair was long and seemed to be covered in grease, his beard was the same. She could not really see his face due to the thickness of his beard,

'Please fetch some more water.' Jamie picked up the buckets and left the room. As he went out into the sunlight, he looked for the well. It was easy to see and he walked to the far end of the yard and started to lower the bucket. As he walked back to the house one of the onlookers took one of the buckets and carried it for him. They did not speak, it felt as if silence had descended over the farm. When he returned to the house, he saw that the body had been dressed in a woollen shroud in accordance with the law of the day. About an hour later Sarah's brother arrived and rushed straight to his sister's side.

'What happened, he was a careful man, he did not take unnecessary risks.'

Sarah's brother, Jacob, was a man not used to waiting for answers. He looked around and saw Jamie,

'And who in god's name is that?'

Jamie felt no bigger than an insect, he knew he smelt and that his clothes hung from his bony frame in tatters. He waited for the response from the farmer's wife.

'He is a man who has been given to us by the captain responsible for the excavation of the drains.'

'He looks as if he needs us more than we need him.' Jamie looked at the man with embarrassment and a degree of anger.

'He is better than nothing and I shall need help in all its shapes over the coming days.'

Jacob took another look at Jamie, and then looked around the faces in the room, he focused on one of the dairy maids.

'Get one of the men that shears the sheep and tell him to bring the tools of his trade.' Both Sarah and Jamie had a vague idea of what was about to happen and they were right. A short wiry figure appeared in the doorway, in his hands he held shears and a sharpening stone, Jacob pointed to Jamie,

'See that thing I want you to do something with it so that I can see what he is thinking.' The man with the shears cast his eye over Jamie,

'I'll do my best but I think it's going to take more than my effort to bring this man back from wherever he is at the moment.'

'Take him outside and get on with it and then don't let him go anywhere until he has been thrown in the river.' With that the shearer grabbed Jamie's arm and led him out of the house. Jacob turned to Sarah,

'Tell me sister what have you been able to do?' His voice had changed, it was now one of concern.

'I have only been able to wash and dress him no more than that.' She had regained her composure and any grief was hidden.

'There are matters to be arranged, you and I will need to speak to those who will be able to organise a church service and internment. Is your church still St Michaels Chapel in the village?'

'Yes, it is and I know the pastor well, he conducted our marriage ceremony and christened William.' Jacob was pleased to hear this, Sarah continued 'I can get a message to him today and hopefully he will be able to come here fairly soon.'

Jacob looked at his sister, in his eyes she was far too young to be a widow and to be left with a one-year-old child would not be easy for her to handle.

'If you are in agreement, I will arrange for a coffin to be made, there is also the matter of informing everyone about the tragedy. I can let our parents and brother know and I am sure they will be here as soon as they can.' Sarah was pleased to have Jacob take control, at the moment she found it very hard to concentrate.

The days that followed David Brooks death were filled with activity. Informing everyone of any changes took time, the tenant farmers, the villagers who depended on David for employment either as day workers or full-time agricultural labourers needed to know who was running the farm. Fortunately, the day workers were in the fields and would be given any instructions during the day. Sarah had worked hand in hand with her husband so she was aware of what was required to run the farm but she could not be in two places at once. Jacob and her other brother Mathew had their own farms to take care of and her parents who lived with Mathew were not in very good health. She had trusted workers, however some things she would need to keep a very close eye on. She looked at the figure of her husband and the tears started to fall. She was not an emotional person but this was becoming too much even for her. What took her mind off matters was the appearance of the man called Jamie, he stepped into the room his hands clutched together in front of him, the change was remarkable. She could see his face, his beard and long hair had gone which left an almost white ring running from his eyes down past his nose and up to his ears. Although he looked odd, she could see that he was younger than first appearance suggested and although still difficult to make out, his face held a lot of interest. He was washed and brushed, whoever had dunked him in the river had managed to find an old smock and a pair of breeches which made him look comical. She smiled at him and for the first time he noticed how lovely she was. He felt himself blushing which Sarah could see but thought it was a result that his changed state had caused.

'I am sorry.' Sarah said as she looked him up and down. 'I have forgotten your name.'

'Jamie, Jamie Dower ma'am.'

'Well Jamie Dower welcome to Brooks Farm, prepare yourself for some hard work, tell me what time do you have to return to the camp?'

'I am to be here for as long as I am needed.'

'And how will you get from the camp to here?'

'I shall walk.'

'How far is it?'

'It is three miles here and three miles back.'

'Not such a long way, each morning you are to speak to me first and carry out the tasks I give you, and if you have any problems, you are to see me first is that clear?'

'Yes, ma'am.' Jamie thought that his life was run by others, do this, do that, never a decision of his own, he just carried out orders.

David Brook's funeral was attended by the farm workers and most of the villagers. He had been a respected young man who had been fair with all who worked for him and those he traded with. After the internment the mourners made their way back to the house where Sarah had laid on food and drink, not too much, just enough to satisfy those that were only there for a free meal. It had been a week since the accident and Jamie had worked every day either tending the livestock or in the fields helping with the crops. It had been hard work but he was happy to be away from the diggings. Sarah had told him that he was welcome to attend the funeral and the wake so out of respect for the family he dutifully made his way to the small chapel and stood with the other mourners.

'What are you doing here?' It was Sarah's brother Jacob.

'I was invited by Mistress Brook.' He stood in his threadbare smock feeling awkward. Jamie stared at the man and he could see that he had been drinking. His speech was a little slurred and his balance was not good.

'Who are you anyway, some sort of prisoner?'

'I have been told to work on Mistress Brooks farm and help in whatever way I can.' Jacob called out to his sister,

'Sarah.' She turned and walked to where he was standing next to Jamie,

'What is it, Jacob.' She could also see that he had been drinking heavily.

'This man, this prisoner, says he works for you is that correct?'

'Yes, he has been sent to help with any work on the farm, he is here from dawn to dusk and only requires feeding. He gets no wage and has proved to be a good worker.'

'Do you really need another mouth to feed, can't you manage with the people you have?'

Jamie could see that things were not going well but all he could do was to watch and listen. Sarah's face was starting to colour. 'I need all the help I can get and if that comes in the form of a prisoner then so be it.' Jacob huffed and turning he pushed passed Jamie knocking him to one side, he muttered something which sounded like 'things will be different when I take over.' Sarah shook her head,

'He has had too much ale and wine he will be different in the morning.

Following the funeral things seemed to settle into a routine. Jamie would appear at dawn, carry out any duties he was given by Sarah and then return to the camp at dusk. He did not see too much of Jacob, which Jamie thought was a blessing, he did not want to be the subject of a family disagreement. After he had been working at the farm for three weeks Sarah asked if he could ask Captain Emery to call on her when he was next in the area. Jamie dutifully delivered the message and Captain Emery appeared at the farmhouse the following day. Sarah had asked Jamie to stay locally as what she had to say to the captain involved his future. Jamie had no idea but dreaded the thought of going back to the constant digging. He needn't have worried. Sarah asked Emery into the house and sent for Jamie,

'I trust you are keeping well, the produce you send to the camp is of good quality and I trust payment is on time and covers your costs.'

Sarah smiled, 'Yes, everything seems to be running according to our discussions.' Jamie appeared at the door, Sarah beckoned him in. 'I have asked Jamie to join us as I want to make you a proposition.' Emery looked quizzically at both Sarah and Jamie. 'I should like to offer Jamie a place to sleep here, in the main barn and the reason for my offer is that by the time he gets here in the morning he has already walked three miles and when he does arrive, he brings with him things from the camp that I do not want on my farm.'

'I don't understand, what things?'

'To start with lice, which tend to enjoy spreading themselves onto any living surface and I am also very concerned to hear that you have outbreaks of disease at the camp and I do not want it to spread amongst my people. So can I have your agreement that Jamie stays at the farm?'

Emery thought for a while.

'I think that may be a good idea, I would have to ask if you could feed and clothe him?'

'That will present no problem, so are we agreed?'

'I think so.' He turned to Jamie. 'Do you want to stay at the farm?' Jamie was a little shocked by the offer made, without hesitation he blurted out 'Yes.' As he looked from the captain to Sarah a broad smile spread across his face the thought of being away from the camp filled him with a sense of relief and joy. Emery then asked Jamie if he had any personal possessions at the camp, Jamie assured him that all he had he carried with him.

'That's settled then, it will not cause me any difficulty in fact it comes at a good time as I have several Dutch naval prisoners arriving later so I shall need the space.'

CHAPTER 3

Jamie was welcomed by the other workers on the farm. They had been suspicious of him when he first started. He had not been one of them and he still wasn't, his fellow workers found it difficult to understand him at times even though his accent had softened since his arrival. The men he stood beside in the field could see that he put everything into his work and at times they did think he overdid it. There were those who became a little jealous of his relationship with the mistress although they were aware that she was his hardest taskmaster. It was the women of the dairy who saw how Sarah treated Jamie. The daily duties she gave him kept him busy, he would run from field to field with instruction and to find out information for Sarah. On rare occasions he would be given permission to take a horse to complete his tasks. At the end of the day Jamie collapsed in the hay loft and slept the sleep of the dead.

  The year flew by and the seasons passed. It was a year after the death of her husband that Sarah's brothers visited. Their parents had been taken from them during the year and had left a large void in their family. Jacob and Mathew rode into the farm and dismounted. Their stride was purposeful as they made their way to the door.

  'We need to see your mistress.' It was a command Jacob issued to Sarah's maid, who scurried off to find her. Sarah had been expecting a visit from her brothers, they were eager to get her married off. She might still be young but the days were passing quickly. Sarah entered the main room where her brothers were waiting. She spoke first,

'What can I do for my illustrious brothers. I hope you're not here to try to get me into the marriage bed with one of your chosen men?' It was Mathew who spoke,

'You have a large farm and a young son they both need a controlling male hand to get the best yields both from crops and livestock and we have several suitors for you.' Sarah was enraged by the thought that she was not getting the best from the land and as for a man being needed to ensure the future of the farm, that was nonsense. She let fly her anger,

'If you think you can enter my house and dictate what I should do with my life you can leave now.' The brothers looked at each other they had not expected such a violent rebuff. Jacob started to speak,

'Sister, you cannot carry on running the farm on your own.'

'Oh, you think not, let me tell you that I have not only improved the yields but have maintained our contract with the army to supply them with foodstuffs which has increased the profits far more than your two farms put together.'

The brothers looked at each other, they were aware that the farm was doing well and they both needed to approach the matter of her marriage in a different way. Mathew started to speak but was interrupted by Jacob who's hot headed approach to everything did not make things any easier,

'Now that our father has passed you will do as we say. We are the head of the family and it would do you well to think on that.' The feeling in the room started to become heated and Sarah slammed her fist down onto the table,

'I will not be pushed into a marriage just so that you can wash your hands of me. I am quite capable of running this farm and will see you two dead before I hand any part of it over to some idiot you select for me to marry.'

The noise of the discussion carried outside of the room and the men and women close by could hear everything.

Jamie had just finished a trip to the men in the fields giving them Sarah's go ahead to start harvesting. He stopped outside the house and listened until there seemed to be a calm period then he knocked on the door.

'Come in.' It was a loud command in three voices as the brothers and their sister spoke together. Jamie cautiously opened the door,

'What do you want?' Jacob shouted at him.

'I have just returned from the barley crop and need to tell the mistress of the progress.'

Sarah stormed across the room and slapped Jacob across the face,

'If the man has anything to say it will be to me.'

Jacob grabbed her hand but she managed to break his grip.

'Now will you please leave my house and do not return until you have something to say other than who you think I should marry.'

Jacob grabbed his hat and took hold of his brother's arm,

'We will be back and you will marry who we tell you to.'

'Over my dead body, I will be sharing my husband's grave before I concede to your choice of a husband for me.'

The brothers left the room slamming the door behind them.

There followed a period of silence between Sarah and her brothers. It was thought inconceivable that she could handle a farm of that size on her own, the brothers thought of getting her a husband and as soon as possible. Sarah carried on with the routine she had established, she would provide the army of diggers with supplies and continue to sell produce at the market. She was not making a fortune but had enough to keep a comfortable life for her and her son. Jamie helped wherever he could and became a valued member of the farm family. His daily meetings with Sarah became more friendly and their familiarity grew stronger. Jamie had become very attached to Sarah's son, William and had spent time with the boy when waiting to see her. William would stagger towards Jamie and clasped his tiny hands around his leg and Jamie would play simple games with him until Sarah was ready to see him.

It was on a summers day that the brothers returned. Their horses galloped up to the house a cloud of summer dirt surrounded them. Sarah looked out from her window only to see her brothers marching towards the door. Her life had been peaceful since their last encounter and she was pleased that she hadn't had to think about her brother's insistence on her marrying. She had just finished her meeting with Jamie, there were various aspects that needed addressing including whether the corn and barley were ready to harvest. Sarah gestured to

Jamie to stay, her brothers burst in and Jacob started in a loud voice to remonstrate,

'You need a husband and we will make sure you have one before the summer is out.'

Sarah stood up and looking at her brother with a face of thunder said,

'You will not get me to the alter with any man you decide upon, I would rather marry this man.' She pointed to Jamie, he is worth ten of any of those you may have in mind.'

'You would not dare to marry such a man and we would withhold our consent preventing you from doing such a thing.' Sarah's face grew redder and she was about to explode.

'I will marry who I want and it will not be so that you can control me or the farm.'

Jamie stood saying nothing, he had become very fond of Sarah over the past months and he would stop any violence the brothers resorted to. Jacob looked at his brother and they both took a step towards Sarah as they did Jamie moved between the brothers and their sister. He turned towards Jacob.

'Please do not raise your hand to strike my mistress.'

'And what would you do, prisoner?' It was a term that Jacob had used before and it hit home hard with Jamie.

'I will do anything to protect her.'

As Jacob moved even closer, he raised his fist and as he was about to land a blow on Jamie, he moved quickly avoiding the fist and at the same time drew his own hand back and with force threw a punch that landed on its target. Jacob staggered back holding his jaw, Mathew held him up, Jacob straightened himself and ran towards Jamie but again Jamie was too quick and stepped aside landing another punch this time to the side of Jacob's head. Jacob fell like a sack of corn. Mathew had moved out of Jacobs way and swiftly lashed out and caught Jamie with a blow to the face. Sarah saw the blood spurt from Jamie's nose and let out a cry. Jamie shook his head but it was too late Mathew had grabbed him by the shoulders and threw him to the floor. Jamie let out a grunt as he hit the solid floor. Mathew then kicked Jamie in the small of the back but as he did Sarah had picked up a cider jug, it came crashing down on Mathew's head and stopped him doing any more damage to Jamie. Jacob was dazed, he tried to regain his balance but fell to his knees and Mathew lay on the floor unconscious from the blow that Sarah had landed. Sarah grabbed a pitcher of water and tipped it over her brother's head, Mathew moved and groaned while Jacob still holding his jaw tried to kick Jamie who quickly moved out of the way, Jamie then kicked Jacob's leg making him fall. He grabbed Jacob by the throat and with hands that were used to long hours of work began to tighten his grip. Sarah could see that Jamie had to be stopped before he killed Jacob, she grasped Jamie's hands and looked into his eyes,

 'That's enough, let him go I do not want my brother's death on my hands or yours.'

 Jamie let his hands slip from Jacob's throat and he stood, his chest was heaving he knew he could have killed Jacob if Sarah had not stopped him. She pulled Jamie away and sat him down, then she poured another pitcher of water over Mathew and tugged at Jacob's arm trying to get him to stand. Eventually the brothers gained their feet and looked at Sarah standing beside Jamie,

    'If you have the slightest thought about marrying this, this prisoner we will move heaven and earth to prevent it.' Jacob's voice although croaky from Jamie's grip still had venom in every word. Sarah moved closer to Jamie and held his arm,

    'If my decision is to marry this man I will do so and I will make sure you cannot prevent it, now get out of my house and never return, I do not want to see either of you again, if you attempt anything I will have my men chase you off do you understand?' The brothers supported each other to the door and turned saying that she had not heard the last of this. Sarah watched them climb onto their horses and gallop out of the yard. She turned to Jamie,

    'That was a brave but foolish thing you did, my brothers could have seriously injured you and believe me they would not have stopped if they thought they could get away with killing you.' Jamie took the cloth that Sarah held out and wiped the blood from his face,

    'You are my mistress and I am beholding to you for many things the least I can do is to try to prevent any harm happening to you.'

    The episode with the brothers left an uneasy relationship behind it. Jamie did not quite know how to approach Sarah, he found himself in an awkward position, was he her worker, her friend, her protector? Sarah had a similar problem the things she had said were 'of the moment' how did she treat Jamie now? They settled into an emotional strained routine, Sarah giving instructions to Jamie and he putting her wishes into operation.

Their feelings towards one another developed albeit in a stuttering way. It was on the occasions when they looked at the plan of the fields and their closeness developed into something more than just mistress and servant. The touching of hands, the brushing of arms became increasingly more difficult to ignore.

It was after the harvest that their relationship really blossomed. The crops had been gathered in and as custom dictated a celebration was arranged following the church harvest service. Sarah and the house staff including the dairy maids produced a fine spread. It was their own produce, everything from the fresh bread to the cold meats with cider and ale. The men produced fiddles and a drum, the singing was of the old songs of the countryside and dancing took place. Men, women and children danced with each other. Some knew the right steps to take others just moved as best they could to the beat of the drum. Sarah stood to the side of the festivities and watch with a certain amount of envy. The women she had become close to over the years taunted her to dance and one who had known her since childhood took her hand and then grabbed Jamie's, she led them both into the centre of the dancing and pushed them together. Jamie took hold of Sarah and with some difficulty moved with her in and around their fellow dancers, and so the evening went on.

As the sun finally dropped beneath the horizon the men and women started to make their way home. They thanked Sarah and what was strange was that they thanked Jamie as well. It was then that Sarah fully realised how important he had become. He was not just another farm labourer, he was someone who had gained the trust and respect of those around him. She moved a little closer to him, their hands touched and then she intertwined her fingers with his. They stood holding hands until the last of the revellers had disappeared then turned to face each other,

    'What do we do now?' She asked. Jamie leant forward and lightly brushed his lips against hers. It was if a dam had burst their feelings took over, they eagerly grasped each other, their bodies searching for fulfilment. She broke away and taking his hand led him up the stairs to her bedroom. Her son was asleep in an adjacent room, Sarah took his hand and pulled him to the bed. Passion took over, clothes were removed almost ripping their material and they fell onto the bed in a state of complete abandonment. Jamie had little or no experience in the art of lovemaking, however Sarah knew exactly what to do, Jamie followed her actions and felt such a surge run through his body that it hurt. He entered her with restrain not wishing to hurt her but she was eager and willing. Their bodies rose and fell together and finally they both collapsed with the satisfaction that love making brings. Jamie looked down at Sarah,

    'Should we marry?'

She smiled and looked at his face and once again saw him in a different light. His face was finely shaped, his eyes soft and welcoming, his lips gentle and full. This was a man who she could easily spend her life with,

    'We may have to if your seed ripens in my belly.'

Jamie gently lifted her shoulders, her face came to his and he kissed her eyes then her lips.

    'I will make you a good husband if you would have me.'

    'It would not just be me you would have to take, William is a part of me I would never let go.'

'He would be our son if you would agree.' At this Sarah smiled reaching up to his face she kissed him with eagerness and their love making continued.

As the sun started to stream through the window Sarah opened her eyes and looked at the man lying next to her. Had she done the right thing? She knew in her heart that everything felt right but in her head thoughts of how her brothers would react and how the community at large would look upon her actions gave her some concern. She got up and went to the window opening it she could see movement and the business of the day taking place. Sarah would embrace Jamie as an equal and they would run the farm together, there would be no doubt in any one's mind about their decision to marry. Her brothers would have to live with the situation and if necessary, she would be quite happy to continue in isolation from them. Turning back to the bed she could see Jamie waking.

'Come on Mister, one night of love does not release you from your duties, now get dressed and be ready for a full day's work.'

Jamie looked through bleary eyes then remembering what had happened quickly reached for his clothes. He was unsure of how to act, had he become something else other than a farm worker, his mind was all over the place. As he dressed Sarah moved back from the window and stood beside him.

'We need to discuss a great deal Jamie.'

He coughed and spluttered.

'Yes, I think we do.'

Sarah looked at him and smiled, 'First we get everyone working and then you and I will meet.' She sounded as if the relationship of farmer and worker had not changed and she could see that he was unsure of what to say or do.

'Mr Dower, you are no longer a person working for me, shall we say that we struct a partnership last night that will hopefully last a very long time.'

The expression on Jamie's face changed and it appeared a little less worried, he became even more sure of his future when Sarah walked to him and reached up planting her lips on his. Their love making felt good but the strain that had been placed upon Sarah by her brothers together with Jamie's status as a prisoner did not make for totally relaxed love making. Sarah thought she may have conceived but it was not to be, her monthly cycle continued.

CHAPTER 4

In the Cambridgeshire fens news of any kind travelled fast and gossip formed the larger part of any news that might circulate through villages and markets. It wasn't long before tales of Sarah and Jamie's relationship reached the ears of Captain Emery. The thought of a prisoner being involved with a respectable farmers wife filled him with a certain amount of horror. He decided to visit and see how close to the truth this gossip was. The sun had risen high in the sky when Emery mounted his horse and headed for Brooks farm. He did not exactly know how he would handle the situation and what right he had to interfere with the lives of those outside his jurisdiction. As he rode into the farm, he could not see the farmer's wife, he could not remember her name, but he was sure she would be somewhere in the house. He dismounted and called to a woman raising water from the well.

'Is your mistress in the house?' His voice carried across the yard and the woman turned in surprise,

'Yes sir, I believe she is, do you want me to fetch her?' Emery looked at the woman who must have been in her late thirties with a full figure and reddish complexion.

'Tell her Captain Emery wishes to speak to her on a matter of some delicacy, and be quick.' The woman disappeared into the farmhouse and minutes later returned followed by the farmer's widow.

'What brings you this way, I haven't seen you for many weeks is there a problem with the produce I send you?' She could tell by the look on his face that it was something else which intrigued her.

'I am here to ask about the man I left with you, Dower I think his name was, do you still have him on the farm?' Curiosity now filled Sarah's reply,

'Yes, he is still working for me, nothing has changed since we last spoke.'

'Are you sure of what you say, I have heard that he has become more than just a 'worker' have you anything to say about that?'

Sarah did not like being asked about her personal life and she knew what Emery was trying to get from her. The serious look on Emery's face told Sarah that he was in no mood for pleasantries.

'Jamie Dower has proved to be a very dependable and knowledgeable addition to the farm for which I owe you many thanks, but I don't fully understand what you want to know.'

Now Emery became hesitant in how he phrased his words.

'Madam it has come to my notice that this man may have become, err shall we say more of a partner than a worker?' Sarah's face was stern as she spoke,

'Are you trying to pry into my personal life Captain Emery?'

Emery's speech faltered, 'I have responsibility for the men under my authority even though they may have been sent to work away from the excavations. If this man has overstepped the mark, I need to know so that I can take the appropriate action.'

Sarah looked at him with eyes that could fell a lessor man at twenty yards. 'The man you speak of has saved me from injury when my brothers attempted to control my life, for which I will be forever grateful to him. If he has become more than a farm labourer it is a matter for me alone to handle and I would be grateful if you would tell your fellow soldiers and the loud mouths you associate with to mind their own business.' Emery was not expecting Sarah's response to be as fierce as that.

'Madam, I will trust that the matters of your life and that of your farm are not in any way affected by the man in question, however I shall have to inform the Adventurers who finance the drainage project of what has happened here and it will be for them to take whatever action they deem necessary.'

'You can tell whoever you want but what happens on my land is my business no one else's.' Sarah drew breath, she was grateful that Jamie had gone to visit the tenant farmers and would be away until dusk. Captain Emery touched the brim of his hat in acknowledgement of what Sarah had said.

'No doubt I shall return fairly quickly once I have been able to seek advice from those in authority.' He mounted his horse, turning to look back at Sarah, he raised his hand in salute and trotted from the farm. Sarah watched him go, she was still seething with the thought that rumours and gossip had reached as far as Emery. She would speak to Jamie on his return and get their relationship sorted out once and for all.

Jamie was unaware of the rumours regarding his relationship had spread, he had no time for such gossip. His mind was on the livestock and the quality of the crops. The men and women he worked with had years of knowledge and experience but his organisational skills developed to a stage where he could assess a situation and place the workers in the most advantageous place thereby creating an efficient and profitable team of people. Those that worked on the farm became reliant on Jamie and their trust in him grew by the day. On returning to the farmhouse, he was unexpectedly grabbed by Sarah who almost dragged him into the parlour,

'We have a serious problem which only we can sort out.'

Jamie did not know what to think as she pushed him onto a chair and then sat opposite him.

'I have had a visit from Captain Emery who has heard that you are now more than just a worker on the farm. He was trying to find out just what position you held here.'

'Does he have to know everything that happens, I thought he was just concerned with getting the drainage finished on time.' Sarah reached across the table and took Jamie's hand in hers,

'You forget you are still a prisoner of war and have very little standing not only in my community but in the law of the land. You have no rights, you are not able to own land or marry, you are a foreigner an outsider and everyone knows it.'

Jamie was stunned, he had become used to being a part of the community and had forgotten his status was that of a prisoner. 'What do you want me to do?' He asked her with a look of uncertainty on his face.

'I don't know, I have allowed you in my bed I have made love to you and fallen in love with you, what do you expect me to do?' He shook his head,

'I think it would be best if I return to the barn to sleep.' He pulled his hand from hers.

'But I don't want to lose you,' Sarah said,' just because some old women spread malicious gossip around the village.'

'You won't lose me, I shall be here to protect and help you in any way I can but I cannot let you suffer in any way because of my position in life. We can continue as we were, you as the mistress and me as just another worker.'

'You will never be just another worker, you are the man I want to father my children, the man I want to grow old with, my protector and hero. I don't care about rumour or tittle tattle, can you not see that?'

Jamie took her shoulders and brought her face close to his,

'You are the woman who saved me, the woman I worship, I do not want to lose you or alter the feelings we have for each other, what I want to do is to guard you from any future pain whether it be from the local population or from your family I am willing to return to my position as a worker or, if need be, to leave the farm altogether.' Sarah gasped,

'You cannot, I will not let you leave, you will stay even if I have to lock you up, you will not leave me.' Jamie tried to prise her fingers from his arm,

'Please let me go, I will be here but not as a lover, it will be for the best, I cannot see any harm come to you or William, please let me return to my duties.' She let him go and slowly he left her and went to the bedroom to collect any clothes he may have left there. When he returned to the door, she was waiting for him.

'I don't know if I can stand this.' Her eyes were filling with tears. Jamie did not know whether to kiss her or just go but his feelings for Sarah got the better of him and he took her in his arms and kissed her. It was a true lovers embrace, their bodies met and clung together the force of their kiss was almost violent and she could feel her lips split and a small trickle of blood mixed in both mouths. Pulling themselves apart they realised that this was not the end of their relationship just a period of time until they were able to return to what they had between them. Jamie left the room and Sarah watched him go. Her son appeared at the door and could see that his mother had been crying he was only three years old but he ran to his mother clutching her skirt he began to cry. She reached down and picked him up,

'Don't cry William all will be well, I will make it so.'

The days and weeks that followed were difficult when Jamie had to inform Sarah of what was happening on the farm, they made sure that they could be seen by her serving girls or the women from the dairy. Counter rumours started to circulate and things appeared to become acceptable to the many nosey busy bodies in the village. It was in late October when Captain Emery rode up to the farm house. Sarah did not see him arrive and was surprised when one of the girl's brought news of his arrival to the dairy where she was checking the cleanliness of the maids and the state of the milking chamber. She made her way back to the house, the captain stood waiting for her.

'Good day to you Captain, what brings you here, I hope it's not more gossip about my private life?'

The captain actually blushed as he thought of the problems he may have been a party to which affected her life. 'I have to ask if you can be available tomorrow at noon, I have a Clerk of Works who is visiting the excavation in this area and has information regarding the prisoners under my command. Can you make sure that both you and the man you know as Jamie Dower are available to speak to the clerk?'

Sarah was curious, what could a clerk want to speak to her about. 'Is it to do with the supplies that we sell to you?' The captain looked at her,

'I have no idea, we are the first site he has visited in this area, it must be something of importance as he has specifically asked to address those prisoners who have been working on the drainage for over a year and I know that the man Dower has been working either on the excavation or on your farm for over two years in fact he has been here almost three years.'

'I will make sure we are both here at midday tomorrow as you request.'

The following day two riders approached Brooks Farm, the man accompanying Emery was dressed in the dark clerical grey robes of his office, a clean, fresh white collar spread around his neck and shoulders. They dismounted and Emery led the way to the farmhouse door. Sarah opened the door and welcomed the two men. They both slightly bowed their heads in respect, Emery looked directly at Sarah,

 'May I introduce you to Mr Adam Percival, who is here to discuss matters arising from various instructions received from parliament.' Percival removed his hat and swept it in an arc in front of Sarah.

 'Madam I have come to discuss matters with you and the man known as Jamie Dower.' Sarah turned and took Jamie's hand.

 'This is Jamie Dower.' Percival's eyes studied Jamie, he looked at him intently looking from Jamie's face to his feet.

 'May we sit,' he asked 'this may take some time to get through.'

 'Please follow me.' Sarah led the way into the parlour, Jamie brought up the rear. 'Can I get you gentlemen refreshment?' Percival looked at Emery then to Sarah,

 'Perhaps later, I would like to commence our discussion as quickly as possible.'

 'As you wish.' Sarah sat opposite the two men and gestured to Jamie to sit next to her. Percival took his satchel from around his shoulders and placed it on the table. As he opened it, he looked at the three faces watching every move he made. Drawing out a sheath of papers he spread them out so that he could clearly read the text which was in his own hand.

 'I will start with the most important message that has been sent by Parliament, it concerns the person, Jamie Dower. Parliament has decreed that prisoners who have served on the digging of the drains in Cambridgeshire, Lincolnshire, Nottinghamshire and Norfolk are to be given their freedom.'

Sarah and Jamie looked at each other, the look of disbelief spread across their faces, Percival continued.

'Those men, who will no longer be seen as prisoners, shall be given the choice of either returning to their place of birth or remaining at their present location. If they decide to return to their place of birth, they will be given passes to enable them to travel freely. If the men in question should decide to remain where they are they shall be taken onto the parish records as members of the community and will be subject to the bylaws of the said parish. They will need to prove to the parish that they are worthy and law-abiding citizens who will contribute to the needs of the parish.'

Sarah reached for Jamie's hand and gripped it tightly, they faced each other and tears welled up in her eyes, no words were needed. Percival cleared his throat,

'I need a decision from you Mr Dower and then we will complete the necessary letters either to allow you to travel or stay.'

It was Jamie's turn to collect his thoughts and try to put into words what was racing through his mind, releasing Sarah's hand he stood,

'I have no reason to go back to the place of my birth, my only family is that of a brother who no doubt will have made a life for himself. I have no doubt where my loyalties lie and whom I have so much debt to repay and it will take the remainder of my life to do so. If it pleases you Mr Percival if we could proceed with the necessary letters to enable me to stay here, I would be most grateful.' Percival looked at Jamie and smiled this had made his life so much easier, letters had already been drafted and all he needed to do was to select the correct one and sign it.

'What is the parish that your place of residence will fall into?'

He didn't know. Fortunately, Sarah interrupted,

'It is the Parish of St Michaels and All Angels.'

Percival smiled and took out his quill and ink from his satchel. As he spread the letter on the table, he smiled, it would be a quick and easy conclusion to this particular episode as far as he was concerned. Emery watched the changing expressions on the faces of the man and woman opposite him and felt some relief at getting the matter resolved so easily. He did harbour a little regret as he had enjoyed dealing with the farm. Percival finished putting the final touches to the documents he had before him,

'I will need your signature Mr Dower.' He hesitated, he did not know if this man could write and looked at him in hope. Jamie took the quill from Percival, who uttered an inward sigh of relief, he scratched his name where Percival indicated then sat back from the table. Percival continued telling them of how the Parish Council would be informed and that if any problems should occur then Jamie should contact Captain Emery in the first instance who would pass any information to his office. The meeting took a lot less time than it was thought and Sarah asked again if drinks were needed.

'A glass of something cool would be more than welcome.' It was Percival who asked. Sarah rose and went to the kitchen to fetch a pitcher of cider and four beakers. She poured the cider into the beakers and they all raised their drinks and toasted Jamie's new found freedom. Sarah and Jamie watched as the two riders rode off in the direction of their next port of call.

'Well, Mr Dower, it appears that you are now a free man.' Her eyes sparkled and her smile made her beauty bloom. They just held each other, it was relief and pleasure together with a feeling of freedom for Jamie. Sarah looked up at him.

'We need to tell the world and especially my brothers.' Jamie laughed.

'I don't know what to do or think, there is so much I want to say and do, my mind is going to explode.' Sarah let go of his hand and spun around her laughter could be heard across the farmyard. Several of those working nearby stopped and looked at the antics going on in front of the house. Sarah said in a loud voice,

'He is free, we are free, we can do what we want.' Jamie grabbed her around the waist and they danced with joy. Sarah called out to those close by,

'We shall eat and drink. We will celebrate, come and get some food and drink and get everyone to come in from the fields and barns.' Those that heard stopped what they were doing and looked at the pair as if they were mad. Jamie looked around,

'Do as your mistress says, we are going to celebrate so all of you join us.'

Women and men started to run around collecting benches, tables, straw bales and anything else they could find to sit on. It took about an hour before most of the men and women had gathered together in front of the house. Sarah stepped forward and addressed those that had gathered,

'We have been told today that Jamie Dower has gained his freedom. He has been offered the choice of either returning to his place of birth or remaining here, he has decided to remain with us.'

There were hoorays and yells of congratulations. From nowhere a fiddle appeared and the dancing began. It was sometime before the party calmed down, Sarah was pleased just to let those around her enjoy themselves. She picked up her son and together with Jamie they danced with those that had come to know Jamie well.

That night, after William had been sent to bed, Sarah and Jamie fell into each other's arms exhausted from the day's events but not that tired to let it interfere with their love making. The sense of freedom engulfed them as they fell into each other's arms, they didn't care who heard them or gossiped about them they could tell the world it didn't matter. As they lay side by side Sarah's body told her that this time she would carry Jamie's child, it felt right, they had moved together and there had been no tension or hesitation it had been wonderful.

'And now you can marry me Mr Dower, that's if you still want to.' He rolled her onto her back and brushed the hair from her face.

'I shall have to think about taking such a big step.' She pushed him over and sitting astride him said,

'You better had Mr Dower or there will be consequences.'

'Oh yes, and what will they be?'

'There would be no more of what we have just enjoyed for a start.'

'In that case I submit, I will marry you at the first opportunity and you will become my wife and I will always worship the ground you walk upon.

'That is exactly the response I wanted to hear, now I think we had better try to get some sleep the farm will need plenty of work in the morning and you my lover will be very busy.' He kissed her neck, there would be little sleep that night.

There appeared to be a lightness in everyone's mood the following day, smiles could be seen as men and women exchanged greetings. Sarah and Jamie rose together and after seeing William they went about their daily tasks. On his return Sarah told Jamie that they needed to visit the church and ensure that the parish had been informed correctly regarding Jamie's status. It would also be a good time to discuss their future as well. They would visit the church and speak to the Parson and decide on the quickest way to arrange their marriage.

It was late in the afternoon when they reached the chapel, they could see the parson in the doorway,

'Good day to you.' The parson's voice was a little hoarse and he coughed to clear his throat. 'What brings you to church at this time, there is no service until this evening.' It was Sarah who spoke,

'I don't know if you have been informed of the good news regarding Jamie?'

'Yes, I have heard, the Clerk of Works and the Captain were here yesterday and I am very pleased to welcome Jamie as a member of the Parish, what more can I do for you?' It was Jamie who spoke,

'We would like to arrange our marriage.' The parson was a little taken aback he knew that there was a relationship between the two who stood before him but this action was sooner than he expected. He looked from Jamie to Sarah and could see that this had been fermenting for some time.

'We had better go to my house and discuss the situation.' With that he led the way from the chapel to his house which was only a hundred yards away.

Robert Fleming had been in the post of cleric to St Michaels for nearly three years. It had been at the start of his association with the local community that he had heard of the prisoners being used as almost slaves in the digging of the drains. He had tried to gain the confidence not only of the local population but also of the prisoners working on the excavation but found it difficult to break into the close-knit community in the village and at the diggings. His predecessor had died in post and had been well respected by all which made his struggle to become accepted by the parishioners a hard road to travel. It had come to his attention that Sarah may have been living in sin with one of the prisoners. He had approached her after a Sunday service but had trouble in broaching the matter. He did not have the experience to give advice or guidance on this situation, his life had been that of a sheltered child with his formative years being spent in college and university. Entering the church had been a calling and he had faith in God but the matter of gossip and conjecture was something he had not been involved in before. Hopefully that particular problem would now be resolved. He looked at Jamie,

'I know little about you Mr Dower and require details of your place of birth for our records.'

It was at this point that Sarah realised how little she knew of Jamie's family and where he originated from, she looked at him promising herself that she would get him to tell her of his past when they had finished at the church.

'My name is Jamie Dower and I was born in a town in Scotland called Livingston which is about twenty miles from Edinburgh.' The parson tried to imagine just where Edinburgh was and had difficulty as he had never ventured that far north.

'Did you attend church there?'

'Yes, my parents were strict believers and covenanters.' This term was one that Robert Fleming had not heard before.

'What are the covenanters?' 'He asked.

'They are followers of King Charles who signed the Solemn League and Covenant. My Mother and Father were Presbyterians and brought me up to be the same.' The parson swallowed, he was not sure that he fully understood the 'ins and outs' of the way the Scots worshipped.

'As you are a Christian, I see no reason why you cannot be married here. There is the matter of the banns being read so I will need an agreed date for the ceremony.' Sarah leant forward,

'How soon can that be arranged.' She asked.

'The banns should be read over several weeks on consecutive Sundays, however if there is any urgency, I am sure that this can be shortened.' Sarah grasp Jamie's hand then looked at the parson,

'As soon as possible, I want to put a stop to the malicious talk surrounding us so that we can live our lives the way we want.' The parson sat back and looked around the chapel. He was trying to plan in his own mind how soon this could be done. He would call the banns during the next week and if agreement was reached the wedding could take place in ten days' time. He explained his thoughts to the couple in front of him. Sarah and Jamie looked at each other, her eyes were gleaming as she nodded at Jamie, they both turned towards the parson and Sarah said with a quiver of joy in her voice that it would be good, very good if he could proceed.

The couple left the chapel in a state of euphoria, all would be well, they would become man and wife and live without the looks of old men and women questioning their right to be together.

CHAPTER 5

When they returned to the farmhouse it was Sarah who first mentioned how they would inform her relations. It would be difficult particularly as far as her brothers were concerned.

'Could we just marry then tell them?' She asked Jamie.

'I think that may make things even more difficult, perhaps we can get a message to them and get them here to tell them face to face. I appreciate that it may result in a great deal of animosity especially towards me but at least it will get things done with rather than have it hanging over us.' Sarah agreed the last thing she wanted was her brothers storming into their lives again. 'My only fear is that they might try to put a stop to the wedding.' Jamie thought for a while,

'Perhaps we could tell them once the banns have been read.'

'Hmm that may be for the best, yes, I think we should do that.'

The work on the farm carried on, the preparations for the wedding were an addition to the labours of the day. Sarah had completely forgotten about asking Jamie for the story of his life and it was not mentioned as the thought of the marriage filled her mind.

It was after the banns had been read that a message was sent to Sarah's brothers and as expected they arrived the same day. Their horses coming to a halt in a cloud of dust they dismounted and ran to the door. There were no niceties as far as they were concerned. Jacob crashed into the door sending it flying, his actions were that of an enraged bull,

'Sarah! Where are you?' Sarah was waiting for them she sat calmly at the table with Jamie by her side.

'We are in here.' She called

Jacob and Mathew came to a standstill in front of them.

'What is the meaning of this.' He waved a sheet of paper at Sarah.

Sarah kept calm, which annoyed her brother even more.

'Have you not read my note?' She said sarcastically.

'I have read it and we,' he gestured between him and Mathew, think that you have lost your mind.'

As he spoke there was movement in the hall of the house. Four men had heard about the visit of the brothers and knew that there may be violence towards their mistress, they had picked up their tools and made their way to the house. The men had a variety of implements from spades to mattocks. The brothers turned and could see that if it came to blows, they would not have the upper hand. Jacob sat at the table talking in a loud and uncontrollable voice verging on the hysterical.

'Do you realise that you will be giving away your land to this man.' He pointed at Jamie. Sarah had not taken her eyes off of her brother and fixed him with a glare that could wilt the toughest of men.

'You do not know what will happen to my land. If you would care to let us draw breath, we will explain what we have in mind. Do you think you could hold your tongue and let us speak?'

Jacob blustered and could see that his sister had more control over the situation than he or his brother had.

'Well, what have you to say?' He sat staring at Sarah with Mathew standing behind him who looked nervously around at the men in the doorway. Mathew rubbed his head remembering what had happened when they last visited. Sarah took a breath.

'Jamie is now a free man and we have talked at length about the land and what is to happen to it after we are wed.' At this point Jamie, standing behind Sarah's chair, spoke,

'I will not lay claim to one yard of your sister's land. As far as I am concerned it will remain hers until it is passed on to William or any other children we may have. She has a gift for the land and knows how to manage it to its fullest advantage. I would not dream of interfering with how she runs it.' Sarah placed her hand on his and told the brothers that future decisions regarding anything to do with the farm would be jointly made that included the provision of supplies to the diggers and the selling of their produce at market or to any other customers. Our contracts will be maintained and our labourers will be treated as they have always been. This speech by Sarah caused Jacob to quieten down. His face was still flushed with his initial anger but he thought a little before responding.

'This is totally against the law of the land and custom. How will you ensure that your wishes are followed?' Jacob had no idea of what sort of reply he would receive. Sarah looked at Jamie and then said,

'We intend to have an agreement drawn up by a member of the legal profession in Ely and together with our wills we hope to cover all aspects of how the farm will be run and who inherits what.'

Their conversation went on for another hour with the brothers bringing up questions that were mundane and irrelevant. Jacob was trying to appear knowledgeable but not succeeding while Mathew remained silent. They reached a point where there seemed to be nothing more to say. Jacob's final contribution was to make Sarah agree that she would show him any agreement drawn up between her and Jamie together with sight of their wills. Sarah thought that this was something that she could agree to but made it quite clear to her brothers, especially Jacob, that once the agreement had been drawn up and signed neither she nor Jamie would change it. Jacob nodded and then sat back in his chair. He did not think he had achieved what he had set out to do which was to stop the marriage of his sister, but he thought that it may be the best outcome for all. This change of heart by Jacob surprised not only his sister and brother but also himself, maybe he was getting old and lacked the fight that he once had. Shaking his head Jacob stood and reluctantly shook Jamie's outstretched hand followed by Mathew, Sarah got up from her chair and walked around the table, her eyes linked with Jacob's and he reached down and kissed her hand and then her cheek. Perhaps, she thought that they may now be a family again however, this was just the start, many bridges would have to be crossed before that could be achieved. Sarah then asked the question which she thought would be the hardest for her brothers to answer,

'Will you come to the wedding?'

Jacob felt drained after their conversation, he looked at Mathew who nodded his head,

'If all is well at my house I shall attend.' Mathew looked at his sister.

'I shall be there.' Sarah then asked which one of them would give her away, perhaps this would be too much but to her surprise Jacob said that as the eldest it would be his duty to perform that role. Sarah was almost speechless, she managed to thank him and said she would send details. The gathering then broke up, the brothers mounting their horses and disappearing into the distance, Sarah and Jamie watched them go. They looked at each other and smiled the outcome could not have been better, with luck the animosity between Sarah and her brothers would now cool to a level that had not been felt for many months.

The days passed quickly the banns were read and arrangements made. Sarah selected a dress from the few that she possessed, there was no time for a new one to be created. With the help of women from the village she managed to put something together which they all thought would show her beauty and form. Jamie would wear new breaches and shirt, it was something that Sarah insisted upon and together with a new hat he would be a picture of a successful farmer.

Any wedding in the area was looked upon as a major event even though those in Westminster had put pay to almost all festivities, they could not stop a wedding celebration. Families would congregate at the chapel and be itching to get to the wedding feast. Jamie had a little difficulty nominating his groomsman however, he had dealt with the farrier in the village on many occasions and they had struck up a friendship. Jamie had approached the farrier, John Barclay, and asked if he would act for him, to which he eagerly agreed.

The day arrived, flowers seemed to appear in every possible corner of the farm. They had been collected by the children and unmarried girls of the village. The blooms ranged from Pennyroyal to Soapwort. Interlaced were herbs of every variety grown in the gardens of the villagers. The air was filled with the scent of celebration and as the community came together there was chatter and laughter which grew to such an extent that the parson had to hush the congregation as they waited for the bride.

Everything went well, vows were taken and a ring was placed on Sarah's finger. As bride and groom left the church wheat was thrown over them to wish them fertility. Family and friends made their way back to the house in a procession led by Sarah and Jamie, the feast awaited them. The day was without doubt a success, yes, there were scuffles and arguments which were expected on such occasions. Sarah and Jamie took Williams hands and lifted him in the air, his squeal of delight was something that filled both their hearts. Sarah had her garters fairly well secured but Jamie managed to remove them and throw them at the waiting Batchelors, who stretched out to catch them. Couples ate their fill and then danced to the drum and fiddle.

Ale, cider and some wine added to the totally relaxed mood of the feast. It was the custom to follow the newlyweds to their bed chamber but on this occasion the guests thought it would be acceptable to give the couple the privacy that they deserved.

Sarah had put her son to bed and then returned to her husband's side. Together they watched the antics of the young and not so young. Sarah had been concerned that her brothers would make a scene but to her amazement they were restrained, she thought that that must be due to their wives being present although that had not stopped them adopting a rowdy behaviour in the past. As the light faded tiredness fell over those that remained. Some had asked if they could sleep in the barn, which Sarah had agreed to, but most made their way to their homes knowing that the following day would demand their energy. Tired, Sarah and Jamie made their way to their bed, the day had been good, friends and families had been together and many a rift had been mended. Their wedding night was one of contented love making. They both knew that their lives would be forever entwined. They lay side by side looking up at the ceiling Sarah thought how blessed she was to have a strong man to protect her. She then turned to Jamie,

'I may be your wife but I still know nothing about you Jamie Dower. You will tell me the tale of your life so that I can pass it on to your son or daughter when he or she is born.' Jamie had been thinking of the things that had happened that day and was startled when he heard Sarah's words,

'What do you mean, I am a simple man can you speak more clearly?'

'Yes, you fool, I am trying to tell you that a child is already forming inside of me and in nine months we shall have a new member of our family, God willing.' Jamie turned to her and drew her close to him.

'I promise I will tell you of every moment of my life and you will be able to tell all our children of their family and where it began.'

The day after the wedding was much the same as any that had gone before. Life in the Cambridgeshire fens took hard work and determination. Sarah had relied on Jamie to seek out improvements to the way they farmed and he had made changes in how they cultivated crops and feed livestock. Although they did not consider themselves wealthy, they were better off than most. Jamie returned to the house as usual to discuss matters with Sarah. Once they had completed their plans for the day Sarah took Jamie's hand and led him to their most comfortable chair and sat him down,

'Now Mr Dower, you will tell me of where you come from and how you managed to worm your way into my life.' Jamie remembered his promise. He did not relish the thought of going over the trials and tribulations of his life before meeting Sarah but a promise was a promise.

'I will tell all, but it is a long and sometimes harrowing tale. It may take some time so you may have to listen over many days before I finish.'

'I am quite prepared to sit here until you have finished, we may have to return each night but if that is what it takes, so be it.' Jamie drew a breath and began his story.

CHAPTER 6

It was in the year 1650 when I left my home at the age of eighteen. I was born in a village in Scotland by the name of Livingston, about twenty miles from Edinburgh. It is a small place surrounded by farms. It has a tower, built many moons ago, called the Livingston Peel which I do not think will last much longer, when I last saw it its walls were not in a good condition. The lords of the manor changed from one family to another. It was under the control of the Murray family and then it passed to the Cunninghams. The village had several houses a mill and a church. My family existed on what it could grow and God willing it would have enough to get them through the winter. I lived with my mother, father and two brothers, Mark, the eldest, then me and finally John the youngest. There had been troubles in the land mainly to do with religion and who ruled the kingdom.

    The time was one of turmoil the kirk had rejected the adoption of the Book of Common Prayer believing that it went against the teachings of the Presbyterian ministers. My family were regulars at the kirk and believed deeply in the ministers preaching and agreed that what was being forced upon them was too close to Rome and its church. Those that rebelled created the National Covenant which supported Presbyterianism and the Covenant was signed by many. The troubles grew stronger when the English killed the King. The Covenanters were against what had happened in London and supported the Kings son, Charles II. The tide then turned and Cromwell's parliament agreed with the Covenant and that Presbyterianism would be adopted throughout the country however, the Royalists in Scotland thought the Covenanters too extreme and sided with Charles. This confusion settled into a war between brothers.

      In the summer of 1650, a call to arms reached Livingston beckoning all men of the kirk to wipe the English king killers from their country. The English Parliament reacted to the Scottish call to arms and an army of some 16,000 was gathered and marched to the borders. Jamie together with his father, brother and cousin, Alex, answered the call and joined the men under the command of General Leslie. They fell in line with almost nine thousand others as they marched alongside three thousand horsemen. Jamie together with his father and brother felt elated to see so many men and guns. Jamie had never seen such things before as they looked at the column of fighting men, they felt they could not and would not be beaten but Jamie had no idea of the force that had been brought to Scotland by Oliver Cromwell. Jamie was given a Pike which he was not used to. His father had been in battle before and tried his best to instruct his son how to use the sixteen-foot-long weapon. A rumour spread through the ranks of the Scots that General Leslie would have an army of thirty-six thousand men to face the English. They thought they had already been victorious without even seeing the enemy.

      As they marched, they sang psalms that boosted their morale. The kirk did have a say in how the army was formed, to the amazement of many of the Scottish military leaders, the kirk carried out a purge of all those willing to fight. Any man considered to be sinful or undesirable was turned away leaving inexperienced officers and poorly trained men. Jamie and his father could not see the reason for sending the men away but kept their spirits up by praying and singing hymns. It was when they reached a point not far from Edinburgh that Jamie was set to work digging large trenches and while he was employed with the shovel, he could see others destroying anything that Cromwell's army could use.

Several times the English army attacked and in late July they managed to capture Arthur's Seat and then turned their guns onto Leith. Jamie had seen the results of these engagements and the reality of battle hit home. Men had been killed and injured, those that had serious wounds would not last long and others would die a lingering death as gangrene entered their bodies. The men around Jamie had their moral boosted when Charles II visited them but the Covenanter government again felt that the men fighting their Godly War would be corrupted by personal loyalty to the king. They asked Charles to leave and then had a second purge of the army reducing their numbers even further. The word spread through the lines of men that the enemy had suffered badly from disease and sickness, some said that they would go back across the border until they were strong enough to face their foes.

Jamie and his father felt a sense of victory when they heard that the English had left the area. Jamie asked his father if they had won, had they defeated the English?

'No, my son, I don't think that the English would go so easily.'

They watched as their cavalry left to harass the English and as Jamie and the rest of the infantry followed, they could see the results of the English fleeing. Equipment and goods were left by the road side and this gave Jamie more hope that the English had been beaten.

Jamie looked around, he could see men with their arms raised giving thanks to the Lord for victory. He put his arm around his cousin's shoulders and cried,

'Thank the Lord.' It was the appearance of a preacher that brought them back to earth. His father looked at his sons and told them not to be so hasty, this had only been a skirmish perhaps the real fight was yet to come. How right he was. They followed the English towards the east finally making camp on Doon Hill. Everything felt as if the battle had been won, Jamie watched as his fellow warriors moved forward trying to confront the English. The night was one in which the Scots slept well and the morning would prove to end the plans of Cromwell.

The day started well, however the Scots seemed to be in some disarray. Jamie had spoken to many others and had been surprised to find that they were not very experienced in warfare nor it appeared were those in command. It was as they opened their eyes that the Scots had an almighty shock. The noise of the English brought the Scots from their sleep and into line, they managed to fight off the enemy but the battle soon moved in favour of the English. The Scottish men of horse were routed and as the foot soldiers saw them disappear, lost heart. Foot soldiers fought bravely but their comrades fell beside them. Jamie had been close to his father, brother and cousin, he could see horsemen getting closer and tried to turn but his pike restricted not only his movement but also of those around him.

The men started to drop their pikes and try to fend off their attackers. Jamie saw his father and brother in the heart of the fight and when they fell, he let out a scream of anguish. As he watched his father collapse to his knees Jamie was struck by a mounted trooper who's sword came down and hit him on the side of the head. The troopers horse then crashed into Jamie sending him flying. He was thrown into the air and landed his head hitting the ground with a mighty thump, then darkness followed.

CHAPTER 7

It was his cousin Alec who came into view as Jamie's eyes slowly opened,

'What has happened? Where is my father?' Alec cradled Jamie's head in his arms,

'They are gone, I am sorry, they are no more.' Jamie struggled to right himself and with effort the two young men got to their feet. Alec had bruises but was not badly marked however, Jamie had blood running down the side of his face. Alec ripped a piece of cloth from his jacket and wiped his cousin's face. They looked around the battle field, it had only been that morning that they marched with confidence towards the English and now after three hours of fighting they stood defeated. Men were wandering around not knowing what to do, they were without leaders and they were mentally lost and physically broken.

'Where is my father, I need to see him.' Jamie's voice croaked and he spat out phlegm that rose in his throat. Alec pointed to several corpses that lay about twenty yards away. They walked towards the bodies, Jamie could see his father, he raised his hands to his face and wept. Alec gently led him forward, Jamie looked again and saw that his father and brother still had their eyes open, they were staring at the sky looking for their god. Kneeling Jamie reached towards his father's face and drew his eyelids closed, bending he kissed his father's forehead and then did the same to his brother. They pulled the bodies away from the others that had fallen with them and laid them out, crossing their arms and straightening their legs.

'What do we do now?' Jamie asked Alec who watched as the men standing were gathered together by some parliamentary soldiers.

'Follow them I suppose.' Alec called to one of the others who looked lost. 'What are you doing, where are you going?' The answer he got was one of dejection.

'Just do as they say.' The man pointed to the English soldiers watching the men gathering weapons into heaps.

A soldier in the red coat of the Cromwellian army walked towards them'

'You two, are you wounded? If you are you are to make your way off the field and seek help.'

Alec looked at Jamie and could see his head was still bleeding.

'Jamie leave the field, get help and make your way home.'

The response from Jamie surprised him.

'No, I'm part of this body of men and I shall stay with my brothers.' It would prove to be one of the worst decisions Jamie made.

'In that case move over there.' He pointed in the direction of a group of men milling around aimlessly. As they moved Alec said to Jamie that they must stick together as he had no idea what the future held for them.

That night the many hundreds of men captured at the battle tried to sleep the best they could. There were bivouacs that they had used the night before which they were able to get hold of, the night was not cold but the shock of battle and the hard ground did not make for a good night.

The sun rose over a battlefield littered with the remnants of those who had fought and died. The survivors were herded into line and told that they would be taken from the area but they were not told to where. They marched, they had not eaten since before the battle and some had been told not to eat even then as it was thought that a hungry soldier fought better than a full one. As they left the area Alec stooped and picked something from the ground. He slipped it beneath his jacket and looked at Jamie and nodded. Jamie looked around at the items that had been strewn about after the battle, he saw a small box and bent down to pick it up. Fortunately, nobody was watching him, it transpired that someone had dropped a tinder box which could be a life saver in the days to come so he did the same as Alec and hid it in his jacket.

The march of thousands of men started, the ragged line moved slowly with troopers watching from horseback and foot soldiers keeping the line moving.

'How many men do you think there are?' Jamie asked Alec,

'It looks like hundreds maybe more, it could be thousands.'

'My god it's the whole army, how did we lose?' Jamie shook his head.

They kept on putting one foot in front of the other some men were limping and were told to leave the column and two men tried to escape and were ridden down by troopers and despatched with the sword. The officer in charge of the column rode up and down giving his men orders that any prisoner attempting to escape was to be shot and no mercy shown. He made sure that the prisoners were in no doubt that if they were to step out of line that they would face death.

The column of bedraggled men marched towards Berwick, no food and only what they had been captured in to keep the rain off, they were not in the best of health. Alec and Jamie agreed that if they were to stay alive, they would have to risk all. The thought of escape was in their minds, Jamie could see that the soldiers guarding them were not a happy band and there were several occasions when they did not give full attention to their role. It was Jamie who said that they should make a dash for freedom that night when their guards were eating. The moment came, Jamie grabbed Alec's arm and they crawled on their bellies towards the edge of the area that the guards had left unattended. The ground was littered with sharp stones which made their progress slow. They had not gone more than thirty yards when there was commotion from where the prisoners were sitting. The guards took up their weapons and started to approach the spot where Jamie and Alec lay, the two men scrambled back towards the column and just made it before the guards reached them.

'We must not give up.' Alec's voice came from a breath seeking body, they were both exhausted. 'We must try again, I don't want to die like a captured animal.'

'But when and how.' Jamie asked.

'We must pick our time and place more carefully.'

They turned their backs against the cold night air and tried to get some sleep. The column reached Newcastle and the two men had not yet come across a good place to make their next attempt at escape. They left Newcastle guarded by foot soldiers and a Troop of Horse. They searched every pause, every stop, every minute of the day for an opportunity to get away from the column. Jamie overheard the soldiers discussing their progress and one said that they were approaching a place call Morpeth. There had been little cover to help them escape as they wearily covered mile after mile but the sun rose in all its glory the following morning. Its blaze of light almost blinded anyone looking into it. Alec could see that the soldiers were shielding their eyes from the suns glare as were the troopers. He pulled on Jamie's sleeve,

'They cannot see us very well, now is our time.' Jamie looked around, he had difficulty in making out soldiers or troopers. Together they dropped to the ground and started to crawl into the grass at the edge of the track that they had been marching on. It was about thirty yards before they reached a small coppice that afforded them some cover. They lay still until they were sure that they had not been seen leaving the line. As the prisoners started to move Jamie and Alec, still on their bellies began to crawl until they were sure they could not be seen by their guards.

The soldiers were looking amongst the prisoners for those that were ill and those that had died. The prisoners had not eaten for five days and some of those a little longer. Men began to suffer from hunger and sickness, their guards did nothing to help as far as they were concerned their job was to get the prisoners as far away from Scotland as possible their condition was of no importance.

The two men raised themselves and started to carefully make their way as far from the route that the prisoners were taking as possible. They moved as silently as possible until they felt safe enough to stand then they ran making as little noise as they could. They carried on through the day and into the night, it was Jamie who staggered to a halt, he had little strength left in his body. Alec turned and took his arm,

'Come on Jamie boy, we can't stop just yet.'

'I'm sorry Alec but my legs won't carry me any further.'

Alec let go of Jamie's arm and they both lay on the damp leaf covered surface of the woodland floor. It was Alec who seemed the most able of the two,

'We need water and food, so the sooner we get to a place where we can eat and drink the better.'

'Can we not rest a wee while here, I have pains in my stomach that are ripping me apart.' Alec looked at his friend and could see he was done in.

'Alright Jamie we will rest, but not for long, we have to find food and water as quickly as possible or we will not get any further.'

As they rested Alec asked Jamie what he thought the outcome of the battle had been.

'It was a defeat for us, the English made us look fools, they had less men and we had god on our side, or so we were told.'

'Do you not think god was with us?'

'If he had been we would not be in the terrible state that we find ourselves in.'

Alec coughed and spat into the bushes.

'We need food Jamie and quickly, there must be something we can eat.'

Jamie slowly got to his feet and made his way to the bushes close by, he reached out and pulled some berries from the branches. He tasted the dark blue fruit, they had some sweetness, he remembered the taste from his childhood pulling some branches towards him he gathered a handful. He put some into his mouth then offered Alec some. Alec greedily grabbed at the fruit.

'It may not do your stomach much good, but anything at the moment is better than nothing.'

They both then started to search around for any other fruits or nuts. Surprisingly they were able to gather a good number and sat eagerly eating what they had picked. Some hazelnuts, wild berries some wild plums and a few early brambles. It was a good feast but did not fill them, they needed something more substantial and to that end they made a move towards the edge of the tree line and looked across the open fields.

Checking the position of the sun they moved northwards, the countryside opened out before them. The heather stretched across the land with outcrops of rocks breaking the surface. They walked on. Both men could feel the pangs of hunger ripping through their stomachs, they both searched the landscape for any signs of life that they could eat. Sometimes God does look kindly on some of his subjects. It was Alec who noticed something, he pulled on Jamie's sleeve and they both stood motionless. Alec slowly raised his arm and pointed to something in a clearing. At first Jamie could not see anything but as his eyes focussed, he could see a stoat dragging an enormous rabbit. The small killer was having difficulty with its prey. Alec looked around and picked up a large rock and started to run towards the struggling stoat. As he drew close the killer looked at him but did not loosen its grip on its kill. Alec brought the stone down on the stoat's head and it smashed like an egg. The stoats jaw still clung to the rabbit and it took a lot to prise it open. Alec drew out the knife he had managed to hide from his captors and started to remove the rabbit's skin. Jamie had watched the action with a sense of triumph. He took from his pocket the tinder box he had smuggled passed the guards, it was still all there. Clearing a spot, he made space for a bed of rocks then looking around he could see nothing immediately to light a fire with, he ran back to the tree line and started to gather dry kindling.

By the time Jamie returned Alec had removed the rabbit's skin and was in the process of gutting the creature. He looked up at Jamie,

'We shall feast today.' He said as the joints of the rabbit were taken apart.

'I can taste it already.' Jamie's mouth was watering at the thought of something to eat. He gathered a handful of dry grass and placed the kindling on top of it. The tinderbox did its trick and a small flame took hold of the grass. Jamie gently blew and the flame grew in size. Alec looked at the blood on his hands and wiped them on the grass then went to the tree line and picked up a few larger dry branches and carried them back to where Jamie was still encouraging the fire to take. Soon they had a fire that would give them their first hot meal in more than six days. Both men looked from the rabbit to each other,

'We have to wait until its cooked.' He saw Alec licking some of the remaining blood from his fingers.

'As long as it cooks quickly.'

Pieces of rabbit were rammed on sticks other pieces were just thrown onto the fire, they couldn't wait. As every moment passed their hunger grew, it reached a stage where they could wait no longer and both men grabbed a piece of the rabbit and started to swallow what they could. Chewing did not matter they just wanted food in their bellies.

The flesh that had been tossed in the fire was blackened but tasted all the better. It seemed to take no time at all until bones were all that was left. Alec stretched back,

'I will never kill another stoat.' He looked at the sky which was clear with wisps of cloud, the day was warm and he had eaten his first meal for some time. 'Do you know where we are?' He asked Jamie.

'I know that we have been heading north but other than that I have no idea.'

'I suppose we had better get on our way, you never know how far away the English are.' Jamie got to his feet,

'You are right, we must move and move quickly if we want to remain free. I am not going back to be treated like an animal by the English whatever happens.' He looked around and then at the suns position he pointed in the direction of some higher ground,

'I think we should head for that hill and then try to find somewhere dry to shelter for the night.'

As they walked, they were alert to anything that might provide their next meal. Alec did see some deer in the far distance but that was just wishful thinking. Before they reached raised ground, they came across a stream which was running clear. The water was cold and refreshing and they drank their fill.

When they reached the top of the high ground they could see for several miles. Jamie saw some smoke in the distance and when he looked closer, he could make out houses, not many just two or three, it was life but was it friendly? Alec spoke first,

'I think we should try to see who lives in those houses and whether there is any food that we can take.'

'Maybe they are farmers of sheep, you couldn't grow many crops on this land.' Alec agreed and they began the decent of the hill towards the houses.

They approached the buildings and both lay on their stomachs and studied the small cluster of stone-built cottages. There was life, they saw two women laying washing on the bushes that ran along the edge of the properties. They listened and what they heard did not please them. The voices were of the English.

'We cannot take the risk even though they probably haven't seen soldiers for many days.' Alec's caution was echoed by Jamie.

Alec led the way around the small hamlet and as they reached the far side, they stood trying to decide on the right direction to take. There was a small river passing close by and that seemed a good enough path to follow. Making sure they were not seen they walked quickly along the river bank. The ground was firm and they made good time. Food was still uppermost in their minds. Jamie stared into the fast-flowing stream he could see no signs of life in the water, no fish to catch not even a frog to eat. On the opposite bank the land rose into rocky granite walls which they would have to climb at some point.

'We need to find something to eat.' It was Jamie stating the obvious. Alec searched the horizon for any signs of life but there was none.

'Let's see if there is anything over there.' He pointed to the wall of grey that loomed up on the opposite bank. 'If we are going to get to the top, we need to do it in daylight so now is a good a time as any.' Alec started to cross the stream with Jamie in his wake. The water was cold and Jamie felt it seeping through his threadbare stockings. They took a risk and started to climb, if they were seen it would not be long before the villagers would raise the alarm. They heard nothing and as they climbed their strength began to leave them. Alec lost his grip and fell back taking Jamie with him. Fortunately, they only dropped a few feet before they regained their hold on the rockface. After what seemed to be an age, they reached the top only to discover it was a false ridge the summit was still above them.

'We must carry on.' Jamie's voice was not full of confidence as he reached out for his next hand hold. Alec followed, then the going became a little easier and progress was made. Hauling themselves over the top of the grey, sharp stone they could see what was before them. The moors stretched out in a never-ending carpet of green, purple, orange and grey, there was nothing, no houses, no rivers, no trees just moor, never ending moors. Jamie lay on his back breathing heavily,

'Where to now, do we know which way is north or do we wait until sunrise?'

Alec was standing looking at the scene before them.

'I think it may be best to wait for the sun. We need to find shelter.' He pointed to the sky, dark clouds had appeared and they both were fully aware of what that meant, rain and by the look of the clouds a great deal of it. Jamie got to his feet, he could see some sort of stone formation not too far in the distance.

'Perhaps that may give us some shelter.' He said indicating to Alec the stones about a mile away. The two men started to walk, their legs were tired and their feet sore but they knew they had to get to shelter of some kind. As they drew closer to the stones they couldn't work out if they were made by man or nature. One huge slab of stone was supported by three others, the fourth side was a rise in the ground. The rain started as they crawled into the stone shelter, it was dry but they could feel the cold as the rain started, it came in torrents running down the slope of the hill carrying with it earth, plants and debris. At least they were dry. The rain continued through the night. Cold seeped into their bones, they had nothing to eat and it looked as if they would not have anything for some time.

'Will this pass by morning.' Alec asked Jamie.

'I don't know, it may be with us for days, so rest while we can.'

As dawn approached the rain eased, the moors were encased in a mist that hid everything. Then a weak sun appeared, Jamie stood in the open and watched where it rose. Looking to his right he tried to identify a point that they could head towards, he could just make out a rise in the ground,

'We should head that way and hope the lord is with us.'

'I hope he is and he is kind enough to lead us to something to eat.'

They made their way carefully across the heather strewn moor being alert to any sharp pieces of stone that could damage their feet even more. With care they ventured forward as they reached the top of the hillock that they were aiming for they could see, in the small valley below quite a large river running through the moor. There were no signs of life to be seen so they cautiously made their way down the slope. Reaching the bank of the river they looked in the rippling water.

'Look,' It was Alec, his voice full of excitement.

'What can you see?'

'Fish, lots of fish.' Jamie looked into the water where Alec was pointing. He could make out several large fish their scales glistening in the pale sunlight. The two men looked at each other and had to restrain themselves from jumping in the water, the thought of fish to eat was almost too much to bear. There were salmon, many salmon struggling to make their way up stream and although the locals would have taken many there were still enough for Alec and Jamie to catch and feast on. They spotted a place where the water was shallow and the fish had difficulty in crossing. Making their way into the river they tried not to disturbed the fish too much. It was Jamie who had success first, he lifted his catch triumphantly before bringing it to the ground then with a large rock smashing its head. He sat on the bank admiring his work. Looking up he saw that Alec was not to be outdone, he lifted a giant of a fish and called out in victory. There was nobody in sight as they made their way from the river with their bounty.

As the fish skin start to curl in the heat Alec's mouth filled with saliva,

'Will it be soon?' He asked eagerly.

'A little longer.' Jamie turned the large salmon over, the smell was intoxicating. He lifted the fish away from the fire they pulled the skin away from the pink flesh. Although it was hot, they didn't care, it was food and they needed it badly. It didn't take long before all that was left was bones. Jamie sat and stretched his feet out in front of him, the sky had cleared and he could see the sun.

'I think that the river may provide for us as long as we are not seen.' Alec stood and looked across the open moor to one side and the river on the other.

'There is more than fish by the river. Look.' He said as his arm swept in an arc. Jamie got to his feet and followed Alec's hand. He could see birds feeding on the grass not far from the river.

'That could be our next meal.'

'If we can catch one.' Alec's answer was not filled with confidence.

'I am sure that we could catch at least one, there must be hundreds down there.'

'But can we get close enough without being seen?'

'We have survived so far and I am sure that we can remain in the shadows for a little longer.'

'Perhaps if we rest until nightfall then make our way in that direction.' Jamie was looking across the river to the next hill.

'How long have we been walking?' Alec was rubbing his legs, 'It seems as if we have never stopped and God knows how many more miles we have to walk until we feel safe.'

'I think it must be seven days so far, as to how many miles we may have travelled, I don't know but we must be getting closer to the border by now.'

They both sat looking at the scene in front of them.

'What would you be doing if you were at home?' Jamie thought for a moment.

'I would be working with the cattle or maybe the sheep. I have a good dog who I could not do without. I could be helping my father …… as he spoke the realisation of what had happened at Dunbar filled his mind and he stopped. Falling silent they both sat in contemplation of the losses that had been suffered in the battle. Alec drew a breath,

'We could have stayed with the column and I hate to think of what would have become of us if we had.' Jamie nodded in agreement.

'I wonder what has happened to the men who were being marched south, no doubt we will find out in the days to come.'

They rested until dusk and then got up and made their way down the hillside and across the river. Alec carried the second fish and clutched it as if it were gold. The river was shallow and they were able to cross without too much bother. On the far bank they scanned the land and could not see any sign of habitation so they started to walk. Their feet had become hardened as their boots began to wear, so far luckily, they had no major problems. As dusk turned into night, they found another rock formation to shelter against. They did not feel as well protected from the elements as they had the previous night. Their sleep was fitful and cold.

The rains did not return the following morning and Jamie was able to clearly see the sun rise. He looked to the north and decided on a hillock with a coppice on its highest point. It was easy to see and they should be able to follow a path to the tree line. Hopefully they would be able to rest there.

It was further than they had anticipated, the good thing was that the rains held off and they were able to keep dry. As they entered the small wood they collapsed on the ground, food was constantly on their minds,

'Shall we have the fish?' Jamie looked at Alec.

'We have nothing else, only berries and nuts.'

Jamie gathered wood and started to make a fire while Alec gutted the salmon. It was another successful meal but what they would eat the following day was in question.

'We must keep on and try to get back across the border, to our own people.'

'How long our journey will be I don't know but I am sure we will make it home.'

The following two days were the most difficult they had experienced so far. They came upon a village and tried as best they could to distinguish whether the people were Scots or English. The accents were unfamiliar so they decided not to stop. They carried on and with only water from a stream to keep them going they walked in a dream. When they reached the next village, which was a little larger, they had no option but to risk all for food. A Kirk stood away from other buildings, they could not see signs of life so they quickly and quietly made their way to the door of the Kirk. Just as they were about to enter a voice seemed to come from nowhere,

'You men, what do you think you're doing?' It was a voice that was used to being obeyed, turning they saw a figure in black approaching. They had no idea where they were or who the figure was but they had come to the end of their tether. It was Alec who spoke,

'We are men from Dunbar, we fought for the kirk and king and are now trying to get home.' Jamie sank to his knees,

'If you want to hand us over to the English then we will not resist.'

The preacher looked at the two figures, they were more like scarecrows than men, their beards covered most of their face and where there was no beard their skin was covered in grime.

'Come with me.' He led the way into the Kirk. Alec and Jamie could hardly stand but managed to follow the tall figure into the Kirk.

CHAPTER 8

In the Kirk the air was cool and clean. There were fresh flowers which was not usual as it might be considered too decadent for a good Presbyterian place of worship. The minister pointed to a row of chairs indicating that they should sit. Both men almost collapsed in front of their host who stood looking them up and down,

'I am John Fraser, the Minister of Southdean and you are not a pretty sight, tell me how you have reached this sorry state?' It was Alec who started to speak,

'We are from a small town near Edinburgh it is called Livingston. We left there many weeks ago.' He turned to Jamie who took up their tale,

'We were at Dunbar when our army of Covenanters was routed by Cromwell. It should not have been so, we had more men, brave men who fought well.' Alec said,

'Aye, they fought well but were not led well.' The minister's eyes widened,

'So, you fought and the battle was lost, what happened then?'

Alec stretched his arms and took a breath.

'There were hundreds, if not thousands of men taken prisoner and we were in that number. We escaped the column and fled trying to make our way home.'

'How long have you been travelling?' Jamie looked at the Minister.

'We have been walking for about ten days, trying to avoid being re-captured by the English.'

They then told the Minister the full story and when they had finished the Minister looked impressed.

'I think what you need is a good meal and a wash, you stink to high heaven, follow me.' He stood and led them to the door of the chapel. I have a small house where you can eat and wash then we must see what is to be done with you.' They followed gratefully behind Reverend Fraser as he headed towards his house. It may have been small in the Reverends eyes but it seemed palatial to Jamie and Alec. The main room of the house was furnished with a table and chairs. A cooking range was against one wall surrounded by various pots pans and cooking utensils. On the top of the range was a large vessel and the smell of simmering pottage filled the room,

'I have a woman from the village who cooks not only for me but for some of those who do work around the chapel and various places in the village.' He took two bowls from a shelf and ladled the thick soup into each of them. Alec and Jamie attacked the food without drawing breath. The Minister reached for some bread and passed it to them. It went faster than he could watch them. A woman appeared at the door and looking at the two vagrants let out a scream of fear. The Minister calmed her down and explained that they were his guests and should be treated as such.

'This is Mrs Bell, I would advise you to heed what she says and do her bidding if you want to get any more to eat and drink.'

Mrs Bell was a woman of small stature however the way she moved and spoke gave the impression that she stood no nonsense. Her full skirt nearly reached the ground, it was of a heavy material that did not make for easy living but would last a lifetime. The bodice was of good wool and topped with a collar of white linen. Her hair was contained in a white bonnet and only a little of her grey locks could be seen, she was definitely a woman not to be questioned.

When they had finished eating the Minister showed them the way to the well. They drew buckets of water then threw it at each other. They were feeling relaxed in their soaking clothes.

'Wait here.' It was a command not a request. 'I will see if I can get some dry clothes for you, I shan't be long. While I'm searching for clothes see if you can do something with your beards and hair.' He left the two men looking and laughing at each other. Alec went back into the house and saw the woman preparing additional food.

'Do you have a sharp knife or even a razor that we could use to cut some of this hair.' He grabbed his hair and pulled it away from his head.

'I will see what I can find.' She disappeared and returned shortly holding a pair of sheep shears. 'You can use these and make sure you wash them after you're done.' Alec took the shears, they were sharp and hopefully would do the trick. He thanked the woman and headed out of the house.

'Look what I have.' He held the shears above his head. 'Now who will be first you or me to have their fleece trimmed?' Jamie was not all that confident about Alec's skill as a barber so he told Alec that as he had some experience in shearing sheep, he would tackle Alec's crown first.

Alec sat on a tree stump and waited for Jamie to begin cutting his hair. Jamie looked at Alec and frowned,

'What am I supposed to do with this stack of twigs?'

'Just get on with it.' Alec turned his back to Jamie who started to cut Alec's dark greasy locks. The hair fell onto the ground and Alec's shoulders,

'Leave me some hair, I need something to keep my head warm.'

'You can always wear a bonnet.' Jamie laughed, he had tried to keep the lines that he cut as straight as he could but the final result did look a little ragged, however, it was a vast improvement.

'Now it's my turn.' Alec swapped places and eagerly got hold of the shears. Hmmm let me see what a mess I can make of these golden locks.' He lifted Jamie's hair which was still in clumps and started to cut. As he began Mrs Bell came out from the house,

'What are you doing.' She said in a concerned voice which did not fill Jamie with confidence.

'I'm cutting his hair.' She grabbed the shears from Alec and pushed him out of the way.

'You have no idea, have you, go and make yourself useful and put some water on the stove and when its boiled stick your head in it to try to remove some of the dirt that's making you look like the devil.'

When John Fraser returned to the Kirk, he was surprised to see the two men with haircut and their faces washed.

'I see Mrs Bell has taken control of you and you look much better for it.' He threw an assortment of clothes in front of them. 'Take your pick, there are various items which may fit you but it will suffice until you have completed your journey.'

Jamie and Alec started to sort through the various pieces of clothing holding them up to see if they would fit. As they rummaged through the clothing the Reverend explained what sort of country they had landed themselves in.

'You are lucky, there is a strong royalist element in these parts. The nearest large town is Jedburgh where any follower of the king would be welcome. I would stress that it is not the same everywhere so you must be on your guard at all times.' John Fraser met their eyes with a steely fix and they could see he was not making any idle threat. 'How far do you think you will have to travel to get to your home village?' Jamie looked at Alec,

'We are unsure but it would be the distance from here to Edinburgh less thirty miles.'

The Reverend paused and took a book from a shelf opening it he turned the pages until he arrived at a map of Scotland, he opened it out so that the two men could see what he was talking about.

'We are about here,' he pointed to an area on the map, 'this is roughly where you want to be.' They followed his finger as it traced a line across the map.

'How far is that?' Jamie asked.

'It would be something like sixty miles, so that means you have a fair distance still to travel.' They looked at each other with a resigned expression knowing that they had no option but to get back to Livingston in the best time and by the quickest route they could. The reverend looked at the map again, I think you will need to plan your journey well. I will list the main towns that you will need to pass through. You will need care and cunning to avoid the parliamentarians, there are still those who put up a resistance and continue the fight, unfortunately there are others who would pass you over to the soldiers without a second thought. Tomorrow we will sit and discuss your route home.

As they picked up the clothes from the floor Mrs Bell noticed their shoes, they were in a bad state of repair, she told them both to take their shoes off which they did without question. Mrs Bell picked them up holding them away from her body, the shoes were wet and stank.

'Stay here and pick out things that fit the best, there is a little more food in the pot but try not to eat it all.' She left in the direction of the village holding the shoes as if they were dead rats.

'You may sleep in the kirk tonight and tomorrow but I think it would be best for all concerned if you were to make your way the day after.' Jamie looked at his friend and nodded, they had a long way to go and the sooner they started the earlier they would get home.

The following morning John Fraser called the men to his house. The kirk had been safe but not particularly warm, both men thought it was better than sleeping in the open or under trees or bushes. The minister took out the book with the map and lay it open in front of them.

'This is the route I think would be best for you.' The path he had chosen followed old roads and drover's tracks. He had made a note of the towns they needed to pass through, he paused, he didn't know if either of the men could read. 'Can you read?' He asked with mild embarrassment.

'We can read the bible but have not had a chance to read anything else.'

'That will be sufficient for you to follow my script. The first town you will need to make for is Jedburgh a distance of eight miles then on to Selkirk, another twenty-one miles, then Peebles.' The he looked up,

'The pace you travel at is up to you, but you should make a little more than twenty miles a day depending on the land that you encounter.' He carried on pointing out the towns and the distance. The first familiar name that Jamie heard was Carnwath which was some sixty miles from Southdean.

'I think I can find my way from Carnwath, what do you think.' He turned to Alec,

'Yes, I think we should be able to get to Livingston from there.'

John Fraser folded the note up and held it out towards the men in front of him. Jamie took it and carefully tucked it into his shirt. The minister made a mental note of how little the men had.

After two good nights sleep the men felt a lot better than they had for weeks. The food and warmth were something they desperately needed. Dressing in the clothes that the minister had given them they felt a little awkward as the clothes were not of a good fit. Long in the leg and a little short in the arm but folding and rolling here and there made the jackets and breeches work. It was a delight for them to have clean blouses next to their skin all they needed was footwear. They watched Mrs Bell approach the kirk and could see that she was carrying their shoes,

'Here you are, and be thankful my brother could make something of the things you were wearing.' She held out the repaired shoes, they looked so much more like shoes than the pieces of leather that she had taken from them. Jamie and Alec pulled them on, they felt comfortable and stable, hopefully they would last until they reached Livingston.

'Thank you, Mrs Bell, I wish we could do something to repay your kindness.'

'You can get yourselves home and stay out of harm's way, that's all I wish for.

Alec held out his hand in thanks and Jamie followed him. John Fraser came into the kirk carrying two satchels,

'These will help you on your way, inside there are letters signed by me asking for all those you meet to give you safe passage. If you have problems go to the nearest kirk and show the minister these letters.'

This was unexpected, Jamie and Alec took the satchels and put the straps over their shoulders. Jamie reached inside his shirt and removed the note with the route that they were to take and put it into his satchel. At this point Mrs Bell came from the house with two sacks and a small iron pot. She gave the pot to Jamie and then handed over the two sacks.

'There are some dried oats, cheese and bread which should give you a good start, I am sure you are able to get berries and other fruit, whatever else you get to eat is up to you.' She made her way back to the house leaving the Reverend Fraser standing before the men.

'I wish you well and hope you find your way home without trouble.' Jamie and Alec thanked the man standing before them, he had given them the hope and strength they needed, they said in unison,

'Thank you Reverend Fraser, we shall remember this day for many years to come.'

'God bless you both.' John Fraser watched the two men walk away from the kirk and he wondered if he would ever see them again or if they would manage to get home.

They set out feeling confident that they were on the last stretch of the path home. The road to Jedburgh was easy to follow and on arrival they found the kirk and after speaking to the Minister were able to confirm the route of the next stage of their journey. When they eventually reached Peebles, they were met with a different attitude, the minister was not as friendly as others and did not take kindly to two strangers invading his kirk. They had travelled forty miles and were in need of food, the oats that Mrs Bell had given them had almost gone. They asked the Minister if he could spare a small amount of oats or barley, the reply was not one they expected from a man of the kirk.

'Are you begging, because if you are we have a punishment for beggars in this town.'

Alec stepped forward.

'All we are asking for is a small amount to help as get back to our home, surely you could spare a handful of oats.' The minister turned on Alec and started to quote the scripture and told them that it would do them good to fast until they returned to their home. Alec knew that it was pointless discussing the matter any further. They thanked the minister for his kind words and left the kirk. As they reached the outer limits of the town, they came across a mill. Treading carefully, they approached the door and were nearly knocked over by the miller who was in no mood to talk to strangers. Jamie turned and followed him,

'Is it possible to work for a meal, we are willing to do anything.' The miller stopped and turned, looking at the two men before him he said,

'For food you can lift sacks of wheat and barley to help me, you're lucky, the boys that normally assist me are unwell and I am far behind with the day's work, so if you want food you will have to work and work quickly.'

Alec and Jamie unslung their satchels and followed the miller. He pointed out a stack of grain sacks which were to be brought into the mill and then be put in place for him to carry on with the day's work. It was not just the sacks that they had to move, the miller gave them other tasks including moving the finished sacks to his storehouse. They brushed and cleaned where the miller told them and worked hard until he was satisfied that they had done enough to warrant a meal.

'Come with me.' The miller said as he headed towards the building next to the mill. They followed and were surprised when he opened the door to his house. They could smell bread and their stomach's rumbled. The miller left them for a moment returning with three loaves of bread, still warm from the oven.

'Here you are now be off with you.' It was not the best of farewells but they had their bread and were keen to get away from the town. As they made their way out of Peebles Alec spoke,

'We are nearly there, it must be only twenty miles to Livingston so as long as god is with us, we should be back to our families tomorrow.' Alec then realised what he had said and looked apologetically at Jamie. 'Sorry, I forgot.' Jamie had not thought about his loss for some time he was too busy surviving.

'I am eager to see my mother and young brother and find out how he has managed the family farm without us.' His younger brother, John, was only thirteen and although eager to follow his father and brothers was not allowed to leave his mother's side, which did not sit well with the young boy.

'Did they have any help?'

'My father and mother would be helped by my uncle and his family.'

'Did you not say that your mother's family lived not far from Livingston?' Jamie could see in his mind's eye his mother and her brother when they were last together and felt a wave of sadness.

'Yes, they would have been given help, I just hope it was enough.'

In the distance Jamie could hear what sounded like horse's hooves hitting the hard ground. He pulled Alec to the side of the path,

'Listen, what's that, can you hear horses?'

Alec stopped in silence listening intently.

'I think it is.' They both jumped from the path they were following and hid as best they could in a thicket. There must have been ten horsemen, Jamie and Alec recognised them as English dragoons, their breast plates and pot helmets glistened in the sunlight.

'Keep still and not a sound.' Alec said as he crouched down pulling Jamie with him. They watched as the horses sped by and they both realised that the closer they got to Edinburgh the more likely they were to meet the English.

Things seemed to happen suddenly. As they pulled themselves out of their hiding place and straightened their limbs, they could hear more horses approaching.

'More soldiers?' It was Jamie asking the question then shaking his head. They leapt back into their hiding place but this time they were seen. The first horseman reigned his horse to a stop and looked in their direction.

'I think we have some animals in the hedgerow.' His voice carried a strong Scottish accent which took a little of the fear from the two men looking up at the mounted man in front of them. They could see he was not English, his jerkin was blue and he wore a blue bonnet. He looked down at the two men in front of him.

'What have we here?'

Alec and Jamie stood up,

'We have no weapons Sir, we are travellers making our way home.'

As Jamie spoke the remaining riders drew up alongside the first.

'And pray tell where is home?'

'Livingston, about twenty miles from here.'

'Why are you not serving your kirk and king?'

'We were, we were at Dunbar and have been making our way back to our homes for many days.' The horses jostled one another as a man of authority pushed his way through to the front of the riders.

'Dunbar you say, and what did you do there.'

Alec stepped forward,

'We were in the battle and then were captured but managed to escape the column of prisoners and have been walking ever since trying to get home.' The man's voice softened,

'That is a long way to walk and now you are nearly home only to be surrounded by the English.' He called out to his men and two horses came forward. 'You can ride with these men for a short way and then you will be on your own again, but first tell me of any troopers you may have seen nearby.' Alec and Jamie started together and the horseman held his hand up, 'one at a time please.' Alec then told of the men they had seen in the last hour.

'Thank you for that, now climb up, we cannot be in one place too long.'

Uncomfortable as it was Jamie and Alec were grateful to be off of their feet for a short while. When the troop of mounted men came to a halt they dismounted and gathered around their leader, who was presumably their officer, and waited for orders. After discussing their next move the men tethered their horses and took out various items of food from their saddlebags. As they sat one man offered Jamie and Alec some of his rations which they took gladly.

'Who are you?' Alec asked. 'You are not part of the army, are you?' The officer looked around at the two young men.

'We have a name it is Mossers, we are also from Dunbar and are currently waging war in our own way. If we can stop Cromwell by attacking his supplies and communications we will. Sometimes that means some are injured or even killed but that is war and we are fighting a war against Cromwell. Now what are we going to do with you two?'

'If you could direct us towards Livingston we will be on our way.'

'Hmm that is easy you are no more than ten miles from your homes but I must warn you that there are many English patrols in this area so be alert and don't take risks.'

Jamie and Alec got to their feet, collected their meagre belongings and started to make their way in the direction indicated by their rescuers. As they were walking away from the horsemen the officer called out,

'Perhaps we will meet again, we men from Dunbar must fight together until our work is done.'

The horsemen disappeared into the distance, Alec and Jamie set out on the last part of their journey.

Alec was growing more excited with each step, they both started to recognise features in the landscape, a hill there, a bend in the stream and even a clump of trees. They felt pleased with what they had achieved.

'I shall be leaving you shortly.' It was Alec he could see the road that led to his father's farm getting closer.

'Shall we meet soon?' Jamie asked.

'Perhaps on Sunday at the kirk.' Alec replied.

The two men felt difficulty in parting, they didn't quite know how to say goodbye. Did they shake hands or just embrace each other. It was if by mutual consent that they both reached out for each other. They had been through an ordeal together, one that would stay with them for the rest of their lives. They straightened up and looked at each other with a friendship that could only be born out of adversity.

'Until Sunday.' Jamie said as Alec turned and headed towards his home.

'Yes, until Sunday.'

Jamie seemed to forget about his empty stomach and felt a lift in his spirits. A source of energy began to flood through his body, his steps began to quicken as he followed a bend in the lane, he saw his father's house and his thoughts then darkened his mood. The sight of his father and brother lying dead on the battlefield appeared before him and his heart sank.

The door to the house was closed and Jamie had difficulty in opening it. He called out as he went inside but there was no sign of his mother or brother.

'Mother, John, where are you, it's me Jamie.'

There was no reply. Jamie thought that they would be outside carrying on with the daily work that every small farm requires. He stopped, something was wrong, there was a smell of stale air and dampness that would not have been there if a fire had been going. The grate was empty, no cooking pot with either water or pottage was evident. He raked the ashes in the stove with his hand, cold, there had not been a fire in this place for some time. He dropped his satchel and started to go into each room of the house. He found nothing, the bed had been stripped of clothing, there were no signs of life anywhere. He began to get very scared, what had happened here, where were his mother and brother? Jamie found no trace of life. Outside it was the same, things that would normally be in the yard were nowhere to be seen. To Jamie it felt as if things had been abandoned. It was then that his mind started to imagine all sorts of things. Could soldiers have been here? Had there been some catastrophe, had there been plague? He sat on the low wall running alongside of the small patch of earth to the rear of the house and tried to think. His only hope was that his mother's brother could help him so he went to the barn and managed to find a few apples that were still edible and then made his way to his uncle's house which was three miles to the north.

CHAPTER 9

Jamie approached his uncle's farm with trepidation. He could see the farmhouse and people going about their daily duties. His aunt looked up from her washing, she could see a figure approaching but did not recognise who it was. It wasn't until Jamie was within a few yards that his aunt recognised him. Her hands left the clothes she was scrubbing and went to her face,

'Jamie, is that really you, we thought you had been killed at Dunbar, where have you been?'

'It is a long story, but what has become of my mother and brother, I have been to my farm and it is deserted, where are they?' His aunt stood and came towards him.

'There is terrible news Jamie things have happened and we have tried our best but have not been able to keep things in the best of order.'

'But where are my mother and brother?' Jamie was starting to get frustrated and angry, he just wanted to know where they were.

'Come, and I will try to tell you of what has happened over the past months.' She went into the house and Jamie followed. Before she entered, she turned and sent a young boy to fetch her husband. They went into the main room of the house. There were several chairs and a large table. 'Sit you down Jamie, 'do you want drink or food', she asked.

'No, no just tell me of my family.'

His aunt nervously folded and unfolded her hands.

'Your mother and brother were told that you, your brother and father had been killed in battle at Dunbar. When she heard this, your mother fell into deep melancholy and although we did all that we could we were unable to help her. She wasted away, she did not eat or drink and no matter what either I or your uncle George did made any difference. I am afraid she sank lower and lower then she passed away. Your brother, John, was at her side constantly until the end. He was then afflicted in the same way, he had lost the will to live. Your uncle tried all he could to bring John back from the dark place he had gone to but could not seem to get him back to reality.' Jamie shook his head,

'Is John dead as well?'

'No, his is alive but has been captured by the same melancholy as your mother. He eats and drinks with us but speaks very little, your uncle finds him small tasks to do and takes him to the fields where he works but still says nothing.'

The door to the room opened and Jamie's uncle George appeared. He was a man with a large frame, his shoulders were broad and his waist narrow. Jamie looked up and could see the family resemblance straight away.

'Jamie.' He took hold of Jamie by the shoulders and nearly crushed him. The two men embraced with joy and sadness. 'Has your aunt told you of the horrors that have visited our family?'

'Yes, but where is John, is he with you?'

Jamie looked over his uncle's shoulder and saw his brother. It came as a shock, the change in his brother was bad, very bad. What Jamie could see was the flaming red of his brother's hair framing a drawn white face with eyes that stared without feeling. Jamie broke away from his uncle and went towards his brother, as he reached to greet his brother John moved away out of Jamie's reach. He grabbed John's arm and turned him,

'It's me, Jamie do you not know your own brother?' Jamie's voice was full of emotion, there seemed to be an instant of recognition in John's face but that passed in the blink of an eye. His uncle placed his hand on Jamie's shoulder,

'He has been like this since your mother passed.'

'Has he not spoken?'

'Only when it is necessary otherwise, he remains in his own silent world.'

'How long has he been with you?'

'Since your mother died, it must be two weeks now and he has not spoken readily since I brought him from your house.'

Jamie could not understand how his brother could get into such a state.

'What happened to my mother?' His uncle put his finger to his lips then turned to his wife,

'Take John and give him something to drink, we will be with you as soon as I have spoken to Jamie.' His aunt took John by the hand and led him towards a room at the back of the house. The two men sat at the table,

'It was a terrible week that led to your mother's death. She had prayed every day that you, your father and brother would walk through the door. She had been told that all three of you had been lost at Dunbar but she would not believe it. John stayed with her as her health deteriorated, he cared for her the best he could, we visited every day to make sure all was well. It was on the Sunday after the kirk service that we visited and found what we dreaded. Your mother had received another message from a man who fought at Dunbar he told her that he had seen you, your brother and father fall in battle. She did not have the strength of mind to cope with such tidings. In her store cupboard she kept various herbs which she used as medicine not only for the family but for any of the villagers who were poorly. She had in her collection some Monkshood, why she had it we do not know, on hearing for the second time that you had been killed, she sat with John in front of the fire and took a fatal amount of the plant. John was with her when she died, we found him still with his head in her lap, he had been like that throughout the night. When I tried to move him, he seemed to gain the strength of twenty men, he fought and raged when I attempted to separate him from your mother. I left him as long as I could then returned with your aunt and together, we managed to ease him away from the body. John did not move from the room even while your aunt and a woman from the village made her ready for burial.' Jamie's eyes started to fill with tears as he tried to imagine what his brother had been through and at such a young age.

'Has John been back to the house since my mother's death?'

'No, we thought it best to keep him away from the place until he had recovered a little more of his senses.'

'I need to go to the house and I would like to try to take John with me, do you think he would come?' His uncle looked worried,

'I don't know, it might send him back to a very dark place which he is slowly leaving, but if you want to try, please do so.' Jamie thought for a moment,

'Could I stay with you until I have cleared my head of all that has happened?'

'You are welcome to stay as long as you have the need to.'

'Thank you uncle, I will do everything I can to help John but I can see it will not be an easy task.'

The days that followed were full of emotion and fear as Jamie tried to coax his brother out of the world that he now occupied. On the third day he asked his uncle if he could use one of his horses to get back to the house,

'That is no problem at all as we have two of your horses here, we have been caring for them together with the cattle and sheep. I have put them with our own stock and they are hardy and well.' His uncle took Jamie to where his horses were kept, they looked in fine fettle, Jamie led the large plough horse to the house and went inside to collect John. He took hold of his brother's hand taking him towards the horse. John stopped in his tracks,

'Come John, you know how to climb on a horse.' His brother started to pull away until Jamie used some force to bring

John to the horse's head. Jamie took John's hand and placed it on the horse's neck slowly taking it up and down gently stroking the animal. Somehow it managed to sooth John's mood, he leant forward and placed his head against the horse. Jamie left him for a short time, he could see that there was some affinity between John and the large plough horse. Jamie placed a bridle over the horse's head and climbed onto the its back. He reached down to take John's hand and was surprised when he reached up and grasped Jamie's. Pulling John up the two brothers sat astride the massive frame of the plough horse, Jamie pulled on the reins and the horse began to walk forward.

Dealing with John proved hard work for Jamie. The days that followed his return were filled with his efforts to try to bring his brother back to reality. Although he loved his brother dearly Jamie could see that all that he had tried was to no avail, John still remained in his own world, the only time he seemed to respond to anything was when he was with the horses. Jamie had not seen his cousin Ian whilst he had been staying with his uncle. That morning as they left to check the livestock Jamie asked his uncle about his cousin.

'I have not seen Ian, is he away somewhere?' His uncle turned from the cow he was trying to get moving,

'He is at another farm across the river, helping a good friend who has been having problems with several of his sheep, not just disease but a plague of rustlers seems to have targeted his flock.' Jamie was surprised at his uncle's answer.

'I didn't think local people would steal sheep.'

'It's not our neighbours, it's those from foreign places who through one thing or another, find themselves here without money. There have been many that have stolen sheep to sell on or in some cases they have just butchered them for their own use. I am expecting him home very soon and I shall be glad to get him back.'

Two days later Ian arrived back at his father's farm. Although the house was fairly substantial it was getting crowded. Jamie moved his things to the barn and slept there. When his aunt protested saying that he should share with Ian, Jamie knew that there was only room for one. He still took his meals with the rest of the family and it was after their main meal on the Sunday that Jamie spoke to his uncle about the future.

'I am at a loss at what to do about my farm and John. He looked at his uncle with a pleading look in his eyes. 'I don't think I can do any more for John and as for the farm, it needs a capable man of the soil which is not me.'

George Dower looked at his nephew and could see the struggle he had in deciding what to do. During the Sunday service the minister had spoken of the Kirk and the King needing men to take up arms and follow the banner of Christ and the King. He had seen Jamie and Alec with their heads together and had an idea of what they were talking about. A little hesitantly he asked Jamie.

'What do you want to do?'

'I still want revenge for the death of my family, their deaths and the state of Johns mind lies with the English and I need to do something. If that means me taking up arms so be it, I will gladly follow the king and kirk.' This did not come as a total surprise to his uncle. They talked into the night, Ian had joined them and eventually they came to a solution that would help solve most of their problems. His uncle summed up what they had been discussing,

'If you want to follow the king then that is your decision, what we will do is take in John here and he can help with the livestock, Ian will take over the running of your farm and any money made he will use to keep him and the farm going, he will in effect be the owner of the farm and will take full responsibility for anything to do with the land, stock and house. Jamie, do you agree to this and are you prepared to give up your rights to the farm.' He looked at Jamie who nodded, deep inside he was still unsure of what he was doing. Could he justify sacrificing his family home to go to war, to fight and hope to win after what he had been through at Dunbar? He just wanted to get away from the problems that he could see mounting up before him, his brother, the farm, the house his future. How he lived his life was up to him, nobody else, no uncle's, no brother's, no farm just his life. He thought this seemed selfish but he knew that it was the only way for him to clear his mind.

The following day Jamie took Ian to the farm, they rode two of the better horses, one of Jamie's and Ian's favourite. They went through everything, Ian was an experienced farmer having worked with his father all his life. When they had finished it was agreed that Ian would bring back all the stock that his father was caring for and keep them on what would be his farm. As they were about to head back, they saw a figure on horseback approaching. As it drew closer Jamie could see Alec in the saddle, when he was in hearing distance Alec started shouting out in an excited voice. His words were unclear, Jamie had difficulty in understanding exactly what he was saying. Then his words rang in Jamie's ears.

'I am going to Stirling to join Leslie's army.' He drew his horse up alongside Jamie's. 'Are you coming with me Jamie?' He looked from Ian to Alec, his eyes lit up the thought of adventure and battle filled him.

'When are you going?'

'Sunrise tomorrow, are you coming?'

Ian looked at the two young men in the saddle, was he jealous, a little perhaps but he was not one to rush into anything especially if it could result in the loss of life.

CHAPTER 10

The two men were in good spirits as they left Livingston, they were to travel on foot even though their experience over the past month had made the decision very difficult. With full bellies and good clothing on their backs they strode out purposefully. It was twenty-six miles to Stirling which they should easily cover in a day. Alec had travelled the road to Stirling several times when taking cattle and sheep to the market there. The halfway point would be Falkirk where they would rest and then once they had crossed Bannockburn it was just a short walk to the town. As Jamie looked around at the countryside, he was grateful for the warmth of the late July sun on his back. A discussion developed between the two as to how they would best serve the kirk and king. Jamie was not in favour of taking up the Pike again, both agreed that the cumbersome weapon made it difficult to move around and if they were to get into any trouble, heaven forbid, they would need to be as free as possible. Alec said that they should not look on the dark side they would not have to suffer the same shame that had befallen them at Dunbar.

'Perhaps we could get Muskets, that would be better than Pike's and would be a useful thing to learn.' Alec pondered a moment,

'But how easy is it to learn and where would we be in a fight?'

'You saw those with muskets at Dunbar, they stood in ranks and fired before the cavalry broke through. I would feel better with a musket than with a pike and as far as learning how to use a musket I am sure that could be achieved quickly if we put our minds to it.'

Alec looked around at the trees on either side of the path they were on,

'Yes, you may be right but we will have to see if we can get someone to accept and train us.' With that decided they continued to talk mainly of those they had left behind. Alec asked Jamie how he thought his brother would fare living with his uncle.

'I think it's the best place for him. I was at a loss as to what to do with him and my aunt and uncle will watch over him. He seemed to be settled when he was with the horses, my hope is that my uncle can make some use of him on the farm without too much trouble. He is not a violent lad just very much affected by my mother's death and that of my father and brother. I could not have brought him with us as he would not understand why and what we were trying to achieve. What about your family how did they feel when you told them you were going to join General Leslie?' Alec said,

'I think my father was proud of what I had decided to do, I have two brothers and a sister so in some ways my not being there helps them, there is more to go round.' He smiled thinking of the way he would argue and sometimes fight over his mother's cooking with his siblings.

They reached Falkirk in good time, the going had been good and after crossing the river they rested and ate what they had brought with them. From their experience during their travels after Dunbar they always made sure that they had enough food for at least the following day if not two. As they left Falkirk they crossed the old Roman wall, it was grassed over but its path could be made out as it stretched to the West. The direction they took was to the North and a clear road and track could be seen running through the lowland fields.

As they walked several men joined them. It seemed that the call had gone out and the response had been good. Their group numbered six and as they approached Stirling their eagerness grew. Jamie looked to see if any had muskets, but none had. He would take his chance and see if he could enter the ranks of the musketeers. The city stood proud on its craggy cliff, the grey stone had hints of shining glass in its rockface. It gave all those approaching the city a sense of pride. When they entered Stirling there was organised confusion, a large number of men were gathered together at various points with banners and standards showing who they were and where they had come from. Jamie talked to one of his fellow volunteers who told him of the last Battle of Stirling when Scot fought Scot, Engagers fought Covenanters. The Engagers who were for Charles I and the Covenanters who were for the Kirk Party. It was settled by the treaty of Stirling and the Covenanters took the lead in the running of the land.

'How long ago was that?' Jamie was aware of the battle but had forgotten when it had been fought.

'It was only three years ago, and now we are together as one under the flag of the Kirk and King.'

Alec had disappeared and returned with a flushed look on his face.

    'Jamie, come with me I think I have found us a place in the ranks of Toquhon's Foot. They need men to train with the musket and I have volunteered the two of us. So come on get your things.' Jamie picked up his satchel and bag and ran after Alec. They arrived slightly out of breath, Alec made his way to a short stocky individual who seemed to be covered in straps and pouches, by his side he had a musket that was almost as tall as him.

    'This is your friend?' He asked Alec.

    'Yes, we are together and wish to join you.'

    'And from where do you hail?'

It was Alec who replied,

    'We are from Livingston.'

    'Good, good and you want to fire a musket.'

    'Yes, we are willing to learn and are at your service.'

    'It is not an easy thing to get to know but I am sure we can use you. My name is Nisbet, Robert Nisbet and these are my men.' He waved at a group standing smoking and chatting. 'Have either of you fired a musket?' Jamie and Alec answered in unison,

    'No.'

    'But you are telling me you are willing to learn, is that right?'

    'Yes.'

'We have some time before we depart so I think we will begin your lessons as soon as we can find you a place to sleep.' He called to one of his men,

'Donald, show these men to our quarters and find them a space then return to me and we will start.' Jamie and Alec followed the man called Donald, he led them through various buildings then came to an open space where there were a number of tents and bivouacs. Alec and Jamie looked at one another with apprehension, they were heartily relieved when Donald passed through the tents and into a large hall.

'This is where you will sleep, we are in this area and there is a little room over there.' He pointed to a space that might just be enough for two men. Jamie and Alec put their satchels down, Jamie turned to Donald,

'Will our things be safe here?'

'As safe as anywhere in this city, there are so many men and I dare say that some are not as Godfearing as you or I.' Jamie shrugged, he had little to lose but what he had was his and he didn't want to be the victim of any petty thief. Donald pointed out where his fellow musketeers slept, lying by their bed rolls were various items that Jamie thought were to do with their use of muskets.

'We must be away back to the Corporal he will be wanting to start you off as soon as possible.' Corporal Nisbet was as good as his word, no sooner had they got back he handed them a musket each and their training began.

Life was not all training, skirmishes still occurred, men both mounted and on foot would leave the city to harass the

English and keep routes open so that supplies could get through to the city. Jamie and Alec were taught how to form up with the pikemen and how they needed them for protection when they were reloading. It was also made clear to the two trainees that orders were given by flags and drums so they had to learn the eight different drum calls.

Their lives went on apace as men were made ready to follow the King and Kirk. Jamie and Alec worked hard at their new found occupation. It was hard going but they enjoyed the thought that they would not be carrying a long heavy pike into battle. Instead of a pike they would be carrying the tools of their new found trade of war, which came in the form of 'Twelve Apostles, which were twelve prepared cartridges in a leather bandolier belt slung across their chest, with it was a powder flask, priming flask, a pouch of bullets and spare matches. They were taught that keeping their equipment dry could mean the difference between life and death, so they copied their fellow musketeers in using a large leather flap hanging over the bandolier belt and to keep spare matches under their hat. It came as a surprise when they were given blue jackets to wear together with a wide brimmed hat. Alec had seen other men of his regiment tying ribbons around the base of the crown of their hats to show which regiment they belonged to. Jamie was a little troubled when Corporal Nisbet explained at great length the danger that went with carrying a musket and its ammunition, one spark and that could mean a serious wound or even death to the unlucky musketeer who had not taken extra care of his powder. The two men now felt part of an army of some magnitude, they were confident and willing to fight.

The year flew by and December ran through to January, things seem to be taking shape and when news arrived that Charles had been crowned King of Scotland on the first of January all the troops were eager for the off. The word reached Jamie and Alec that the Parliamentarian Army had stalled due to the fierce defence of Stirling. Alec had heard that some fighting had taken place in various towns, the Scottish army had not been able to defend strongholds at Tantallon and Blackness on hearing this news Alec and Jamie lost a little of their confidence.

The defence of Stirling was outstanding and the Scottish army prepared itself to march, Alec and Jamie thought that they would be heading towards London but there was a change and the army prepared to travel through Lancashire and along the Welsh border gathering men as they went. Jamie marched with confidence, his new found skill with the musket gave him pride and courage although he had not yet fired his weapon in anger. Jamie, with the rest of his company crossed into England in early August, it felt as if they were taking the battle to the English and would be fighting on their ground. It would not be the same as Dunbar, Jamie and Alec would be the attacking force and they would drive their enemy back and win the day. There was talk that their numbers would swell as they marched but Jamie could not really see any sign of many men joining the column. As he looked back, he thought that they were many and he was sure that with God on their side they would be strong enough to defeat any force that they would meet. The army marched on, the weather was getting hotter, summer reached its zenith they had passed through Carlisle and then Penrith, English soil felt good beneath their feet and as they approached the River Ribble their hopes were high. There must have been well over ten thousand men in their column and it was a sight to behold, totally different from the ragged line of men that Jamie and Alec had been part of after the battle of Dunbar and that was a situation that Alec and Jamie had vowed never to be caught up in again.

They marched long and hard, Jamie with Alec stepped out and with the words of the psalms ringing in their ears the English countryside of green pastures and woodlands covered in the full leaves of summer cast shadows over them as they passed. Corporal Nisbet gave them any news that he could find, in some instances it was not good. At Wigan there had been a fight and the Kings army had not performed well, however, that was not going to deter them.

One foot in front of the other, each foot a little nearer to battle. The mood was high and voices rang out in praise of God and the King. The column was brought to a halt for rest and water. Jamie sat looking across the fields on either side of the road. He thought he could see movement in the grass which stood tall on the verge. He got up and started to investigate, to his surprise he could see the figure of a child, a small girl about six or seven years of age. He approached the girl who immediately started to cry. Jamie tried to calm her with soft words but seemed to be getting nowhere. A woman appeared and snatched the child away from Jamie,

'Don't handle my child.' Jamie was taken aback, all he tried to do was comfort her.

'I'm sorry, I thought she was in distress.'

'The only distress here is the likes of you.' Jamie looked around and could see no other men in earshot.

'What do you mean, we are here to put the rightful king on the throne and bring god to you all.' She looked at him with venom in her eyes,

'You have come from a foreign land bringing with you talk of kings and God and what do you do, you take all we have. Our harvest has been poor, we have only enough to survive and then you and your men demand all we have. You do not fight with shot and sword, you fight with hunger and disease. You do not leave dead soldiers behind, you leave the old and children starving. Is this your gods work? Jamie looked around again, this was blasphemy, if any other heard what she was saying she would be dealt with severely.

'I mean you no harm, I don't want to take the food from your mouth or your child's but we march to afford you better things, a better life, a better future.' Jamie said these things without thinking, it was what he believed and if he wavered in that belief there would be no point in going on. The woman spat and looked at Jamie with scorn,

'Look around you, do you know anything about harvest? Look into the fields and see how dry and stale the earth is.' Jamie followed the woman's arm as she waved around the fields that bordered the road.

'I am sorry that your harvest was poor but I am sure we will not deprive you of so much that you will starve.'

'You think so, you and your fellows are like locusts everywhere you go you strip the land of any goodness it might have had and do not care what you leave in your wake.'

'Where is your man, does he follow the kings banner or is he for parliament?'

'My man, as with most, is trying to gather anything he can to keep his family alive.'

'But there are many men who would join our ranks and fight for the King.'

'You think so, I do not know of one man who has left his home to fight for anyone, king or parliament.' Jamie thought for a moment,

'You have not seen our ranks that swell as we march through this part of the country. It is where the king's father had great support when he did battle.' She looked at Jamie and raised her hand,

'I know of no more than the fingers of one hand the numbers that have joined your ranks.' As she said this Alec approached them,

'What's this, Jamie are you trying to get women to join us?' The woman picked up her daughter and started to make her way quickly towards the cottage about half a mile in the distance.

'No, I was just giving her back her lost child.' He turned to join Alec and as they walked back to the column he asked, 'how many others have joined us from this area?' Alec looked up and down the rows of men getting ready to march,

'I don't know, they would have joined various companies and be absorbed into the column or joined at the back, but we have good numbers as far as I can see and we shall be able to account well when we meet parliaments army.'

Corporal Nisbet had been summoned by his officer and returned with news.

'We are to head for Worcester and there we will make ready for whatever awaits us.' A voice called out,

'How much further is this place called Worcester.' The corporal replied,

'About another day's march and then we will rest.'

There was a murmur of approval as they made ready to move off. The towns they passed through were strange to Jamie and Alec, names such as Hagley and Muston Green meant nothing to them only that they were hopefully getting closer to their destination.

CHAPTER 11

The city of Worcester is dominated by its cathedral. The square tower watched over the cities half-timbered houses stretching along its broad streets. The suburbs had been taken down during the last occupation by royalist forces making it easier to defend. The two friends took stock of the area that they found themselves in. As they entered Jamie and Alec noticed the traders with their baskets of fruit, particularly apples and pears, together with fowl, fish and meat. In their eyes it was a thriving place especially when compared with some of the small villages and towns they had passed through.

    Men and carts began to fill the streets as the Royalists army took over areas considered to be strategic. A call had gone out to all the parishes in and around Worcester for them each to supply thirty men to work on the reinforcement of walls, buildings and any other points that could be used to repel any attack by the parliamentarians. The men from the parishes brought with them spades, shovels and pickaxes and were put to task in building earthworks and repairing gates and walls. Corporal Nisbet gave Jamie and his fellow musketeers the good news that the Worcester Council had decided to surrender the city thereby preventing any more damage to its buildings. Jamie asked.

    'Where are the enemy, are they close?' Corporal Nisbet looked around at his men, in his eyes they were as good as he could make them and he would be with them no matter what General Cromwell threw at them. Nisbet cleared his throat,

    'I have been told they have withdrawn out of the city but that is not our main enemy that was only the small city garrison which would have been no match for our troops.'

    'So where is our foe, are they close, when will we do battle?' The corporal shook his head,

    'Be patient my brave lad, you will soon have more than enough to keep you busy.'

Jamie and the men from Tolquhon's Foot and Horse rested regaining their strength after the long march from their homeland. It was, rumour had it, that there were men joining them from the area, many Royalists who would fight with them. Jamie could see no sign of any great numbers, yes there were maybe two dozen that he had seen but no more than that. Jamie had arrived with the main royalist army on the 22nd of August and had been employed on various tasks around the city. It wasn't until eleven days later that he heard of any movement by the enemy. The word arrived, Jamie together with Alec and their cohort were ordered to make their way to a bridge and there they were to stop the parliamentarians crossing. Collecting their weapons and ammunition they made their way to the bridge which bore the name Powick, it was a name that had already featured in battle, men said that it was at the very start of when Prince Rupert had fought there.

    The men around Jamie walked tall and proud, they would give a good account of themselves no matter what the enemy threw at them. Nisbet called to Jamie and his fellow musketeers to make sure that they were in position with pikemen protecting them. Jamie could feel a sense of excitement welling up inside him, turning towards Alec he said in a loud voice,

'We are to do battle, we can avenge those who fell at Dunbar.' Alec shouted back.

'It will be for your father and brother that we take the enemy's blood.'

Then it began, Jamie held his musket high and could see the faces of the men he was about to kill get closer. The pikemen stood firm they would protect him when he had to reload, his hands trembled then became steady. He could see his target and hoped he would hit it, then the noise started. Muskets fired, smoked filled the air stinging eyes and choking throats, Jamie had taken aim but could not be sure if he had been successful in hitting his target. Pikes were lowered and a fierce wall of sharpened steel prevented the enemy getting close while Jamie and his fellow musketeers reloaded. It took time for Jamie to bring his musket into the firing position but he could see that the first volley had halted the parliamentarians. The command was given to fire and he felt his weapon let loose its deadly charge. The enemy seemed to falter and stop and even fall back, their dead were few but the shock of the first taste of battle caused them to hesitate. Alec had lifted his weapon in victory but he was premature, the parliamentarians rallied and returned a deadly hail of shot. Men fell close by and Jamie saw the first dead of the battle.

The musketeers and pikemen held the bridge. Not many men had fallen and those around Jamie and Alec stood firm, their courage boosted by the wavering line of the Parliamentary men. There seemed to be a great deal of movement along the river banks and in the distance, men could be seen dragging what appeared to be boats towards the river. A call went out for Scots to make ready to move. Jamie and Alec took their places and made their way with their comrades to an open space where the ground flattened out. It became obvious to Jamie that the day was going to get tougher. The pike heads of the enemy glinted in the morning sun as they drew closer. Jamie could hear and feel the lead shot as the opposing musketeers fired, intent on killing or wounding him or his fellow Scots. The shouts of the enemy drew ever closer, Jamie had no time to reload, his hand went to the short sword he carried, as he pulled it from its scabbard, he felt the wind of shot whistle passed his right ear, he turned to see Alec standing with his sword held high waiting for the advancing soldiers to get close enough to fight. The English troops pushed forward but King Charles' men stood firm and then the English wavered and fell back, Jamie with the men of Toquhons Foot had seen off the English. The men around Jamie let out a cheer as they saw the Parliamentarians come to a halt. Jamie with Alec formed up into their respective lines and were told in no uncertain terms by Corporal Nisbet that this was only the beginning. How right he was. Cromwell's men appeared from nowhere, their numbers were increasing all the time,

'Where have they come from.' Asked Jamie.

'They've crossed the river.'

'But how, did they swim?'

'It's the boats, they have used the boats as a bridge.' Alec's response had a tinge of panic as Cromwell's men moved ever closer. 'Our horse will be with us soon, I am sure.' Jamie looked around the field of battle but could see no sign of their cavalry. Noon had come and gone the men were thirsty and the long marches of recent weeks had taken their toll. The noise of battle ebbed and flowed one moment it felt as if victory was in the hands of Jamie and his fellows then they were falling back trying to protect themselves from what seemed to be an ever-increasing wave of Parliamentary forces. Alec screamed at Jamie,

'They are coming from the side!' Jamie turned to see yet another body of men fighting their way towards him, he looked around, only to see men that were standing by him only a few moments ago trying to leave the field of battle. Their leaders were yelling out orders to remain and hold fast but it was to no avail. Corporal Nisbet walked amongst his men pulling them back and turning them to face the enemy, his efforts did not have the desired effect, the men were now beginning to panic. Nisbet finally managed to regain some control and steadied his men. No longer were they running but no matter what they did they still fell back towards the city walls.

'Why haven't our horse attacked?' Jamie asked anyone who could hear. A voice answered that they were cowards and had no stomach for the fight.

Jamie and Alec now found themselves inside the city walls with men who were running in all directions. Their muskets were useless as they ran from street to street. A troop of Parliamentary horse appeared and galloped into the group containing the two friends. Men darted down alleys and side streets trying to flee from the lances and pistols of the troopers. Screams could be heard as Scots men were lanced or struck down with the sword. Injuries were bloody and frightening, limbs and blood littered the streets as the fighting increased.

Cromwell's men were in the ascendance and there appeared to be no stopping them. Jamie had lost sight of Alec during the attack by the horsemen, he looked around him but the cries of the wounded made him feel sick. He could not see Alec and then he heard the sound of more riders, he dived into a small alley between two houses and dropped to his knees, he could feel sweat pouring down his back, it dripped from his forehead his eyes began to sting.

  Jamie had no idea of where he was or where his fellow Scots were, he ran until his lungs were burning, stopping he knelt down and tried to regain his breath and composure, every muscle in his body began to ache, what was he to do, where were the men that he began the day with, how many were still alive? He leant back against a wall and tried to calm down. Somehow, he had lost his sword and was now without any means of defending himself, he looked around but there was nothing he could use. Taking a deep breath, he got to his feet and steadying himself he started to make his way carefully along the passage way. As he reached the street, he could see the dead and there were many of them, his foot trod on something that gave way under his weight, he looked down, it was the body of a young boy, no more that thirteen or fourteen, his head had been blown apart by a musket ball, Jamie retched, the small amount of food that was in his stomach spewed from his mouth making him gag. Alongside the dead boy was a shattered pikestaff, the head was intact but the shaft was split, Jamie wiped his mouth and bent to pick up the pikestaff as he did, he heard the clatter of a horse's hooves approaching, looking up he saw a mounted trooper in the buff-coloured coat of the Parliamentarians, the rider pulled on the reins of his horse bringing it to a halt just in front of Jamie, the trooper pulled his pistol and aimed it at Jamie's head. Jamie was transfixed he could not move as the trooper levelled his pistol and took aim. Jamie prepared himself for death but then there was a muffled noise as the pistol misfired, then came a curse from the trooper, Jamie grabbed the damaged pike and stepped forward bringing the sharp point of the pike up towards the rider. The trooper had leant forward to get his best shot leaving an area to his side unprotected, Jamie took hold of the splintered shaft of the pike and drove it with all the force he could muster into the trooper's side. It entered his body below his breastplate, the trooper's hands dropped the pistol and grasped at the head of the pike trying to remove the weapon that had entered his body. As the trooper leant forward, he fell from his saddle, the pike head hitting the ground first as he fell which drove the metal further into his body. Jamie watched as the trooper's body crashed onto the ground, he could see the point of the pike trying to punch through the trooper's coat. On the ground the troopers body lay in a position that was hard to explain, but for the pike shaft he would have been on his side but his body was being held up by Jamie's weapon, as he lay there the last movements of a dying man made the body jerk.

      Frightened for his life Jamie looked around for an escape route, each corner he turned there seemed to be more enemy troops waiting for him. He was determined not to be taken prisoner and go through the same demoralising days that he had undergone after Dunbar but it was not to be. There would be no escape for him this time, too many of Cromwell's men roamed around the city of Worcester gathering up the remaining Scottish infantry. Jamie picked an alleyway which looked like it would lead him away from the chasing troops, he ran into the darkness of the narrow passageway, he had no time to fear anything or anyone, his legs still held firm and his confidence still high. Then he was hit by what felt like a hammer smashing into his face, his head spun and tears flooded into his eyes. As he fell backwards, a booted foot struck him in the stomach which made him wince with pain. Through the tears he could see a giant of a man standing over him, the man's fists were clenched ready to land another blow if needed however, he looked at Jamie's face and realised that he was going nowhere, he grabbed Jamie by the shoulder and lifted him to his feet,

'I think your day is done.' The voice was heavily accented. 'Come on my lad you can join your fellows.' Jamie tried to wipe the tears from his eyes, his nose felt as if it was about to burst and his lips began to swell, he was not going to argue. He tried to speak,

'What has happened?' His voice quaked as the giant pulled him along like a dead lamb.

'What has happened.' He echoed. 'The king has lost the day, that's what has happened, and you my lad are going to join your fellows until we find out what is to be done with you.' Jamie's thoughts went back to Dunbar, was he a prisoner again? He did not try to resist the soldier, who seemed to have the strength of several men and was not to be challenged. Jamie found himself amongst a throng of bewildered men not knowing what their fate would be, how many lost souls aimlessly milled around he did not know. He asked the blue bonneted soldier next to him,

'How did this happen? Did many avoid capture? The response he received was tired with defeat etched into every word.

'Our men, foot soldiers, did not stand a chance, their horse rode us down and herded us like sheep into this place.' He shook his head, another standing nearby clenched his fist and waved it in the air,

'We had no lancers or dragoons, we were abandoned by Leslie.' There was a murmur of agreement from those close by. 'Many good men and those of high birth have been killed or now await their fate, we stand here without hope or faith, our lives in the hands of the English.'

The day was drawing to a close, the sky had darkened and there was a chill in the air. For Jamie and his fellow prisoners, for that is what they were, their hearts had been cut out of their bodies along with their will to resist. The night fell, Jamie tried to keep warm, he managed to find a space in the lee of a building which had been damaged but had some walls remaining upright. He dozed, in his waking moments he wondered where Alec was, had he been injured or killed? Was he a prisoner like himself? Would they ever meet again? He felt alone even amongst what seemed like a thousand men and he felt isolated in his thoughts.

As daylight broke Jamie stretched his limbs and tried to stand. The physical effort of the battle had tied his muscles in knots, not only did he have difficulty in getting his body to move, his mind was in turmoil. He asked himself. Would he be made to march as he did after Dunbar? Would he escape again, but this time he was nearly 300 miles from his home so returning would be almost impossible and could he do anything on his own, at Dunbar he had the fellowship of Alec to support him but now he was by himself. Alone, he thought as he turned and tried to gauge how many men were waking from disturbed sleep, there must be hundreds. The sound of horses hooves made him look to the right of where he stood, more men were being brought in by the horsemen, how many more and what was to be their fate? The day drew on, they had no food and it had been two days since Jamie had anything to eat, his mouth was dry and his throat sore but there was nothing, no food or water, he heard one man ask for water, a soldier laughed and told him that water was for the victors not the vanquished. As the sun gained height the warmth eased his aching body, Jamie thought he caught sight of Alec but it was only for a fleeting moment and then the image disappeared into a crowd of men, perhaps he had survived and they would meet again or would their next meeting be in a higher place. During the day several mounted troopers separated a number of men into areas, for what, they were not told. Jamie moved along with the others without thought or feeling, his will power was low, for the moment he would just do what he was told.

There were hundreds of men waiting for their guards to tell them what was to happen. Talk was not common amongst men who had just been beaten in battle, the only discussion was why they had been so let down by their cavalry and left to the mercy of Cromwell's men. Morning slowly passed into afternoon and still no word of what was to become of them. Towards evening a Captain of horse rode up and gave instructions to the troopers guarding the Scots,

'You are to make ready to depart at first light tomorrow, get all the men in column, those unable to march are to be left, sort them out, I do not want any delay in moving out of this ruin of a city.' A voice beside Jamie said,

'So, it is another miserable and hungry night we have to spend here.' Jamie looked around at his fellow soldiers who were now prisoners and his heart sank, what would become of them and where would they be marching to? A dry spot by a partially collapsed wall would be his bed for the night, as he tried to make the best of the ground he was about to lay on he smelt the air, the sweet sickly aroma of dead horses and men came from the bodies in the streets, he had become used to the battles aftermath and no longer felt pity for the dead. Those around him talked of where their next meal would come from it had already been nearly three days since they had eaten and that was just thin pottage, their stomachs grumbled with hunger, although it was something that they had experienced in the past, it still caused them a great deal of concern. Little sleep was had by Jamie and the men lying in doorways and against walls. The dawn broke to reveal several soldiers with swords and long poles getting the men to their feet,

'Come on you lazy Scotsmen wake up you are going for a walk.'

The soldiers laughed as they prodded and poked the men who had tried to sleep on the cold earth of Worcester city streets and alley ways.

Jamie followed the instructions of the loud-mouthed soldiers and formed up with the rest of the prisoners into a column which stretched into the distance. Jamie thought there were hundreds of men, some with bandaged wounds others coughing and some being sick. Soldiers would pull those that they thought would be unable to march out of the ranks, what fate awaited them Jamie did not want to dwell on, he just straightened himself and stood in line. There were several mounted officers who rode up and down inspecting what their soldiers had allowed into the column. Jamie thought it was the senior officer who addressed the column,

'You men will march as directed by my men, you will keep with the column, those who stray abroad will be shot or put to the sword. You will not speak to those you see on the road, you will not try to gather food and you will rest when you are given permission. Any man seen to disobey orders will suffer the severest penalty. You will have three ministers to give you the comfort of prayer and you will be allowed to join in the psalms. That is all.' He looked around at his men. 'Get ready to march, Sergeant Harrison go to the head of the column and lead off, take a drummer with you to get the men started.' A soldier stepped forward, presumably Sergeant Harrison, who caught a drummer boy by the sleeve and dragged him to the head of the column. The officer waited until he was sure Harrison was in position then took his sword from its scabbard and raised it above his head, as he brought it down the drummer started and the column moved slowly forward.

There would be no attempted escapers, the Scottish soldiers were tired, hungry and dispirited. Word had spread that some men had been selected for trial, as many as one in ten of the multitude of prisoners captured. These men were found guilty of rebellion and subsequently put to death. It was a grim reminder to Jamie and his fellows that the war with the English continued but not on the battlefield.

CHAPTER 12

Jamie walked with his head down placing one foot in front of the other, what had happened to Alec? In his mind he pictured the adventure they had when escaping from the column after Dunbar. He had no close friend to share his thoughts with, he listened to others speaking of what had happened to them in battle, some men talked of their homes and families, this only made Jamie sink further into a depressed state, he had resigned himself to a life as a prisoner and if death should come then the sooner the better.

There was a guard who had a little sympathy for his charges, a man from the border country. Although he didn't speak a great deal the information he imparted was like gold dust to Jamie. The soldier was called John, as they marched Jamie asked,

'Do you know where we are bound?' John said that as far as he was aware they were headed for London. Jamie's next question was,

'How far is that?'

'It is over one hundred miles.'

'How long will it take us to get there?'

'We should be there in no more than ten days as long as the pace is kept.'

Jamie asked if the soldier knew what their fate would be once they arrived in London but the soldier did not know. Jamie would keep on asking but not so much as to anger the soldier.

    The column was made up of hundreds of men, there were several wagons which had been taken from the Scottish baggage train and were now used for items that would be necessary to keep the men going. There were some cooking implements such as pots and skillets but very little to put into them. As the column left Worcester behind the countryside opened out. There were farmsteads and Jamie could see livestock in the fields, crops would not be easy to grow on the hills that they marched through but the flatlands and valleys were fertile and were well cultivated. Any slowing down of the line gave those in the column the opportunity to scavenge for any berries on bushes and brambles by the side of the old road that they tramped along. What was needed was good weather but God did not smile upon them, it rained, not just an autumn shower but a downpour that soaked all that they had. Everything from caps to boots suffered and together with a chill breeze most of the men started to shudder. It rained without let for the rest of the day. Jamie tried to make out the cottages that lay back from their path, he hoped that a kindly soul might take pity on him and his fellow prisoners, perhaps even some scraps of food would come his way but alas nothing. They marched with the ground beneath their feet starting to turn into mud. After over a thousand pairs of feet had passed their boots sank into mud and lifting each foot became an effort.

    As daylight began to fade Jamie sought out the soldier John, he asked,

      'Where is this place?' The soldier turned to face him,

'I don't know, I'm not from these parts, it's a strange land to me.'

Through the heavy rain Jamie could see honey-coloured cottages with thatched roofs, there were people moving around, women gathering washing in from the rain and children being children, Jamie watched their antics and how their mothers shood them into their homes when the column came close. The friendly soldier called to one of the women,

'What is this place?' She did not want to tarry and yelled back at him,

'This is Evesham.' That was all she said, she hurried back into her dry cottage leaving the men standing drenched to the skin. The command to march echoed down the column, they started to move this time slower as the cold started to penetrate through their skin.

The second day of the march was much the same as the first, it rained. The men had no chance of drying out, Jamie's clothes were still wet from the previous day, his bones ached and his stomach rumbled. He could see some of the men scrambling to the road side looking for anything to eat. He did exactly the same and managed to gather a handful of berries which he eagerly devoured, carefully guarding them from any of his fellow marchers. As night fell Jamie made note of a strip with green leaves which must have some root vegetable growing beneath it. He waited until the men had gathered together for warmth and the guards had reduced their numbers as some went to a nearby barn to eat and sleep, carefully he crawled from the column and slid through the mud and onto the strip which he had seen earlier. Grasping a bunch of leaves, he pulled and success! at the end of the plant a glorious round shape appeared, it was a turnip. He made sure he was not being watched, the men were huddled together trying to keep dry, he slid back and made a space for himself under a small bush. His hands had difficulty in breaking the hard turnip, he seemed to have no strength and together with the cold he nearly gave up but hunger was his master. Trying again he managed to break the turnip with the aid of a sharp piece of stone he managed to dig from the soil. He smashed into the hard vegetable and as he did it broke down making it more pliable, his teeth sank into the root taking chunks into his mouth. Chewing was difficult the lack of food had weakened almost all of his body but he persisted. Slowly he swallowed pieces of the vegetable, he could feel it sliding down his gullet with some difficulty, he did not care, it was food. Jamie ate half the turnip and carefully broke the remainder into small pieces which he would eat whenever the opportunity arose. His stomach began to ache but he was determined to keep the food inside him.

   The sun rose through the mist and rain its dull outline did not bring any joy to those in the column. To their amazement some bread was distributed to the men, it was stale and carried mould on its surface. Those that could reached for it, anything was better than starving, some did not have the energy to stand let alone fight for bread. Jamie managed to secure a chunk and with the others he greedily stuffed it into his mouth, he also took a piece of the turnip and ate that as well. Then they marched through the rain for a second day. One man close to Jamie stopped and was sick bringing up whatever he had tried to swallow, it was not just being sick, his bowels emptied he had lost control of his bodily functions, a stream of foul liquid fell from his body soiling his breeches. The poor man looked around but nobody was willing to assist him. As they marched off Jamie watched as the man collapsed at the side of the road, a guard walked over to him and poked him with his staff. The man groaned and turned to look at the soldier who shook his head, turned and walked away. The column moved off and the man was left where he had fallen, no help was offered not by the guards or by his fellow prisoners, he was left to die.

As Jamie marched on, he passed several others laying by the roadside in a terrible state, it was the bloody flux that had taken them and it would not stop there, Jamie knew that once this started many would succumb to the disease. The column moved on.

The column passed by a series of orchards full of apple and pear trees and there were some fruits still unpicked and others laying on the ground. Men took the risk, they ran swiftly into the first rows of trees picking up as much as they could then turning with hands full of fruit re-joined the rest of the men who clustered around them hoping for something to bite on. The fruit that the men snatched disappeared, stalks and all. Jamie managed to get four good apples which he jealously guarded. In times gone by he believed in sharing and helping his fellow man but this was a matter of survival and he was determined to live and not end up as a corpse on the side of the road. Then he stopped, the sound of a musket echoed along the ranks of men, turning to face where he thought the shot had come from, he could see men staring in the direction of a soldier standing in the field at the side of the path, his musket still had some smoke drifting from its barrel. In the field lay one of the prisoners, his tattered clothing loosely covering his body, Jamie could see that in his hand he still held an apple, was that all that a life was worth, an apple he thought. Jamie tried to conceal the four apples he had managed to pick up, fortunately all eyes were on the scene surrounding the dead man and the musketeer, he quickly fell into the column making sure his apples were secure.

    The line of march followed a drover's road which seemed to stretch for miles. The cattle, sheep and other livestock had left firm compacted soil interspersed with stone and gravel. The column marched on until the light began to fade, as they came to a halt Jamie managed to eat one of his apples which was like nectar, any worms or magots only added to the flavour. The night was like all others, cold damp and miserable, trying to sleep was difficult laying on cold ground he managed to leave the world behind for several hours, his sleep was light with his precious food held close to his body. And so, life continued one foot in front of the other, the fields and forests passed by, handfuls of berries were hurriedly picked and eaten, blisters were burst and lice cracked under finger nails.

    Miles covered were getting fewer, the captain leading the column was not in the best of humours. He needed to make good time and get the men to London so that he could be rid of them. It was not a job for an experienced soldier who had fought well at Worcester however, he knew that his face had not been in the correct place for him to have been given a better position. Looking at the strange array of men in his column he did not feel any compassion or sympathy toward them, if they broke the rules, they would pay the penalty and that meant their lives would be taken either by shot or sword. He knew very well that they were on the edge of starvation but he could do nothing other than try to get anything he could from the towns they passed through. It had been difficult enough trying to obtain rations for his men, as for the prisoners they would have to get by on anything they could scavage but bearing in mind that stealing would be punished by death, many did not have the courage to seek out food and became weaker with every step taken.

  The column arrived at Morton in the Marsh, which Jamie had heard from his friendly soldier, had been a loyal royalist town. Perhaps there might be friendly faces that could spare food and drink he wondered. The town seemed to stop as the column crossed its boundary, heads turned and low voices muttered. It was not what Jamie had expected, there were no smiles to greet them or offers of food, the townsfolk just turned away from them. It was only the children who looked with interest at the men invading their streets and they were rushed away by their mothers, away from the ragged, evil smelling men that now crowded their main street. At the Church of Saint David, the officer in charge sought out the parish parson, he found him in the vestry of the church,

  'I have many men on the road to London, they are in need of some form of sustenance and water, can you help?' The parson shook his head,

  'We have had a poor harvest, any food that may have been surplus the people need to see them through to next spring.' The officer shook his head in frustration,

  'I can pay, and pay well. Is there any bread, how many mills do you have in Morton?' He looked around the vestry he could see the fine garments that the priest would ware for service and he thought how his men would not take kindly to any person from the church imitating Rome. 'I see you like the robes of

Rome.' His voice carried with it a tone of ridicule and threat. The parson looked up,

'We are good followers of the Church of England.'

The officer replied,

'I have with me men who are very strict Presbyterian in their belief of how the church should act and there services be carried out. In fact, they have been known to take umbridge at the sight of signs that the Protestant faith may not be being adhered to and I would hate to see what they would do to your very well kept and beautifully adorned church.' The parson physically shuddered, he had seen and heard of the destruction the soldiers had done to churches they thought 'ungodly'.

'You cannot intimidate me with your threats.'

'My dear man I am not threatening you only asking for you to do your Christian duty and help feed the poor. I can control my men to a point but they have minds of their own and will act as their faith demands.' The parson was almost in tears,

'I will see what can be done, how many men do you have?' A look of success spread across the officer's face,

'I have nearly eight hundred, I had more but death and desertion have reduced the numbers, so if you can give me assistance you will be saving so many lives and you will surely get the approval of our lord.'

'We cannot feed all that number, it's impossible, I will speak to the mayor and the council but you must keep your charges under control and leave as soon as possible.' With that he scurried away and the officer returned to the column. It was a sorry sight, men were sitting or lying too tired and too weak to stand. The smell was overpowering, sweat, disease and death filled the nostrils of any that passed by.

The officer heard the approach of horses, it was not just the parson who was returning. Then they came into sight, four men dressed in the finery of the day.

'What in god's name do you think you are doing?' It was the main character of the party who spoke.

'I am resting my charges and trying to get something for them to eat, and who may I ask are you?' The leader of the party leant forward and spoke with a clear voice full of its own importance.

'I am the mayor of this town and I do not want you or your band of disease-ridden sots anywhere near it.' The officer did not need some self-important idiot telling him what he should do.

'I am not proceeding any further until these men are rested and fed.' He waved his arm around indicating to the men of the column.

'You cannot remain here, if you want food and rest it will have to be taken away from my town. There are a number of fields where you can rest your men.' He pointed to the east. 'Take the road to the Four Shire Stone, there is a place where your charges can rest away from my people.' The officer began to get agitated,

'And food what about food?'

'Get your rabble out of the town and I will get food to you but only when you have left the town boundary.'

'Do I have your word that you will supply food for the men?' The mayor coughed and spluttered, he turned and looked at those that accompanied him. His followers conversed in low tones then the mayor turned back to the officer.

'Yes, you have my word, we will get some rations to you and your men, now please go before the miasma that surrounds you and your men settles on my town.' The officer gave the order to get ready to march, he looked at the sorry state of the men as they got into column, they were in poor condition now, what would they be like when they reach their final destination, he thought and shuddered. It was about two miles to the Four Shire Stone, the column entered a field which appeared fallow, the men sat and lay down they spoke little but their thoughts were many. Some of the sick collapsed not able to hold themselves up and in one group two of the prisoners drew their last breaths. From his saddle the officer called to a corporal,

'See if you can find three men who are able to handle a spade and pick and bring them to me.' The corporal nodded and left to seek out the fittest he could find.

Jamie was laying looking into the sky his legs had started to ache even though they had only marched a few miles. He stood and stretched as he did the corporal spotted him,

'You'll do, come with me lad.' Jamie had a look of surprise on his face as he turned to follow the corporal. '

'Why do you want me?'

'The officer has a job for you, now look sharp and follow me.' Jamie shrugged and followed in the corporal's wake. He could see the corporal looking as if he was searching for one particular individual. He came to an abrupt halt as he saw two men squaring up to fight each other.

'You men stop right where you are.' The men both turned towards the voice, the corporal grabbed them both by the sleeve,

'You two will not use any strength you may have fighting each other, the officer is in need of two men with energy and spirit so follow me.' They fell in line with the corporal and Jamie. A questioning look appeared on their faces when they looked at Jamie, he just shrugged his shoulders and continued to follow the corporal. When they reached the officer there was a soldier standing close by with three spades,

'Good work corporal, you three men are to seek out the bodies of those who have died and bury them. You are to dig their graves no more than four feet in depth, there will be a preacher to say some words over them and then you will fill the graves. Is that understood?' The three men felt a cold chill run down their backs, one man asked.

'And what if we refuse?' The officer was surprised at the question.

'Do you see the musket that soldier is cleaning?' The man looked in the direction that the officer was pointing, a musketeer had a cloth and some oil, he stopped what he was doing and looked at Jamie and his new companions.

'Yes, I see him.'

'Well, he will have to clean his musket again after he uses it on you if you refuse an order. Does that answer your question?' The man nodded as the soldier handed the spades to

Jamie and the two others. 'You will dig the graves over there.' He pointed to the edge of the field where a hedge created a boundary. 'Now go with the corporal and collect the bodies and to show you I have a heart there may be some bread for you when you have completed your work.' This did not seem to encourage the men, they knew that the bodies would carry illness which they may contract but if they refused a shot in the head would be all they would gain. There was a silent agreement between the three and they dutifully followed the corporal.

    There had been four deaths in the column, the bodies had been pulled away from the main body of men and left without clothes. Anything that could be used had been taken, rags to bind feet jackets if they could provide warmth or protection were now on somebody else's back. Not a word was spoken as Jamie and the two fighters lifted and sometimes dragged the bodies to the place where the officer had indicated. The smell of death mixed with their own fear filled their nostrils as they manhandled the corpses towards the place where they were to dig the graves. They stood looking at each other waiting for the first one to make a move, the corporal shouted,

    'What are you waiting for, get on with it.' Jamie took up his spade and rammed it into the earth. The spade bit into the grassy surface and sank under the pressure he applied. The other two picked up their spades and joined in, the taller of the two said.

    'There had better be bread for us or I swear I will take the shot rather than do this work.' He looked at Jamie, 'what are you called?' he asked. Jamie could feel the sweat starting to form rivulets down his face,

'I am called Jamie.' He did not wish to enter into conversation with the man or anybody else he just wanted to keep his own peace.

'Well Jamie, I am Robert and this unfortunate creature is Ian.' Jamie looked from one man to the other, they were completely different in stature and looks. One man, the one called Robert, was tall and slim with a shock of red hair with beard to match. His eyes were green and looked out at the world without blinking. The other, Ian, was short with a dark brooding look about him. What was once a stocky body had lost weight, what he was wearing hung loosely about him. Jamie noticed that as he gripped the spade, he had a finger missing from his right hand and having seen the men fighting he thought that the finger was probably lost in a fight not a battle. His two companions lifted their spades and dug with what strength they could muster.

When they had dug four graves down to about chest level in depth the corporal called a halt. Jamie with his two fellow diggers scrambled out of the grave they had just finished.

'Put the bodies in the graves then wait for me, I shall be back as soon as I have found the preacher.' They watched him head off in the direction where a gathering of prisoners was listening to a central figure. On his return the corporal was accompanied by a tall man clothed in black, he walked with an unsteady gate favouring his right leg, his left looked a little shorter. As he approached Jamie could see that below his hat the preacher was gaunt with sunken eyes, Jamie did not think it would not be long before they were preparing a grave for him.

The preacher glanced down at the naked bodies and shook his head,

'Have you nothing to cover these men?' The corporal looked a little embarrassed,

'We have no cloth or spare clothing they will have to leave this world the same way they entered, naked.' He turned to the grave diggers. 'Get them into the graves and be quick about it.' Jamie took an arm of the first corpse Robert grabbed the other, Ian took hold of the legs and they carried the body as gently as they could, then laid it into the first grave. The preacher turned to the corporal,

'What are their names, and where do they hail from.' The corporal shook his head again,

'We have few details but I think their names are,' as he pointed to each corpse, he called out their names. 'This is William Thompson.' His finger then moved to the second corpse, 'this is John Ashkirk, that is Andrew Urie and the last is John Wynet, as to where they come from, I do not know, is that important?' The preacher looked from corpse to corpse and shook his head,

'No, I don't think it matters, not to us and not to them.' John Wynet's body was the last to be placed in a grave, the corporal made a gesture to the men to start to cover the bodies. As they started to shovel the earth onto the naked form of Wynet the preacher opened his arms and looked skyward his voice was hoarse and trembled.

'The Lord is my shepherd; I shall not want.

He maketh me to lie down in green pastures; he leadeth me beside the still waters.'

As he began men nearby stopped what they were doing and stood bowing their heads in respect. The preacher continued,

'He restoreth my soul; he leadeth me in the paths of righteousness for his name's sake.

Yea, though I walk through the valley of the shadow of death, I will fear no evil; for thou art with me; thy rod and thy staff they comfort me.

Thou preparest a table before me in the presence of mine enemies; thou anointest my head with oil; my cup runneth over.

Surely goodness and mercy shall follow me all the days of my life; and I will dwell in the house of the Lord for ever.'

As he finished the psalm those around the graves said 'Amen' then turned away not wishing to think of who would follow the four men into early graves. Jamie and his two companions smoothed the soil on the graves then rested on their spades,

'You three come with me.' Jamie shrugged his shoulders and followed the corporal.

'What is it they will have us do now?' It was Robert, never to look on the bright side, dropped his spade and started to follow the corporal who turned,

'Pick that up.' He pointed to Robert's spade. 'You'll be needing that in the days to come.' Robert stooped down and collected the tool that he had now become a friend with. They walked into the adjoining field where tents had been pitched to give the soldiers some protection against the elements. A fire was burning bright and several men were sitting eating their first meal of the day.

'Sit over there.' The corporal pointed to a flat piece of ground, the three walked the few yards to where the corporal had indicated and sat. Jamie casually started to clean his spade which he soon dropped when he saw a soldier approach with three bowls with steam rising from whatever was inside. They were given a bowl each containing what appeared to be some form of pottage, grease floated on the surface which could mean that there was meat beneath the cabbage they could see. Even more surprisingly a second soldier came to them with a loaf of bread, he broke it into three and dropped each portion into their bowls.

'Eat.' The soldier said. 'It may be the last you get for many a day.' Jamie, Robert and Ian could not believe what they had in their hands. The bread was dark, almost black, and as hard as rock. Each man put the bread into the watery pottage and as it softened, they wolfed it down. Jamie could find no meat in his bowl but was happy to get something to put in his gut. The three men finished by licking every morsel from their bowls, it was the first food they had been given in what seemed like months. The corporal came to them,

'It may be in your best interest not to tell anyone about this.' He gestured to the bowls lying next to them. 'You may find the resentment leads to something more than you can handle. Just tell anyone who asks that you had a further body to bury.' The three men nodded in agreement. 'Anyway, there may be some more food coming this way later in the morning and if I were you, I would take whatever I could. We, 'he pointed to those soldiers around him, 'do not get much more than you, now let's get you back, on your feet.' The three plus the corporal made their way back to the main column.

It was late afternoon when the prisoners heard the sound of wagons approaching. Through the entrance to the field where they had been kept overnight came four wagons and with them the smell of food. Jamie could see the prisoners get to their feet as the aroma of something edible reached them. Each man had been carrying a bowl, plate or beaker with him and as the wagons came to a halt, they all took hold of their various utensils and started to crowd around the carts as they drew closer. There was a shot fired and everyone stopped. An officer on horseback rode in front of the first wagon.

'You men will form a line, anyone leaving that line will be shot. Is that understood?' There was a mumbled response, he rode along the row of men repeating his warning. Jamie had given the bowl he had used earlier back to the soldiers but he and the two others still had their own battered bowls which they clutched as the row of men straightened. The wagons came to a halt, on the back of each one was several large cooking vessels, Jamie could see that the lids had been secured with flour and water forming a seal. The soldiers split the line into four, each line being allocated to a wagon. The drivers and their assistants climbed onto the back, broke the seal and lifted the lids. They were armed with large ladles which they plunged into the pots and stirred. Each large pot contained mainly stewed barley with vegetables. There had been pieces of meat but that had disappeared into the broth. Jamie tried to see if there was any bread but could see no sign. Still clutching their spades, the three followed the line until they arrived at the back of the wagon.

'Hold your bowl up, higher.' Jamie lifted his bowl and saw the contents of the ladle spill out. Carefully he balanced his bowl whilst trying to carry his spade, he eventually reached a space where he dropped his spade and very gently sat not spilling a drop of the precious liquid. His two companions followed him, as they sat, they looked knowingly at each other then started to devour their second meal of the day. When the cooking pots were nearly empty two preachers approached the mounted officer and asked if they might take some food to those who were too ill to get to the wagons.

'You may do as you wish, but don't you think the food would be better served to those who have a chance of living than to those who are most likely to depart this world shortly?' The preachers shook their heads and one said.

'Perhaps one last mouthful of kindness will see them on their journey to the promised land in peace.'

'As you wish.' He called to a trooper who escorted the preachers to the wagon and then to the dying. Jamie watched this and found himself thinking that he may be burying those men the following day and how the living needed sustenance. He cruelly thought to himself that those near to death should be abandoned, they had little time left on this earth and they would be doing far better in helping those around them to survive. Life had become cheaper as the miles passed under their feet.

The following three days became harder with each step, Jamie and his two companions were kept busy and thankfully received bread for their labours. Bodies that were left for them to inter were a gruesome sight. Sores appeared all over the dead who were rolled away from their once friends and kinsmen ready for burial, Jamie together with Robert dragged the dead to the ground allocated for burial, Ian carried the spades, when they reach a clear area the bodies were laid to one side and they began to dig. Where the ground was soft and without too many stones their work went well, they could complete their task before the night was fully upon them, however when the ground was hard and full of rock's they would have little sleep but it was worth it if they were to get food.

From the guards Jamie found out that they were only a day's march from Oxford and that word had been sent ahead to prepare some food for the column,

'It could be that we are fed in Oxford.' He had never been this far south and had no idea if Oxford would be friendly towards them or not. He, with Robert and Ian, made their way to where the bodies of the dead were laid, Jamie could see a pile of dark rags and with a certain amount of curiosity lifted the edge of the rotten cloth. What he saw did not shock him, it was the preacher. His clothes and hat had not been removed, probably out of respect Jamie thought, as Robert took one of the preachers arms Jamie grabbed the other but two men were not needed, the body weighed nothing, the arm that Jamie had taken hold of was nothing but bone, the preacher was no heavier than a child. The wide brimmed black hat fell away from the head of the preacher revealing a skull with very little hair and virtually no flesh, the eyes were sunken but still stared towards heaven. They dug the grave all the time looking at the lifeless figure with its grin of death. As they were finishing another black robed individual arrived at the graveside, he stood holding his bible, Jamie thought he could see tears in the man's eyes,

'When you have completed your work, I will say a prayer for my brother preacher.' Jamie didn't know if he meant that the dead man was his blood brother or if he was just a brother in God.

The last days march into Oxford proved painful. Men were now nearing the end of their tether. Clothes that had once covered their bodies were now in rags their footwear was almost non-existent, cloth had been bound around the feet of many. Men limped and struggled to keep up, they all knew that the only way to keep alive was to doggedly keep in line.

The outskirts of Oxford held little for them. The town buildings loomed up before them its honey-coloured stone looked soft in the sunlight but for those in the column the world had lost its beauty their only thoughts were on food. The officer in charge had ridden ahead, he reined his horse in, Jamie could clearly hear the instructions he gave to his men,

'We will travel North of the city and then turn to the East, a number of the soldiers from the garrison will accompany us as guides. As soon as we have cleared the city provision has been made to feed the prisoners.' He stretched up in his saddle and scanned the column. 'The prisoners are to be kept under tight supervision at all times, if any try to run then they are to be shot. There will be a change of guards, men from the garrison will replace those that have been with the column since Worcester and they will stay with the column until London.' There was a cheer from the soldiers who had been with prisoners since they started the march following the battle. Jamie looked around at Robert and Ian,

'I don't know if we will be employed when the new officer takes over.' Ian coughed,

'If we lose our bread we will surely starve.'

'We will have to see what those who replace these soldiers want, we may be able to carry on, just take care of your spades and we will seek guidance from the replacement soldiers.

CHAPTER 13

The column marched off making their way around the city. Although the buildings were such as the men had never seen before, the place had the same aroma as any other town, it stank. The column moved away from the buildings and then into green fields and fresher air. Jamie could tell by the position of the sun that they had turned to the east they crossed a river and as they did the men eagerly bent down to take as much water as they could, it was cool and clear and even those nearing the end felt better for the taste of the liquid running down their faces and throats. The guides led the way to a large open space where there stood several tents outside of which were fires with cooking vessels bubbling. Every man could smell and taste the food at least a mile before they arrived.

A quiet descended over the men as a figure on horseback made his way into the centre of the column. He pulled on his reins and looked around at the mass of men, he removed his helmet, the men could see a shock of dark hair, not long like the cavaliers of the royalist army, neatly cut at the white collar that was bordered with what appeared to be a line of lace. He put his weight in his stirrups and took a position where all could see him.

'I am Captain Stanton.' His voice was loud and clear he spoke without accent so it was difficult to place where he originated. 'I will be in command from here until we reach our destination, which is London. I have been tasked with getting you there within the week so you will be pushed hard. You will be fed and watered with whatever can be obtained from the towns we pass through, rest assured I will make it my business that you receive something it may not be much but I will keep you alive.' There was a ripple of approval from the prisoners, however they knew that times were hard for the townsfolk and getting anything would be difficult. The captain replaced his helmet and turning his horse shouted to a foot soldier,

'Pass the message that I shall be viewing the column within the hour so get the men ready.' The soldier ran off to find the sergeants and corporals who were responsible for parts of the column. Jamie sat with Robert and Ian, they said little there was not much to say, they would have to wait and see if they were to continue burying the dead.

Captain Stanton hated the thought of being ordered to get these wretches from Oxford to London. It was about sixty miles and he would normally expect a fit body of men to cover the distance in three days without any problem but looking and the poor specimens before him he realised it would take possibly double that time, if not longer. He had been told of the problems that had existed so far on the prisoner's journey by the officer he was relieving. He did not value the information given very highly. It appeared that the man he was replacing could not wait to handover his duties and return to the West Country. Stanton had not been given much information about his charges, only that they were starving and poorly clad. What surprised him was the casual way he had been informed about the deaths on the march. He had difficulty in understanding how men could perish in such high numbers until he saw those who faced him as he drew close to them for the first time. The gaunt faces and damaged bodies clothed only in rags, some without footwear, did not fill him with confidence in carrying out his orders.

The route he would take passed through some reasonably large towns. He would send a trooper ahead to inform those in authority of their approach and to ensure that bread together with anything they could collect should be made ready for their arrival. They would pass through places such as Tetsworth and Stokenchurch then the Wycombes before reaching Uxbridge when they would only have another fifteen to twenty miles to cover before reaching their destination. Stanton needed the men to be strong enough to cover that last stretch in good time, he hoped to make it in a maximum of two days, he would have to assess their fitness as they progressed.

Jamie could just see the new officer with his men gathered around him, he gave his orders, the foot soldiers and troopers dispersed to their sections of the column. A soldier, who looked as if he had seen many a battle, came towards the group in which Jamie, Robert and Ian were standing.

'My name is Ford, Jerimiah Ford and you will call me Sir! You will do as I say and not drag your feet. You will march when I tell you, sit when I tell you, eat when I tell you and sleep when I tell you. Do you understand? Any man who does not speak English will be told what I am saying by those that can.' The soldier walked up and down the line of prisoners, 'My god you are a sorry lot.' He reached where Jamie was standing with Robert and Ian. 'Why have you men got spades?' Robert spoke first.

'We dig graves, we bury those that fall on the march.' It was at this point that Captain Stanton reached the part of the line where the prisoners were being spoken to by Ford. He had just caught the last part of the conversation. He looked at Jamie,

'Where do you bury those that fall?' Nervously Jamie replied,

'Wherever there is space, sometimes to the side of a field, sometimes on the side of the road, anywhere we can.'

'Are you telling me that the men that die on the march do not have a Christian burial?'

'They have words spoken over them by a preacher but that is all.'

'So, you are telling me there is no record of where the men fall or where they are buried?'

'No, sir, only what others can remember.' Jamie saw Captain Stanton physically shudder.

'While I am in command no man will be interred unless it is in consecrated ground. I will speak to you three when I have made arrangements to deal with the dead. Keep your spades I may need you to continue with your work. See to it that these men are brought to me tomorrow at midday.' The soldier, Ford, touched the tip of his cap,

'Yes sir.'

There was an audible sigh of relief from Jamie and his two companions, hopefully they would continue to get additional bread but they would have to wait until the following day and hear what the officer had decided.

The column started to move at sunrise, men staggard to their feet, legs aching and feet tender. At the head of the long line of prisoners rode Captain Stanton, he turned in his saddle and was satisfied that all the prisoners were on the move. The road they followed had been used over many years and was well worn. The men stumbled on, they had been over worse tracks and pathways although their feet did blister for all the hard skin that had developed over their long marches from Scotland. At midday the column rested, Jamie with Robert and Ian were taken to the captain, they carried their spades as if they were pikes resting on their shoulders the blades of the spades glinting in the sunlight. Stanton saw them approach,

'I believe there has been one poor devil who lost his battle with disease this morning, you men will take him to the church of St Giles in this town, I have spoken to the minister who has agreed to the body being buried in the churchyard.' He pointed to the soldier, 'You will find out his name or at least the name of his clan and then place the body on that handcart.' he pointed to a two wheeled cart that had been used for the transport of some rations, 'You will then go with these men to the church and give my compliments to the minister who will give you further instructions. After the body has been interred you will return to the column with all haste, is that understood?' The soldier stuttered,

'Sir how am I supposed to catch the column it may take some time to dig a grave and have the minister say his words.'

'It is one body and those men,' he pointed to Jamie, Robert and Ian, 'are in relatively good health so it will be up to you to make it back. The column will remain on this road without deviation so all you will need to do is follow it until you see the main body which will be rested for the night in a field adjacent to the road.' With that he turned his horses head and galloped off. The soldier kicked the earth and then glared at the three men in his charge.

'Bring the cart and follow me.' Ian, together with Robert and Jamie managed to get the cart moving. It had not been taken care of and needed its axels greasing, the noise it made as they pulled it into life was that of a screaming banshee and made their teeth ache. They dragged the cart as they followed in the tracks of the soldier. The prisoners cleared a pathway for them to get to the body, it was the same as they had seen many times in the past, the body had been stripped of anything that could be used and left alone. This time there was some clothing covering from the waist down, Jamie could see that the sores on the man's torso were deep red, almost purple, the ribs were clear to see and the stomach was bloated.

'What clan is this man from?' The soldiers voice echoed around the men standing looking on. The reply was clear,

'He is of Clan Fraser.'

'Do you know how he was called?'

'I think his name was Gregor but it could have been Graham.' The soldier shook his head,

'Graham Fraser will do, you three get the body onto the cart and be quick about it.'

The three men picked up the body in a way that they had become accustomed to using, one on each arm and one to carry the legs. They quickly got it onto the cart and started to pull it towards the main track. From the road they could see the church about half a mile in the distance,

'This way, follow me.' The soldier stepped out purposefully and the three men tried to keep pace as best they could. The ruts in the path made it difficult to manoeuvre the cart but somehow, they managed to get it on to more solid ground. The tower of the church they were headed for got closer,

'You will have little time to get your work done so do not slack for a moment otherwise we will all miss our rations, is that clear?' The three said in unison.

'Yes, sir.

As they reached the church its shape became clearer. It looked as if it had been standing for a hundred years. It was the colour of other buildings they had passed, a rich honey hue of the area. It had windows with arches pointing towards heaven and doors that looked as if they could withstand anything that the weather could throw against them. The minister had seen them coming towards the church as he was trying to find a suitable place to bury the corpse being brought from the column. The officer had visited him on the previous day had said that he wanted a grave dug and a prayer said but nothing more and the good thing was he also said that he would send men to dig the grave. He instructed his sexton to mark a patch of earth and to get ready to tell the men where to dig. The soldier, Ford, approached the minister,

'I have been told to report to you, where shall these men start to dig?' The black clad minister pointed to where the sexton was standing,

'There, where Mr Prentice is standing.' The cart was manhandled across the grassy churchyard and positioned close to where the sexton stood. 'You will tell Mr Prentice when you have completed your work and he will fetch me and I will pray for the man and carry out a small service. Give Mr Prentice his name and date of birth.' The soldier coughed,

'We know his name but that is all.' The minister looked sternly at Ford,

'I suppose that will have to do.'

Three spades started their work, the ground was soft which made the weed filled top soil easy to remove. Jamie and Ian started to dig, Robert made sure that the earth that was removed was piled so that it would not fall back into where the other two were working. Although the autumn chill could be felt, the men started to sweat. They removed their ragged jackets and threw them to one side, the soldier and the sexton watched for a short while then the sexton made to go back to his duties.

'When they are nearing the end of their work fetch me, I shall be inside the church.' Ford grunted and sat on the wall that bordered the churchyard. He watched as the men slowly sank as they dug, Jamie and Robert were the first to swap roles, Jamie jumped out of the partially dug grave passing Robert as he almost fell on top of him. It took them almost an hour to get to the required depth, Ford could see they were almost there, he then went in search of the sexton all the while making sure he could still see the three men. He banged on the church door which was opened by a slightly startled sexton,

'We are nearly done.' The soldier told him.

'I shall be with you shortly.' The sexton went back into the depths of the church to finish off what he was doing. when he returned, he followed the soldier back to where the grave was being dug.

'Your men have made good time.' The sexton was pleased. He looked from the soldier to the three men stripped to the waste and covered in sweat. He could see that they were in need of a good meal their arms were thin and almost stick like,

'I will fetch the minister,' he then looked at the body that was to be interred and held his nose, 'I will bring some cloth to wrap the poor man in, we cannot bury him in that state.' Robert looked at his two companions, they had put many men into their graves without a thread of covering and were amused by the approach taken by the sexton. The sexton left them and made his way to the cottage a few hundred yards from the church. Ford told the men to take a rest, they collapsed on the soft grass that surrounded several graves. It was not long before the sexton returned, he surprised the men, he was with a woman and two children, they were carrying something. Jamie could see that one had a jug but what it contained was anybody's guess.

'After the minister has carried out his service you will be able to eat and drink before you return to your fellow prisoners.' The three men and the soldier looked at each other with a smile on their faces. As the sexton and his little party came closer Jamie could see that the two children were a boy and a girl. The boy was about eleven years old and the girl a little younger, they were carrying something wrapped in a clean white cloth. Jamie hoped that it was food that they were carrying. They returned from their thoughts of food and looked up saw the minister turn the corner of the church, he was carrying a large bible and looked as if he had changed his robes. The three men and the soldier stood as he approached, they watched as he neared the grave and took his place at the head of the opening.

    'I shall say but a few words for this departing soul and pray that he is resurrected in the presence of the creator and his soul rest with those who have gone before him.' The minister's voice filled the still air of the graveyard and as he reached the end of his prayer, he lifted a hand full of soil and gently let it drop onto the body of a man he had never known. He nodded to the three men who started to fill the grave. It took them no time at all to return the earth from where they had lifted it. As they smoothed the surface the minister recited death, the leveller's poem,

> 'The glories of our blood and state
>
> Are shadows, not substantial things;
>
> There is no armour against fate;
>
> Death lays his icy hand on kings:
>
> Sceptre and crown
>
> Must tumble down,
>
> And in the dust be equal made
>
> With the poor crooked scythe and spade.'

    As he ended the verse he turned to the sexton, 'I see you have brought food and drink for the men, please carry on as they must be back to their column as quickly as possible.' The sexton with his wife and children opened up the cloths they had brought, there was bread, cheese and apples. The jug that the boy had was full to the brim with small beer, he carefully poured the liquid into the beakers his sister had been carrying. The sexton's wife unwrapped the bread and cheese and beckoned the men to help themselves. The soldier was first to the food followed cautiously by Jamie, Robert then Ian followed. It was enough for them to take a half loaf each with a large wedge of cheese. They sat eating and drinking, the men were in heaven, if they could expect this every time, they buried a prisoner then they might just survive. When they had finished, they thanked the sexton, his wife and children. The minister had left the scene and disappeared into the church. As the men took hold of the handcart the girl ran to them holding out four apples which they gratefully took and hid them under their shirts.

    It had been an easy day for the grave diggers, they had got on with their work without interruption and managed to get handsomely paid for it. The bread and cheese sat well in their stomachs. When they caught up with the column the sun had set and all was in darkness. Lights from fires shone and guided them back to their places. Jamie could see the faces of men he had seen during the march, they were a ghostly pale in the moonlight. The soldier told them to wait as he made his way to his own area. After speaking to a corporal, he returned and guided Jamie and his fellow diggers to where some rations had been set aside for them. They ate quickly, all three not saying anything, every morsel went into their mouths without a breath being taken. It was Ian who mumbled as he ate the last pieces of bread soaked in the greasy fluid in the bottom of his bowl,

    'It has been a fine day and we should thank the lord that we have benefited from our toil.'

    'I pray that we have more days like this,' was Jamie's reply. Robert's answer was to belch loudly and rub his stomach,

'Now we can get some sleep.' They settled down the best they could on the hard earth with little to keep off the nights cold air.

The day started with a fine mist which developed into heavier rain. Jamie went to the hand cart and tried to manoeuvre it into a position where they could easily take it to any part of the column. The soldier who had been with them the previous day appeared with rain dripping from the tip of his nose.

'We have work to do, so look lively.'

The three men took their positions, one to each shaft with one at the rear to push. The soldier led them along the column. Men parted as they saw the death cart approaching then the first body came in sight. There was not much to show for a life and as Robert and Ian lifted the corpse the head lolled to one side and the mouth dropped open as if it was about to speak. A shudder ran through Jamie as he turned the cart slightly to allow the body to be slung on its wooden floor. The soldier looked at those standing by,

'Is there a name for this poor fellow?' No reply came forth. 'Well, what can we call him?' Still silence, then a low voice said,

'I think he came from Montrose.' The soldier looked at the man speaking,

'Nothing more, no Clan name or Christian name?' The same voice said,

'No, no relatives, no home, no life.' The soldier looked mournfully at the thin lifeless form in front of him.

'Well, what's your name of calling?' The voice responded with some hesitation, nobody wanted a dead man called after themselves,

'I am known as Duncan.'

'That will do, he shall be called Duncan Montrose and god rest his soul.'

They were called for several times and by the time they had finished there were four bodies on the cart which became difficult to handle. As the column made ready to march Captain Stanton rode up to them, glancing at the load in the cart he told the soldier to fetch some harness from the baggage wagon, he then rode off and within minutes a trooper rode up to them.

'Captain Stanton has ordered me to help you.' He dismounted and inspected the cart.

'I am supposed to help you get these creatures to the nearest church how I do that is a challenge but somehow I have to use my horse and I warn you if anything should happen that will harm her,' he patted the horse's neck, 'I will not hold back in administering punishment.' The soldier, Ford, reappeared carrying harness and rope,

'I hope this will do.' He said looking from the tangle he carried to the cart and then to the horse. The trooper swore under his breath, he was not a happy man, he was a trooper not a purveyor of corpses. He unsaddled his mount and together with the soldier tried to attach the harness from the cart to his horse. Eventually they managed to make things secure, as the trooper started to lead his horse there was a cry and another trooper came trotting towards them,

'Wait, there may be more for you to bury.' The trooper now standing by the head of his horse responded,

'What do you mean more, how many more, there are four on the cart already.' The mounted trooper looked a little sheepish,

'I have seen another five bodies back there.' He turned in his saddle and pointed to the rear of the column. 'You are to take the wagon and collect the corpses and then make your way to the village of West Wycombe, there you are to contact the minister at the church of St Lawrence. He will be expecting you but I don't think he will have been told about the number of bodies you will be carrying.'

The trooper standing next to the cart and the soldier, glared angrily at the man looking down at them from his saddle. He pulled on his reins and galloped off the report back to Captain Stanton. There were now five men in the burial party the soldier looked at the trooper,

'If you are to stay with your horse there is no need for me to accompany the prisoners.' As soon as the words were out of his mouth he regretted it, if he remained, he may get additional food similar to that of the previous day. Before he could say any more the trooper told him in no uncertain terms that he would remain with the column and would put the care of his horse in the hands of the soldier and woe betide him if his mount were injured or damaged in anyway. The trooper bent down and removed his spurs, he moved towards his horse's head and brushed its flank with his hand.

'I expect to see you at the head of the column before dusk and then I will make sure my mount is in good order, if she is not then you will have to pay in whatever form I decide upon.' The three prisoners together with the foot soldier moved the horse and cart to where the bodies lay.

The last of the nine bodies were placed upon the flat bed of the cart, Jamie had been detailed to lead the horse so he took hold of the reins and pulled forward. He had handled horses before but this one was not accustomed to being hitched to a cart and it took some persuading to get it to move.

Their journey to West Wycombe was fairly short and with the horse pulling the cart Jamie and his fellow diggers had a relatively effortless time. It was an easy church to find as it was on the top of a hill and its tower stood proud for all to see. As they drew closer to the building a woman stepped out from the church yard.

'You.' Her voice was directed at the soldier, 'yes you.' She pointed viciously at Ford who was taken aback at her actions and tone of voice.

'Me.' His reply was filled with surprise.

'Are you the burial party?'

'We are.' She looked at the cart and stepped back holding her mouth and nose.

'The minister was told that you would have four to bury, I can see more than that.'

'God called another five during the night so we now have nine graves to dig and nine new parishioners for you to care for although they will not need much looking after once they are in the ground.'

'This is not good, not good at all, I shall have to fetch the minister, no this will not do at all.' She spoke to herself as she hurried off in the direction of the church. The four men sat and waited, there was nothing they could do until they were given permission to dig the graves. As they waited the soldier took out a pipe, long and thin with a very small bowl. He struck a light and puffed, the smell of the tobacco reached Jamie who had not smoked but the look on Robert's face was one of desire as he tried to breath in the smoke. Jamie looked from Robert to Ian who was coughing, not hard raking coughs but something he had not done before. As his bout of coughing finished, he looked down at his hand and could see traces of blood, Jamie noticed the blood and it was not a good sign. Ian looked from his hand to Jamie they both knew that this could be the beginning of something serious and without gods' mercy Ian could be in for a terrible time if he had contracted the bloody flux. The look that passed between the two men was one of understanding, they would tread carefully over the coming days and pray that it would not develop.

The men heard voices coming from the interior of the church, the door opened and the Minister stood in his black gowns staring at them.

'I can't have this, this is not what your officer told me the number would be.' He almost ran to the cart and stared down at the bodies. 'This is far too many, far too many.' The soldier took the pipe from his mouth.

'What would you have us do with them, take them back?' He was not in the mood to be pleasant to any man, let alone the minister.

'Bring me the sexton and the verger and be quick.' The woman ran towards the church all skirts and mumbles. 'How many have you?' His voice did not have the welcome of a man of the church.

'There are nine bodies to bury, you seem to have room enough.' The soldier raised his pipe making an arc around the graveyard.

'This is ground that is for those who worship at this church not for prisoners.' Jamie could see that the soldier was getting annoyed by the minister's reluctance to receive them.

'Surely god would not begrudge these poor creatures a resting place in your church, there must be a corner you could allow us to do our work.' The minister huffed and puffed, just then the woman returned with two men by her side. Jamie thought one must be the sexton and the other the verger, the church must have a goodly congregation to support the two of them plus the minister and whoever the woman was.

'Mr Holstead and Mr Granger, we have a problem, these men wish to bury nine bodies in our churchyard, is there any where we can place the graves?' There was a brief exchange of words then one of the men, possibly the sexton said,

'The only way we can accommodate nine bodies is to bury them together either in one large grave or three lesser ones.' This pleased the minister.

'Where would you suggest we site the graves?' He asked the sexton.

'I would suggest on the west side of the church as close to the wall as possible. Will they have any markers?'

'They will not, I shall record their names but that is all. Please take the men and cart to the place you suggest and set them to work.' He then turned and addressed the soldier. I have been advised that you require no payment only bread and ale, is that correct?' The soldier knocked his pipe on the sole of his boot then looked up at the minister.

'Whatever you can spare would be gratefully received.' He spoke in an aggravated voice then told the three diggers to take the cart and follow the sexton.

The area that the sexton pointed out was next to the wall of the churchyard and looked the worst of the land available. The three men took their spades and started to dig. It had been decided to bury the corpses three to a grave so that meant that Jamie and the others had their work cut out trying to reach a suitable depth. With Ian starting to struggle this would not be a good day. The sexton disappeared again but fortunately for the diggers he returned accompanied by two men who's physical appearance was that of men who were not unused to hard work.

'You, soldier.' Ford looked at the sexton and grunted.

'Yes, now what is it?' The sexton walked forward with the two men.

'These men are to help you, they are used to the work as they usually dig the graves for the church and are employed by the local parish to keep the area clean.' Jamie and Robert heard the conversation and let out a sigh of relief. The men had brought their own spades and without being told too, they started to dig alongside Jamie. As they removed the earth, they found first gravel and then clay, it was not easy going and by the time the sun had reached its highest point the men were in need of a rest and some form of sustenance. The woman that had first met them brought a jug of ale and some bread together with a surprisingly large chunk of good cheese. The men ate in near silence, they had nothing in common except the graves and that did not make for good conversation. Jamie watched as Ian ate his bread,

    'How are you?' He could see that Ian was not getting any better, his shoulders shook has he coughed and again wiped the blood from his lips. Ian looked back at Jamie with a shrug gestured that there was nothing he could do to improve his condition. They went back to work eventually reaching sufficient depth for the bodies to be buried. Thankfully the sexton's men had taken on most of the work. They had seen the condition that Jamie, Robert and especially Ian were in. Few words passed between them but the sextons men took the lion's share of the work. The bodies were placed in the graves, each grave had only enough room for the three, one of the sexton's men left the graveside to fetch the minister. The minister looked into the graves and was satisfied that they could do no better. As the graves started to be filled the minister read the lord's prayer and then the psalm that had been used at the last burial. Once the graves had been completely filled and the earth smoothed the minister thanked the sexton's men but only glanced at the prisoners. They knew it would be highly unlikely that they would get any further food from the man. Jamie looked around the churchyard to see if there were any fruit trees or even a hedgerow that might prove to be a source of food. He could see that there was a very small orchard that ran along the side of the church, there were apples just waiting to be picked and several bramble bushes that were heavy with ripe black fruit. Jamie plucked up courage,

'Could you spare an apple or two?' The sexton turned towards him then looked to see where the minister had gone, he saw the black robes disappearing into the church,

'I think we could spare the windfalls if you are quick and your guard is in agreement.' The soldier nodded,

'As long as there are apples for me, go ahead.' Jamie, Robert and Ian climbed over the wall and started to gather the fallen apples. The condition did not matter any worms would just add flavour, the blackberries were sweet and the juice trickled down their chins.

'Come on you three it's time to go.' The men reluctantly left the orchard making sure that any apples they had were secured beneath their jackets. The horse had been taking advantage of the grass which ran between the graves, they checked the harness and turned the cart in the direction of the column. The soldier sat in the back while the others leant on the body of the cart.

By the time they caught up with the column it was preparing to halt for the night, the horse was taken from between the shafts of the cart just in time for the trooper to take possession of it. He looked over every inch of his precious beast and only when he had finished inspecting its hooves he was satisfied.

The nights rest was again in another open field, no cover, no warmth and very little food. Jamie knew that without the extra bread and fruit that they had been able to gather in the churchyard, they would be in a poor state. He looked again at Ian and could tell that the man was getting worse. His hacking cough was louder and the blood from his mouth had increased, hopefully, Jamie thought things would be better in the morning but he had little confidence in his thoughts.

As he woke Jamie felt the morning dew soaking his body, his clothes did not give him any protection. He looked over to where Ian lay there was movement but not much. He stood and stretched then walked to where Ian was still sleeping. Kneeling down he spoke gently to his friend,

'It's time to go Ian, we will have our work to do.' There was no reply, Jamie touched his friend's forehead, it was on fire. He called to Robert who dragged himself to his feet then staggered over to his fellow diggers,

'What is it?' He asked, then after looking closely at Ian he looked at Jamie and held his eyes. Jamie shook his head, Robert came closer, he could see that his friend had deteriorated a great deal overnight. There was nothing they could do for Ian, he could not stand and as for work, that was out of the question. Ian looked at Jamie,

'I know I have little time left, will you make sure I am treated well.' Jamie could see that Ian's face had taken on the pallor of someone close to death. Ian's skin was almost translucent, his eyes were circled with black and a film of sweat covered his features. 'You have been good to me and I will wait for you.' Jamie understood that Ian was preparing himself,

'Yes, we will see each other again in a better place, we will sit with each other and eat the best of meat and bread. We will taste the finest wines and tell stories and we will laugh together.' Jamie saw a smile appear on Ian's lips,

'Yes, we will tell of the times we have been together and how we fought for the king and the kirk. We will forget the hunger and the thirst, we will be under clear blue skies surrounded by the hills and heather, it will be so good.' As Ian spoke Jamie felt his hand slip from his own. The rattle of death came from Ian's mouth, his last words had been spoken, he was now at rest. No words were needed between the two men looking down at their friends still body. They would stay with Ian until it was time to take him to the nearest church, they would make sure his last possessions were not stolen.

Their soldier escort appeared and stopped when he saw Jamie and Robert next to the body of Ian.

'Is he gone?' Robert cleared his throat,

'Yes, he is in a better place now.' The soldier looked from the body to the cart that stood close by.

'We have work to do and now there are just the two of you.' Both Jamie and Robert turned and fixed their eyes onto those of the soldier. He shuffled his feet, 'I will speak to Captain Stanton, wait here.' With that he set off towards the head of the column. They waited in silence not wishing to speak of Ian, they just stood by his body making sure nothing or nobody disturbed him. The soldier returned followed by a boy of about fifteen years of age. He was skinny with a shock of red hair, his knees did not meet one another and Jamie thought that he would have difficulty stopping anything that tried to get beyond him. There was no smile of welcome on any of their faces,

'This is your new friend.' He pushed the boy forward. 'Tell them your name lad.' The boy's eyes searched the two figures in front of him, he did not speak immediately it was almost as if he was dumb, then the words started. Slowly he seemed to gather himself,

'I am Thomas, but I answer to Tom.'

Robert pointed to Ian's spade,

'That's your new friend, pick it up and make sure it never leaves your side.' The boy looked at the spade with a puzzled look on his face.

'Why do I need a spade?'

'It is what you will be using in the coming days and it may keep you alive.' Tom bent down and picked up the spade. Jamie walked to his side,

'Follow us and do as we say, you may find things sickening but that's our work.' The three went to the cart and pulled it closer to Ian's inert form. Jamie went to his usual place, at the feet of the body whilst Robert took hold of one arm.

'Take the other arm and lift, be gentle mind you this is our friend.'

'But I could catch his disease.' At this point the soldier drew his sword and prodded Tom in the back,

'You could catch the point of this if you don't do as you are told.' Tom took hold of Ian's other arm and the three lifted the corpse onto the bed of the cart.

'Today we have only two to take, so follow me and the sooner we get started the better. It is a long haul to the next church and we will be lucky to keep up with the column.' They took hold of the cart with Ian's body in the back and wheeled it some two hundred yards to where the second body lay. As Jamie and Robert took their positions Tom looked at the corpse and was almost sick, the body was naked and covered in sores, the face had a grotesque grin with eyes that stared into nothing, as Tom looked at the face, he thought it was staring at him. He bent to take hold of an arm, as he touched the skin its cold clammy feel made him drop it and step away. Robert glowered at the boy, you will see worse sights than this.' He nodded at the body. 'So, you had better get used to the feel of dead flesh.' Tom gagged as he bent forward again and grasped the arm of the dead man. The soldier went through the same ritual asking if anyone knew this man and what was his name. The reply was the that he came from Dundee but his name of calling was not known.

'And what is your name of calling.' The answer was Joseph. 'So that is what he will be buried as, Joseph Dundee.'

Once they had loaded the bodies on the cart Jamie asked the soldier how far they had to travel to get to the next church.

'We are directed to go to St Margarets Chapel in a town known as Uxbridge which is about seventeen miles from here and when we have finished, we will have to go a further mile to reach the place where the column will be resting for the night.' Robert glance at Jamie and then turning to the soldier asked.

'Can we not get the use of a trooper's horse, it's a long way and although we have only two bodies, we will have trouble joining the column after we have completed our work. The soldier told them to wait then disappeared returning some minutes later pulling on the reins of a tired bedraggled beast which was definitely not a trooper's mount.

'Here you are, a fine-looking animal that we have the use of for the remainder of the march.' They managed to harness the poor old beast and set off towards St Margarets Chapel.

The minister at St Margarets was a long serving, dyed in the wool puritan. He had no time for those who did not follow the gospel as he did. When he was approached by a rather dishevelled soldier asking where he should dig two graves, he was taken aback. There had been an officer who called on him the previous day but he did not expect the scene before him. The vision of the soldier and three men standing by a rather poor specimen of a horse and a cart that could do with some repairs presented a sorry picture.

'What do you have there?' The way his arm shot out and his index finger stabbed the air led the soldier to believe that this was not going to be an easy day.

'Sir, we have two bodies to bury in your churchyard, they are the bodies of poor unfortunates who have breathed their last during the night. Do you have a plot for us to carry out our duties?' It was as if the minister had been struck by lightning, coughing he managed to get out some words that were laced with a certain amount of angst,

'Two bodies you say, bodies of who, where are they from?' The soldiers face said it all, this was not going to be a friendly chat,

'As I have said, they are from the column of prisoners that is being taken to London. They are Scottish and far from the land of their birth. I have been ordered to bring them to this place where, I have been told, that the minister has been made aware of our requirements.' The minister's face grew red as his blood pressure rose,

'The person who visited me did not make it clear at all, prisoners you say.' It was if he was speaking to himself. 'Wait, do not do anything.' He marched off with a determined stride. The men by the cart stood and looked around the churchyard, fortunately the weather was dry and the sun's warmth relaxed their tired muscles. It was almost an hour before the minister returned, he had another man with him also in the clerical grey who turned out to be his assistant.

'This is my associate Mr Truman, he will direct you to a place and answer any questions you may have.' With that he swung his body round and made off in the direction of the chapel.

'I am afraid the minister has some matters of trust he has yet to come to terms with. His body is sound but his mind can sometimes wonder. Now what is it you need?' The soldier explained again why he had brought two bodies to be buried and asked where his men could start digging the graves.

'Follow me.' He walked around the side of the chapel and led them to an area well away from the entrance to the churchyard. Pointing to a space at the furthest end of the land surrounding the church he told the soldier, 'This will be yours to do your work, but tell me who are these men, do they have names, dates of birth, names of relations?'

'I'm sorry, we have only names and some of those may not be correct. One of the bodies is that of Ian of Cononbridge and the other, well we think he may be called Joseph of Dundee and that is all we have.

'Do you know when they were born?'

'No sir, we have no knowledge other that what I have just told you.'

'I shall enter them into the parish records as that, so there will be something to note their burial.'

Jamie walked back to the cart and took hold of the poor horse's bridle, pulling it he got the nag to walk back to where the graves were to be dug. The three men started to dig, it was easier ground than that of the previous day. Robert told Tom what to do and they tackled the earth. They made good time, it was before noon when they stood by the side of the two graves and waited for the minister to return. Fortunately, it was the younger of the two, the soldier let out a quiet sigh of relief as the young minister took his place at the side of the grave. Prayers were said and the three men together with the soldier threw handfuls of soil onto the cold figures at the bottom of the graves. Jamie and Robert stood in silence as the others left the area, they bowed their heads then slowly turned and walked back to the cart. The young minister looked at each of the men and could see they were tired and thirsty,

'Come with me and I will see what food and drink can be spared.' They followed the black coated figure. When they arrived at the cottage, situated not far from the chapel, they were met by a rather portly female figure, she almost waddled towards them.

'Mrs Strode have you managed to find something for these men?' Her round face, which was slightly flushed, looked at the men,

'I have some cold meats left over from last night's supper and that together with some small beer should see them right.' She waved her arm towards the cottage, 'Come, follow me.' They trooped along behind her to a table that had been set up outside the main door of the cottage. On it the men could see several plates with what appeared to be chicken on one and pork on the other. In the centre was a large basket with chunks of fresh bread which made all four men lick their lips.

'You had better get this down you as quickly as possible.' It was the soldier who looked anxiously around the table. 'We have a good few miles to cover before we reach the column and when we get back there will be little left for us, so eat well. Tom stood with his mouth open,

'Is this for us?' he said with both surprise and hunger. 'Did you get things to eat in every church you visited?' Robert looked sternly at the lad,

'What we received is for us to know and for you to keep silent about. Is that clear?'

Tom knew when to follow what he was told.

'It will stay with me.' He lifted a chunk of bread in one hand and a piece of pork in the other and started to fill his mouth. When their plates were empty and the ale drunk the soldier called them together and after thanking the minister and Mrs Strode, they took their leave.

They managed to catch up with the column in good time, the road that they followed was one used by many travelling from Oxford to London. Signs of the column were clear to see, a trampled verge to the side of the road made by the hundreds of men led them in the right direction. The column had halted for the night in fields close to the small town of Hayes, the burial party arrived in time to receive more bread and a small amount of cheese. As the ate their ration Tom smiled knowingly but nothing about what they had been given at the chapel was mentioned.

The morning that followed proved to be one of trauma and frustration. The soldier appeared calling their names, when he could see that they were getting to their feet he gave them their work for the day.

'Its bad news I'm afraid, any that have passed during the night are to be buried in the church close by and we are to catch the column as fast as we can.'

'What is the reason for that?' Jamie asked.

'We are nearing the end of our journey, we have one more day then we will be in London. It is there that I and my fellow soldiers and troopers will leave you.' Robert looked worried and asked,

'What place are we going to?'

'I am not sure but it is in the city of Westminster that's all I can tell you.'

'What work do we have this day, how many met their maker during the night?' It was Jamie asking the question his hands grasping the handle of his spade.

'There have been four deaths which means we are to work hard and fast so be quick in what you are doing.' The three took their spades and made their way to the cart and the old horse. Harnessing the horse was fairly easy but locating the four bodies was a little more difficult as they had been moved by the other prisoners. Eventually Jamie found the bodies and the three men loaded them onto the cart.

'Where are we to take them?' It was Robert asking the question as he folded the arm of the final body onto the cart.

'We are to go to St Mary's church, now hurry we must be quick.'

With the bodies secured on the back of the cart the men followed the soldier who had been given the directions to St Mary's. On reaching the church the soldier told them that there would be no time for eating anything,

'If we are given bread make haste in eating it.' He seemed to be a lot more worried than usual. 'I have been ordered to join the column without delay as they need every man to be in the column as it reaches London.' With that he took hold of the horse's bridle and started to pull. This was unlike the soldier who would never do more than guide the men to the churchyard. They set off at a goodly pace and within no time at all were at the gate of St Mary's. The minister stood waiting for them,

'Follow me.' He gestured to the entrance to the churchyard. He paused at a spot that should be adequate for four graves as long as they were positioned close together. 'This is where you will dig and once you have completed your task you are to fetch me.' He spoke to the soldier who appeared to be very uneasy by the way he was being spoken too. They brought the cart to the spot indicated by the minister and began to excavate the graves. They worked hard and fast, not taking any rest. The soldier kept on at them to hurry which did not encourage them but nevertheless they finished in less time than usual. The soldier banged on the church door from which the minister appeared,

  'We are done.' The soldier said wiping the sweat from his brow although he had not helped with the digging. His sweat was that of a nervous man, his eyes followed the minister as he took his bible in one hand and started to recite the Lord's prayer. It was over very quickly, the minister did not ask for details of the dead which was fortunate as the soldier did not have names or places of birth. The three men looked expectantly at the minister who on seeing their stares told them to wait. He did not return but two young boys of some twelve years of age appeared from around a corner of the church, they were carrying a large loaf of bread, as small amount of cheese and a jug of ale. The four men ate the bread and cheese as fast as they could and washed it down with mouthfuls of ale. The two boys had never seen food disappear so quickly, they were handed back the plates and jug as the men pulled the old nag around and headed towards the road.

  It was a hurried journey back to the column, they reached it where the road passed close to a river. Before taking their places, they drank, the water may not be good but their thirst made them take the risk of catching something. Captain Stanton rode up to the burial party and told them what they were to do.

  'You are to follow at the rear of the column and place any man who cannot walk onto the cart. If the numbers become too great then send word to me and I will decide on who is to be taken, some will have to be left to fend for themselves.' To Jamie and his two companions this was a sentence of death to anyone left behind but as they were probably near to the end of their lives it would not matter. Life had become very cheap along the road from Worcester, the many that had died would lay in the graves dug by the three men and be forgotten by the world. Robert took hold of the horse's bridle and began to pull the beast towards the rear of the column.

CHAPTER 14

Although they were headed towards the largest city in the kingdom the fields seemed to continue. Corn, barley and wheat had been grown and harvested in the acres that they passed. Travelling in the wake of the column was not easy, the pathways were cut up by the hundreds of feet walking, stumbling along the route leading them to heaven knows where. The worst of it all was when they came across bodies that could not go any further. The soldier would have to make the decision, did they place the body onto the cart or did he encourage them with his staff to get up and march. Jeremiah Ford had been a soldier for seven years, he had seen sights that would make a sane man go mad. Killings on the battlefield were one thing but deciding who should live and who should die on this journey was something he did not wish to take responsibility for however, his orders were to leave some and take others, so that is what he would do no matter how much he hated it. Would his god blame him for their deaths or would he understand that this human was not responsible for their deaths it was those, like Captain Stanton, who should carry the burden of blame.

      Ford managed to get most back on their feet but the pace set was getting faster as the captain had been given a time to get the men to their final destination. The old nag pulling the cart was not in the best of health and required Jamie, Robert and Tom to use all their strength to get it to keep up with the column, sometimes they wondered if they could do a better job without the horse. Small villages came and went, fields of sheep grazing looked as if they were in a different world to that of the ragged stream of humanity that passed by.

The change of scenery seemed to come all of a sudden. Houses started to increase in number and there were more people to be seen. The column was taken to the west and approached the City of Westminster at a slow pace. Soldiers and troopers were trying to keep the men in some form of column but as the buildings closed in it became ever more difficult. Captain Stanton had explored the route the previous day and knew that he would have to direct the prisoners along the widest of roads. He called a halt to enable the men to catch up. He took the opportunity to visit the rear and speak to the burial party.

'How many do you have on the cart?' Ford looked up at the captain whose horse was not in the mood for standing still, it moved suddenly nearly knocking Ford off of his feet.

'We have but two bodies and they are alive but I think they have little time left in this world, others I have been able to get to stay on their feet and march with the rest.'

'Good work, we are not far now from the end of our journey, keep them moving as best you can.' As he turned his horse Jamie could see a man struggling to remain upright, his legs buckled leaving him on his knees. Ford took his staff and gently prodded the exhausted creature,

'Get up, we are almost done, soon you will be able to rest and get food so be a good fellow and rise up.' The man tried to lift himself to his feet but as soon as he had managed to raise his head above waist level he fell back. The man's chest was heaving and a rattle of a breath left his lips, his head turned towards Ford,

'Let me go to meet my maker.' His words were hardly distinguishable as the fluid from his lungs welled up into his mouth. Ford bent towards the man not wishing to get too close for fear of catching his disease.

'Stay where you are, we will get you onto the cart where you will be able to rest.' Ford knew that the man had only a very short time left and that he would not live out the day or even the hour but he was in a mind to let the man die somewhere other than on the side of the road. Robert and Tom took the man's arms and Jamie got onto the cart ready to lift the man onto its creaking wooden floor. Between them they managed to get him in the best position they could, Robert looked down at him, his face was white with purple lips, his cheek bones were clearly visible, his eyes wide and lifeless. Turning to the soldier Robert said,

'He is gone.' He closed the man's eyes and turned the body to face the side of the cart, Tom followed him.

'Will there be many more today?' Tom's question was only met with blank looks. It made their total three so far but they knew there would be others.

The city engulfed them before they realised it. Houses became closer together, the streets narrower and the stench grew with every step taken. To Jamie it was a different world to the one he had left behind in Scotland, in fact it was as close to his home as the moon. The column worked its way forward, the space between houses almost disappeared, it was as if he was looking into the mouth of a monster. What was the white of the plaster on the houses was now a dirty grey or brown they looked like the teeth of one of the corpses they had recently put onto the cart, the slime that ran down the centre of the alleys and pathways was nothing more than piss and puke thrown out by those that lived in the upper floors. Jamie almost trod on a rat that scurried into a crack at the side of a doorway, life could not get any worse, could it? He asked himself.

Strangers passed them, turning their heads not wishing to acknowledge the prisoners, they had enough worries eking out a living and trying to avoid sickness and disease.

'Keep moving, stay in line, keep together.' The voice of Ford was straining to be heard, even he felt the overpowering miasma of the city. As they reached the end on one street an opening gave way to an expanse of green, Jamie looked from the lush grass to Robert,

'Are we back into the country? The city was not big, just filthy.' The soldier heard the comments,

'I am told this is a royal park, it is where the wealthy play.' Jamie could see the other side of life, houses came into view, large ones, with clean white stone shining in the watery light. The column was halted and then turned away from the park and the aristocratic houses that lined its borders. They were forced back into the gloom of the decaying life of the poor. Tom was amazed,

'How can this be, the starving, the dying surrounded by such wealth.' Robert touched his shoulder,

'It is the way of the world, life leads us along a path that the good lord has set for us and we must make the best of what we have. So, it is for those in this city and all those that struggle for life.' They continued in silence, looking and watching at what was happening around them. Jamie was surprised that the faces of those who first saw the column looked at them with pity, he thought that it was they who needed the pity. He then looked at those walking through the shit that covered the cobbles, those men that had been marching for days, those men who had fought at Worcester, they had been so proud to fight for their Kirk and King now they were looked down upon by the lowest members of city society. Jamie heard the clatter of hooves and then saw the captain approach,

'You with the cart make haste I do not want any bodies left for the rats, is that clear? Ford touched the brim of his cap,

'Yes sir.' He struck the poor old nag on the back trying to get it to move a little faster. 'Come on you three get behind and push or we will all be in for a beating.' They passed from squalor to fresh air, from one open green space to another and then Jamie looked up at the building in front of them,

'What is this?' His voice trailed off.

'That, I have been told is the Abbey of Westminster and it marks a place close to the end of our march.' Jamie, Robert and Tom stood with their mouths open admiring what was before them. Robert turned with scorn,

'If god can allow this to be built in his name, how can he bless those who watch people die of hunger.' His life had been moulded by the kirk and he still had strong beliefs that men were created equal in the eyes of the lord. During the time he had been, first with the king's army and then with the prisoner column, he had felt his faith being tested to its limit but as he saw how man could survive almost anything placed in his path his resolve grew stronger. That resolve was now at its lowest ebb, the bodies he had lifted onto the cart and then into graves sickened him and now what was left, he had two men who he now called friends and a spade. He lifted the spade and with all his strength brought it down with a crash onto the back of the cart.

'What's this.' the soldier stopped in his tracks, are you mad, you have come all this way and now you place yourself in jeopardy?' Robert had about as much as he could take, the days, weeks and months had finally caught up with him. Although a strong man physically, he leant on the back of the cart and wept in anger and frustration. Tom looked on not knowing what to do, Jamie placed his arm around Robert's shoulders and gently pulled him upright.

'We are almost at the end of our journey, be strong not only for yourself but for us, we need you Robert, we need you and your faith, help us to survive.' Robert wiped a grimy sleeve across his face leaving lines through the dirt and sweat that covered it.

The column had come to a halt, men were bunched together not knowing what to do, Captain Stanton rode up to the main body of prisoners,

'This is where you will be quartered until your final disposition has been decided. You will be told what to do and where to go by the governors of this place.' He turned his horse and rode off to where several men were eyeing the mass of wretched humanity that was awaiting its fate. Jeremiah Ford had been away from the column for about an hour when he returned, he immediately called the three men he had been responsible for to come to him. When they reached the place where he stood Jamie could see that he was not in the best of moods.

'You three men have worked well for me, I have been gathering news about this place which is not good. I shall be returning to my home now that my duty is done but I could not leave without passing to you what I have discovered. You will be kept in this place, which is called Tothill Fields, there are many already here some from the battle of Dunbar others from various other skirmishes.' He looked even more concerned when he saw the condition of the three standing before him. 'It is a place that few leave and those lucky enough to get away to foreign places may not be better off. What I have been told is that beyond these gates lay nothing but sorrow so if you have any chance to leave do so.' His face had a stern look upon it, this was not idle advice. 'I shall be taking the horse and cart once the bodies have been removed. You will not be required to bury them, they will be taken to where others lay.' Jamie felt a shudder ripple down his spine, it can't be worse than that they had experienced since Worcester, he thought. 'Place your spades on the cart then join the rest of the column.' The three spades clattered onto the back of the cart then Jamie, Robert and Tom watched as the soldier led the old nag away. He turned as he grasped the horse's bridle,

'Mark my words, this is not a place for you to stay, get away as soon as you can.'

Jamie stood with his two colleagues as they wondered exactly what the soldier was trying to tell them. It was the young voice of Tom that stated what they were all thinking,

'It can't be worse than that of the road and the punishment of the march that we have just completed, can it?'

'We shall see very soon.'

A strange group of soldiers and others started to herd the men towards a gate beyond which was a place that would dictate how the rest of their lives would be lived.

CHAPTER 15

The sight that met the three friends was one that could only have been created by the devil himself. Men were in a state of near starvation, they had very little in the way of clothing and as Jamie tried to pass through a group some of the skeletal figure pleaded for food. What could be seen of their flesh was covered in sores, as they spoke Jamie could see that their teeth that remained were black and broken. Tom turned to a guard,

'Where do we sleep?' It was a question of innocence that only Tom could show.

'You will sleep wherever there is a space.'

'But is there no shelter, no rooms for us to lay in?'

'Rooms are for the dying, and you appear to be far from that.'

A sense of sickness filled all three, the soldier had been right, this was a place to get out of as quickly as possible. Jamie asked,

'What are we to do?' The soldier had become annoyed at the questions being asked,

'You will do what you are told to do, now move on, make way for others.'

Jamie led the way past the begging hands and finally reached a space where they could try to take in what their new surroundings had install for them. Tom held his hand to his mouth and nose, the stench was overpowering, he mumbled,

'What is this place, no man should be kept in this filth.' He retched and felt what little he had in his stomach rise into his throat. Robert's eyes were searching through the mass of men trying to make sense of what was happening to them, his shoulders slumped,

'We should have tried to leave the column, death would have been better that this.'

The day was coming to an end and as darkness descended they tried to find a space to sleep. Night brought with it few comforts only that if sleep did come then they would not have to watch the morass of sickness and death that surrounded them. Jamie had closed his eyes but his dreams only followed the agony of the day. Visions of black angels taking his breath and food, shouting move, make way for others. He woke with a start, Tom and Robert were close to him trying to share each other's warmth, Roberts eyes were open, his voice was dry and he croaked,

'Can we get out of this place Jamie, or will this be where we meet our end?'

'I don't know, whatever the day brings we must try to find a way to get out and if it means that we would be killed in an attempt then so be it. Let's believe that the heaven that awaits us would be glorious compared to this hell.

Dawn broke and with it the vision of purgatory flooded back into Jamie's mind. There was a commotion towards a building at the far end of the field. Men started to form lines with bowls in their hands.

'Quick you two get your bowls, I think there is food being given out.'

They waited in line, those in front and behind had the bodies and faces of the starving, eyes staring at nothing their frail bodies hardly able to stand. Some had horrific sores on their necks and faces, Jamie could see puss seeping from the edges of the red swellings that covered their skin. The thought of the disease that everybody dreaded filled his mind. He turned to the man behind him,

'Do they have the plague?'

'No, it is sometimes worse, they have the kings evil and it will kill them.' Jamie took a step back not wanting to be infected, he made the sign of the cross not realising what he was doing but if God could help him avoid this disease, he would make the sign of the cross as many times that was needed to keep him from the pestulance. Others stood near and Jamie could see that they were in a place of pain, he could see that the legs and feet of several of his fellow prisoners were almost black, and this was not dirt that coloured them, the sores had started to rot the flesh and spoil the blood, the rot would spread and the men would die.

Jamie reached the place where he could see bread being handed out, again he turned to the man behind,

'What food is this?'

'We are given one pound of bread and half a pound of cheese every day, the bread is mostly rye and it is as black as night, the cheese is not the best I have ever tasted but it is the only food we are given so eat what you can.' Jamie reached the point where bread was given out, he took what was handed to him. The hard pound of bread felt solid in his hand and as for the cheese, there may have been added ingredients that no man would usually stand for but it was food and if it kept him alive, he would eat every morsel. The three men took their food and found a space next to the boundary wall, leaning back they looked across the field at their fellow prisoners. Robert was surprised and shamed as he saw nature take over some of the men. Those with some strength left would grab bread and cheese from the weakest of the prisoners, leaving them with virtually nothing to survive on. It was those poor wretches that would find their way into the grave pits. Tom greedily stuffed bread and cheese into his mouth,

'Be careful you don't choke.' Jamie advised him.

'I'd rather choke than die the way some of these men will end their time on this earth.' Jamie understood that after seeing men collapsing in front of them and that if they could achieve peace in any form by whatever means they would take it. They finished their food and stood up, their bodies were stiff and their bellies still empty. Around them they could see the morass of men mingling and merging, there was little for them to do. Noise started to spread, Robert could see something happening at the far side of the field. There were men, not guards or soldiers looking at the prisoners. Jamie turned in the direction where Robert was pointing, he could see men being singled out for something, they were being taken to one side by the guards and then strangers seemed to be inspecting each one in turn, starting with the prisoner's heads, checking their hair, if they had any left, then their eyes. Mouths were then forced open and teeth checked, it was as if they were buying animals at market not dealing with human beings. Those that passed the inspection were taken off to one side where they waited. Once the number had reached about one hundred the men were marched off leaving the hell hole that was Tothill Fields behind. Tom, in his naive way, asked a fellow prisoner where the men were being taken.

'It could be anywhere, there are stories of those leaving here and going to work in tanneries and mines and some even being sold as slaves, it is unlikely that any of those men will see their homes or families again. Perhaps they will never reach the shores of Scotland in their lifetimes and I feel sure that many will die alone no matter where they end up.'

Tom looked from the person speaking to Jamie,

'Will we be picked to leave or will we be sentenced to death by starvation in this terrible place.'

'We will do all we can to get out of here and live our lives, we must believe that we can survive and that we will not perish in this place.'

Every day Tom looked around the prison trying to figure out from where the next group of men would be chosen. After the bread and cheese was distributed the three men anxiously waited, perhaps it would be their turn today. The situation grew worse, if that was possible, the rain started and there was nowhere to shelter. Most had been without water for many hours, they lifted their heads and opened their mouths. The rain quenched their sore and dry throats, bowls were held out to catch as much as possible. Jamie knew that no matter how much the rain was like liquid gold, they would suffer later. The few clothes they had on their backs would be drenched and that would add to the misery of the night.

The guards and soldiers moved around the prisoners, not getting too close. They were men who did not want to be there. The soldiers were annoyed and frustrated their role in life was to fight the enemy not look after the dying. In their eyes that is what the men before them were. Other guards had been taken from the gaols and workhouses, they were not happy with their lot although they were used to dealing with the poor and in some cases the dying. Both sets of men did not wish to be anywhere near these prisoners whose bodies were nothing but human cess pits, the likelihood of catching a deadly disease was great enough for many to beg to be released from this duty. Unfortunately, there seemed to be few others willing to carry out the role of gaoler which resulted in very unhappy guards who carried out their role under sufferance.

For five days they waited, eating the hard black bread and the rancid cheese before they had a chance to get chosen by the strangers. Their opportunity came just after they had received their ration of bread and cheese, a stranger approached, he was accompanied by two guards and a soldier, he would point to an individual who was then brought to him for inspection. Just before he reached where they were standing, Robert felt the contents of his stomach start to trickle down his legs, he touched Jamie's arm,

'I must go, I can't jeopardise your chances.' With that he clutched his stomach and hurried away.

'Robert wait!' Jamie's cry was in vain, he saw Robert nearly bent double as he rushed to empty his bowels as far away from his two friends as he could. Before Jamie knew it, he had been turned to face the stranger.

'Stand there.' He was told, and don't move.' Jamie did as he was told and suffered the indignity of being prodded and poked but if this meant a chance of getting out of this place, he was willing to undergo any humiliation. The soldier pointed to where a group of prisoners were standing,

'Over there with the others, be quick.' Jamie moved and as he did, he could see that Tom was in front of the stranger who had started looking into his eyes. It was with a great deal of relief that filled Jamie when Tom joined him but he couldn't help thinking that he had left Robert to a fate that may result in his death.

The group of men numbered upwards of one hundred and fifty. They appeared to be the healthiest of those in the confines of Tothill Fields. Jamie and Tom moved slowly in the direction of the gate leading from their prison, those men who had been chosen considered themselves lucky at this point without knowing what the future held for them. A soldier was pushing them into some semblance of order when a Gentleman approached,

'You men.' He looked at the faces before him, they were hollow and their eyes showed no interest. 'You will be under the command of this man.' He pointed to a tall, well-built individual standing next to him. 'He will lead you to your place of work which will take three or four days for you to reach. He will ensure that you receive food and drink during your journey. I have instructed him to deal with any of you who should try to run or fall on the march with the severest of punishment. He has the authority to bring any man down with either shot or sword and if this should be your punishment, he will not be held responsible for your deaths.' There was a murmur from those around Jamie and Tom,

'As long as we are out of that place I do not care.' It was Jamie who spoke to Tom who nodded in agreement.

The soldier stepped forward.

'I am Corporal Hadley, and I shall be leading you to your place of work. I shall have two soldiers to assist me. You will obey all commands given, any man who does not will be punished. This may mean loss of food or lashes, I will decide on the punishment and I will make sure that it is carried out.' The prisoners looked at the corporal and knew that all that he said he would carry out without hesitation. 'You will march in column, four abreast, if necessary, I will tell you to change formation when we pass through villages or towns.' He looked at the faces of the men before him they appeared to be taking in what he was saying. 'Our march will be in stages but I will be asking for a minimum of fifteen miles a day and depending on the country this may rise to twenty.' Again, there was a rumble of noise from the men. The corporal then looked at the prisoners directly in front of him, their clothes were in tatters, only rags and they did not cover their bodies sufficiently to hide the sores and bruises that each man had. The Gentleman who had spoken first took the corporal to one side,

'There is food set for the men at the stages we have discussed and there will be fresh clothing for them when you reach Cambridge. I realise this will be a drain on the men but you will have to do the best you can. If there is any possibility of getting the clothing to you any earlier I will. Are you sure of the route you are to take?' The corporal was not enamoured with what he had been told but he had no choice in the matter,

'Yes, I know the route well, I have journeyed down it many times and I know the places that will provide food and shelter.' The corporal still had an anxious look on his face.

'Is there something else you wish to discuss?' The corporal was only too well aware that whatever he asked for he would have to wait. He had been given wages and promised a bounty when he reached his destination and for that he was content, how he would achieve his goal was yet to be seen.

'I suggest you make a start, you still have most of the day which will hopefully see you out of the city.' Corporal Hadley turned to the men, his confidence was still with him but how long would that last, he did not know.

'You men line up here.' He pointed his staff at four men who walked towards the place he was indicating. 'The rest of you follow them and make four ranks.' He watched the men, luckily, they seemed to have little problem with their feet which he thought was a god send.

The prisoners marched on feet that had taken a million steps since leaving their homeland. Dreams of returning had long since faded it was only the thought of survival, and that meant food, that kept most men going. The rain, that had fallen earlier, had stopped although there was little heat from the sun. Jamie tried to position the sun, by his reckoning they were moving to the east, the men were not in the best of moods as the food that had been mentioned may yet be many miles from them. Jamie noted the change as they quickly left the mix of squalor and wealth that was the city behind and started to march along roads bordered by fields that held sheep and cattle. Some of the more level land had been harvested and there were hay stacks in rows across the fields. The air was fresh and no rain made the going easier. There was an air of escape as the men marched on, the corporal had little to do except keeping the men in line, the incentive was with them, food.

CHAPTER 16

David Hadley was familiar with the road, it was Ermine Street, a road that led from London to Lincoln. He had made a careful study of not only the road and its condition but the places that had been identified as resting points where he would get the prisoners fed and a place to sleep. Some were religious houses others were farms both had the ability to provide enough food for the one hundred and fifty men in his column. The route that he would be taking was straight forward and with luck and a following wind he would make it on time and qualify for his bounty. He dropped back and walked alongside one of his assistants,

'How are they doing?' He asked his colleague,

'So far they are keeping the pace.' His accent was one of Lincolnshire and could be hard to understand at times.

'Have you seen any serious signs of sickness?' It was the one thing that prayed on Hadley's mind, if he was to get all his charges to their destination it would be mainly due to keeping the men as healthy as possible.

'They could do with a good scrub and fresh clothing.' He pointed with his staff at the tatters that some of the men called clothing. 'The thought of food is on all their minds, how long will it be before we reach our first stop?' He studied the corporals face, he had only known him for a short time but it had been long enough for him to decide that Hadley was a man of his word and a straight talker.

'We should be at Waltham by sundown and then the men can eat and rest. We will be fed in the abbey and I have made sure that our food is of good quality.' With that Hadley made his way to his second assistant who was further back.

'Will, how are things with you.' Will was an experienced soldier who, Hadley knew, would rather be with his regiment than shepherding prisoners for days. There was a grunt,

'I know of better ways to spend my time, I have little love for my fellow man especially when I look at these creatures.' He waved his hand at the men marching alongside him. 'I would dearly love to be in battle rather than carrying out the duties of a gaoler.'

'This is your last duty the same as Henry and me.'

'It is and I can't wait to be released so that I may return to what's left of my family.'

'What do you mean 'What's left of your family?' It was difficult for Will to continue, he did not like discussing his problems with anyone. It was his belief that it was only he that could tackle his problems.

'The fighting took a number of my family, I have only two sisters and their children now, before the fighting I was the third of five brothers and we were successful with our land. What is left of it I am not sure but I will go back and try to make a life for my family.' Hadley had known many men whose families had been torn apart by the civil war and those that had suffered during the battles fought. He was one of the fortunate soldiers who, along with his family had remained intact throughout the troubled years. He looked at the weather worn features of the man next to him, it was men like Will who deserved peace now not to be ordered to escort prisoners.

'It will be over as soon as these devils are delivered to the adventurers in Cambridge and that is no more than three days from now.' With that Hadley patted Will on the shoulder then headed back to resume his position at the head of the column.

The fields rolled by and although the men did not march as they had when they first left Scotland, their progress was good. Jamie and Tom spoke little as they placed one foot in front of the other. They had been marching for many months their resolve had weakened especially when they were incarcerated in Tothill Fields but hopefully they were heading to a better place. The soldiers guarding them were strict, and no doubt would have brought them down with the sword if they tried to run, but they were treated more like human beings than walking corpses.

As the column neared their resting place villagers came out to watch them pass. One woman in particular approached Corporal Hadley,

'You can't bring that rabble into our village, what are you to do with them? She was becoming increasingly agitated as she walked alongside the prisoners shaking her head. These animals can't stay here, there is no room or food enough for them.' Hadley looked at the woman, she was no picture, her dank hair and visible stubble on her chin did not make her an appealing sight.

'You can rest assured, madam, that these 'animals' as you call them will not be in your village for longer than one night.' The woman's face changed slightly but still remained ugly in Hadley's mind and it wasn't just her looks it was her whole being that repulsed him. He would rather have the prisoners as friends than this hag.

A mile further on the column came to a halt outside a large building that had seen better days. The corporal disappeared through the main door. As the door was opened a smell reached the men, it was a blend of vegetables and ale, their mouths watered and stomachs rumbled. Each man took hold of his bowl with expectation, they all looked to the corporal as he returned,

'There is food for you all, you will form a line and wait, each man will receive one bowl of pottage, one piece of bread and when you have finished eating your bowls will be filled with ale.' There was almost a cheer as Hadley and his men started to get the prisoners into line. There was some jostling and pushing but on the whole the men had a certain amount of patience that surprised Hadley. The first man looked longingly as the steaming stream of liquid containing barley and oats with roots which would normally be fed to the cattle splashed into his bowl. One man thought he saw some fragments of meat but couldn't be sure. The men took their first meal for what seemed months and sat greedily stuffing the bread into their mouths which proved easier to eat if it was first soaked in the pottage.

It took an hour to feed one hundred and fifty men, which was quick. The men's hunger moved them along at speed. As they finished their bread and pottage, they licked their bowls clean and then went to a table that had several casks upon them.

Each man received a bowl of ale and sat drinking it slowly. It was a banquet for the men whose last meal was rotten bread and mouldy cheese. The corporal told his two men to go into the building were they would receive their rations, he would wait until they had been fed before he relaxed. Hadley looked at the men sitting against walls wolfing down their meagre bowls of food, he wondered if this would be enough to sustain them until they reached their next stop, he hoped so.

The house that had provided their feast was the 'Spital house'. Hadley had stopped here on his way to London from Cambridge. It was he who confirmed that food would be available for the men and that they would be able to spend the night under cover. Once he had finished his meal, he got the men to their feet and started them off in the direction of two very large barns. As they drew closer the men could see through the doors that there was plenty of straw inside the buildings.

'This will be your sleeping quarters for the night. You will be dry and warm. Do not create a nuisance by noise or mess. I will inspect the area in the morning and any man responsible for causing problems will have his rations either cut or stopped. Is that clear?' A rumble of acceptance ran around the men. Once the men had been ushered into the barn the doors closed and chained securely. The three soldiers headed to a building no more than fifty yards from the barn. It was a coaching inn and it was there that the three hoped they would be able to relax whilst still being within earshot of the prisoners. The three sat with good beer and each man lit a pipe. As the smoke drifted up towards the ceiling they sighed collectively. Will looked at his colleagues,

'Well, that is the first day, do you think the remaining days will be as easy?' Hadley drew a mouthful of tobacco smoke,

'I think so, as long as we can feed and quarter them, they should remain relatively easy to handle.' Henry then exhaled,

'How long until they receive better clothing?' Hadley leant back in his chair,

'That won't be until we reach Cambridge, perhaps a little before it depends on the time it takes to manufacture enough breeches, smocks, stockings and boots for over one hundred and fifty men.' With that they sat and just enjoyed being away from the column. They left the Inn and made their way to their sleeping quarters, they were to sleep on a floor above the men and would have to climb a stairway on the outside of the barn to get there. They were pleasantly surprised, it was not just a case of sleeping on hay, there were three trestle beds with a blanket on each, this was luxury they thought. Before disrobing Corporal Hadley reached into his jacket pocket and took out his copy of the Soldiers Pocket Bible, as he did so each man dropped to his knees. Together they recited the Soldiers Catechism, the words were etched into their brains, the sound gave the men a sense of comfort and purpose. The corporals voice led the way,

'What are the principle things required of a soldier?' The others joined in with the response,

'That he be religious and godly.

That he be courteous and valiant.

That he be skilful in the military profession. The corporals voice raised a little as he asked.

'How do you prove that our soldiers should be religious?' The joint response was,

'By scripture.'

'Because they lie open to death.'

'They stand in continual need of Gods alliance.'

'They fight for Religion and Reformation.'

'God hath raised them up to execute justice.'

'Men may be as religious in this profession as in any other.'

'We read of brave soldiers that have been very religious.'

'A well-ordered Camp is a School of Vertue.' The corporal's voice was raised again with further questions.

'What is taught in this school?'

'Preparation for death.'

'Continuence.'

'Vigilance.'

'Obedience.'

'Hardness.'

'Temperance.'

'Humility.'

'Devotion.'

The corporal asked the question. 'Who do chiefly offend against these rules?' They responded together,

'Such soldiers as give themselves to whoring and uncleannesse.'

'Such as use to swear and blaspheme the name of God.'

'Such as follow the swinish sin of drunkenness.'

'Such as plunder and steal whatever they come near.' The next question came in a stern voice from Hadley

'Are these things tolerable in soldiers?' The answer came with some force.

'No more in them than other men, the scripture saith generally to and of all men whatsoever:

'That whoremongers and adulterers God will judge.'

'That the Lord will not hold him guilty that taketh his name in vain.'

'That drunkards shall not inherit the kingdom of God.'

'That he that doth wrong shall receive for the wrong he has done, and there is no respect of persons.

They finished on that note and Corporal Hadley ended with a resolute 'Amen' which the others echoed. The three men had become accustomed to reading from the Soldiers Pocket Bible each night unless battle had been engaged. Each man disrobed and settled down for the night, the noise from below was one of snoring and farting, nothing more and they slept well.

Hadley was woken by noise from below, he could hear men calling out for the door to be opened. He shook Henry and Will, the three made their way to the front of the barn and unchained the door. There was a rush of men, not trying to escape but desperate to empty their bladders. Once those in need had carried out what was necessary Corporal Hadley had them remove any soiled straw, making sure it was carried to the place where it would be left to rot down later to be used on the land. A surprise waited for the men as they filed out of the barn, there was more food. It was from the same large cooking vessels as the night before but it had been added to. There were more vegetables and more barley which thickened what was almost a broth. The prisoners were given a ladle full each which was quickly consumed. After licking their bowls clean, they formed up ready to march. Hadley looked at his charges, they looked better for food, drink and sleep but he could see that they remained in a bad state. If they were animals they would be killed as they would be no use to work the land or for meat. Hadley led the men from the place that had been good to them and headed north.

He was following the old Roman road which was straight and as roads go not in very bad condition, although the potholes and crumbling verges did not make for easy going. Jamie had spent a night of what he thought was luxury. To sleep under a roof where it was dry and comparatively warm gave him hope of survival. He looked towards Tom who was walking stiffly, the sun had not burnt its way through the autumn morning mist yet and his limbs ached.

'Are you better for a night's rest?' He looked at his young companion, his red hair was a mess and his eyes hardly open.

'It is better than anything I have had for weeks, my belly still feels empty even though we have had two bowls of food.' His arms reached around his shoulders as he scratched himself.

'How far to you think we will have to march today?' Jamie looked at the sky,

'I think it may be more than yesterday as the corporal may think that now we have eaten we can march many more miles, but we shall see.' They joined the ranks of the others and started to march. It was clear to Tom that the smell of the abused bodies was still with them, the clothes they wore were in tatters and the footwear hardly gave their feet any protection.

'What is this place called?' Tom asked the soldier who walked alongside him.

'This is Waltham it is famous for having a cross placed here in the time of the first king Edward and is named after his wife, Elanor, which is all I know.' As they marched from the village Jamie saw at least four Inns,

'Are there many travellers on this road?'

'There are many, it is the main link from London to Lincoln and beyond.'

'So, are we headed to Lincoln?' The soldier looked at Jamie thinking that this man, like many others, should not be heading for a land that they knew nothing of. The soldier knew that the prisoners had fought against Parliament but now the fighting had finished surely, they should be set free to return to their families. He sighed inwardly aware that his orders were just to accompany Corporal Hadley and get these men to their given destination.

'We are headed north and that is as much as you need to know.'

The day wore on and the column kept a steady pace stopping only at a river that the corporal had been told had clean water. The prisoners came to a halt they broke ranks to plunge themselves in to the river. They drank deeply then after pissing in the field alongside the river they reformed in column and began again placing one foot in front of the other. Corporal Hadley had travelled the route and had made allowances for not going through the centre of the towns and villages wherever possible. He guided the men around places such as Broxbourne and Hoddeston but as they reached Ware things became a little more difficult. There was no suitable road around the town so the Corporal led them straight through the middle. It was a gamble as this was one of the main coaching stops on the London to Cambridge Road and it was a town that had a chequered history. He had been told when he was last there that it was in Ware that soldiers mutinied over pay and other grievances. He had been told that the place of mutiny was called Corkbush and that it remained a place of some dispute in the hearts and minds of many soldiers.

Jamie had Tom marching beside him and they looked longingly at the many Inns they passed. The smell of beer filled the air and when bread was being baked their hearts and stomachs almost burst. They spoke little except when they were trying to discover where they were and how far they had travelled. Jamie kept a watch on the sun's movements in the sky and could tell they were still heading in a northerly direction. The land was a mix of flat fields where he could see various crops growing and some were almost covered in sheep. He had seen cattle, long horned animals standing tall at the shoulder, he thought that they would make good eating. Tom sometimes mentioned Robert and they both wondered what had happened to their friend. Was he still alive and if so, had he been sent on a similar march to them? They had no answer, their desire was to stay alive and finish this march and hopefully regain some of their self-respect. They marched on, aching feet started to blister and the muscles in their legs tightened, they needed rest and good food neither of which would be coming their way. Tom, with his usual quest for answers, looked at Jamie.

'If this place is called Ware, are we closer to our home land?' Jamie smiled,

'We are many miles from Scotland that is all I can tell you, we may be travelling north but our homes are too far beyond the horizon for you to think that we are within marching distance. It will be many years before you or I see the land of our birth again.' Tom turned his head, he did not want to think that home was a place he would never return too.

The column passed through a small village which for its size supported two well-kept inns, as they left the small collection of cottages Corporal Hadley could see several riders approaching. They were in no hurry, as they drew closer Hadley could make out five horsemen each wearing the red jackets of the foot soldier but these men were on horseback 'they must be dragoons' Hadley thought. He started to bring the column to a halt and as the first rider came close the men in the column rested. Hadley looked up as a rider came up to him. His horse did not appear to have been ridden hard there was little sweat that Hadley could see.

'Are you the column of prisoners for Cambridge?' Hadley looked at the man, he was wearing a helmet which hid some of his features.

'Yes, I am Corporal Hadley, who are you?'

'I am Sergeant Chapman and I ride with Parliaments Dragoons. My men, he waved a hand at the other riders, have been sent to see if you require any assistance and to give you a message.'

'What is the message.' Hadley was a little impatient.

'The good news is that the men in your charge are to receive new clothing and boots just after Cambridge. You are to halt your men at the village of Milton where you will be met by the provider of the clothing.'

'How far is Milton from Cambridge?' Hadley did not wish to go further than he had to.

'No more than four miles and it is flat land so you should do it easily at the end of your days march.'

'We still have to reach Royston which is some distance from here, I believe.'

'Your journey has still a good twenty miles to go, do you plan to rest the men in Puckeridge which is less than ten miles ahead?'

'Why do you ask, is there a problem? All that was needed was a problem with food or the planned rest place.' he thought.

'No, just the opposite, I have spoken to the Inn keeper where you will be resting, he has confirmed that he will provide food and good water and that they are to be quartered in the two barns that are but a mile from his Inn.' A wave of relief washed over Hadley, things were going to plan and that made him feel good. He approached the dragoon's horse and patted its neck, looking up he asked,

'How long do you think it will take us to reach the Inn?'

'You are almost there you will be there well before dark, now we must continue on our patrol of these parts.'

'Why do you patrol this road?'

'We are just an advance patrol my captain requires full details of the road ahead and any trouble that may await us but so far all has been well.' With that he turned his horse, called to his men and they walked their horses down the road that Hadley and the prisoners had just trodden.

Puckeridge was reached easily, the men were tired and hungry, now they knew that food would be given out when they stopped, the prisoners were eager to get to their destination. The Falcon Inn was a large white building with a thatched roof. The sign that swung outside the building showed a falcon in flight, what sort of falcon Hadley could not determine. He entered the building and was greeted by the Innkeeper. After going over what had been arranged Hadley returned to the column, he climbed onto a table,

'You will be split into halves, there are two barns, my two men will take charge of a barn each, he pointed unnecessarily at Will and Henry. I shall be passing between each barn to make sure all is well. You will receive your food at the rear of the inn where you will form ranks, you will be given rations in good order any man not following my orders will lose his rations, is that understood?' There was a rumble of agreement from the prisoners.

Jamie and Tom stood together in line waiting for their food,

'What will we be served today, I wonder.' Jamie had a smile on his face as he tried to look beyond the line to where the food was being ladled out. 'I have a feeling it will be much the same as yesterday but we must thank the lord that we are getting some form of nourishment and not being starved as we were in London.' Tom moved forward eagerly with his bowl in hand he started to breath in the aroma of stewed vegetables. What was given to them was similar to the previous day, the broth like mix had barley, peas, corn with a hint of some sort of animal, possibly sheep, thought Tom but when he asked Jamie what he thought it could be he said it was more likely to be cattle bones, the marrow from them would give the mixture a better flavour than they had for a long time. When they had finished licking their bowls clean, they were separated into two. One half taken to the far barn led by the soldier called Will, the others were marched to a closer building. Corporal Hadley watched as the men entered the buildings. He would make sure the doors were fastened. They looked sturdy enough but the prisoners had been fed and watered which may give them ideas of escape so with this in mind he followed the first group into their barn. Hadley climbed onto the hay to a height where he could see all the men and he hoped that they could hear him.

'You men have had food and ale, you will sleep in the dry and warm this night, if you have any thoughts of running, I would remind you that the Dragoons that visited the column earlier, patrol the road and the area on either side. To them you remain their enemy and if you run, they will hunt you down and strike you dead. They will show you no mercy because you are their foe.' The faces of the men below him looked surprised, they were in no fit state to run from the column. Jamie had listened and knew that any man trying to leave the column would be a fool. There was no way they could evade capture or death, any man travelling this country would be spotted immediately, they would have no food very little clothing and shelter would be out of the question. He remembered the plight when he ran from the column after the battle of Dunbar and how difficult it had been for him and Alec to survive. He thought that the only reason that they made their escape good was that they were closer to their homes and had met friendly faces especially when they had crossed the border back into Scotland. Trying to escape from the column when they were in the heart of England would be madness. He turned to Tom,

'We should be careful and not be dragged into any foolhardy plans others may have, our path is set and we should see where it leads.' Tom was a little disappointed he would be only too eager to join anyone trying to leave but he knew Jamie had been in this situation before and was willing to take his advice.

Corporal Hadley addressed the second half of the men with the same forceful tone as he had used on the first. When they had settled the men, he called Will and Henry to him,

'You will patrol around the barns at times you feel that are needed, we will keep vigilant watch on the men four hours each, when we sleep it will be in the back room of the Inn.' Will asked,

'Do you think they will try to run?' Hadley shook his head,

'I don't think so but if we lose any it will be reflected in our pay, so look sharp and lets not have any runners. Will, you are to take the first watch and I will take the second, Henry you will get the men ready to march at the end of your watch. If there are any difficulties you are to wake me immediately. Do you have any questions?' Will and Henry shook their heads and so the night began.

Jamie spent a troubled night, he ached in every part of his body. The food they had been given he found hard to keep in his stomach but he knew that it was all he was going to get so somehow, he managed to keep it inside him. The bodies in the barn tossed and turned, there were strange screams from some men, their dreams were probably of the things they had seen and lived with over the past months. There were men who, like Jamie, had fought bravely at Dunbar and again at Worcester, they had also suffered badly on the march and when they had been incarcerated at Tothill Fields. He also thought he could hear men sobbing, he did not know if this was in pain or anger, probably a mixture of both. He looked at Tom's face as he lay snoring in the hay, what would become of this young man, what awaited him, would he ever return to his home?'

The morning was clear, the sun shone through a blue sky, as the men rose and left the barn's they were given bread and cheese, a handful of each. The ate what they were given as they took their places in the column. When the count had been completed Corporal Hadley gave the command to move off. As they passed through Puckeridge Jamie saw how this village gained its wealth. There were livery stables that could accommodate a change of coaching horses, a blacksmiths forge was close by and a little further a chandler's shop looked as if it sold most things from rope to fodder. There was a pond that sat in the centre of the village green on which floated several ducks that would have to take care as they could make a nice addition to some eager family's pot. Leaving the village, the fields opened up and Jamie could see what appeared to be common land. It had several horses and a few cattle grazing quietly, he could see several women collecting wood, their full skirts made it difficult for them to carry a great deal but somehow, they managed.

The column slowly made its way along Ermine Street, it had been the one saving grace for Hadley as there was not much deviation from his route. The old Roman road. although battered and full of pot holes, still marked the quickest route from London to Lincoln and he only needed to branch off the road when he got closer to Cambridge.

As they marched Tom asked Jamie so many questions,

'How far had they come? What was the next town or village called? How many men had they lost? When would they next eat?' Jamie answered some but not all. He would fix his gaze on a point in the distance and try to concentrate his own thoughts on what was to become of him and the others. Tom asked yet another question and Jamie looked at him and smiled,

'Do you dream Tom?' Tom was a little confused, Jamie rarely asked questions and this was a strange one.

'I have thoughts at night but perhaps not dreams.'

'Maybe you do not have dreams but do you have nightmares?' This really flummoxed Tom,

'Sometimes I suppose when I am very hungry or thirsty or when I am in pain.' Jamie looked at Tom again, they were only two years apart in age but Jamie felt so much older, it was if Tom was a younger brother who always sought guidance from those older than him.

'What do you wish for Tom, do you wish for your home and family, do you long for the hills and heather?'

'I have lost sight of what you speak of,' Tom replied, 'I can only see the road in my mind and hear the Corporal giving orders. My wishes are for a dry place to sleep and food to fill my belly.' Jamie smiled again and looked from Tom to the fields where men had started to tend to the crops and animals.

CHAPTER 17

It was after the sun had passed its highest point when Jamie heard the pounding of horses. The noise slowly increased until it was joined with the jangle of many harnesses. A troop of Dragoons came close to the column, this time it was not just four or five troopers but what seemed to be a whole company. As they drew level with the column Jamie thought he counted twenty-five riders. Leading them was an upright figure sat upon a rather splendid mount. Jamie could see his spurs and that his uniform was a cut better than most he had seen. The rider drew up alongside Corporal Hadley, he bent in the saddle and started to talk. Hadley brought the column to a halt then turned to the rider to listen to what he was saying.

'Are you Hadley?' He asked in a voice that was used to being obeyed.

'Yes, I am Corporal Hadley, what is it that you want?' Hadley had become tired and he just wanted to get this march over so that he could end his service and return to his family.

'I am told by my sergeant that you are headed for Cambridge and beyond, is that correct?'

'Yes, that is my destination, I am to deliver the column to Milton where I believe the prisoners will receive new clothing.'

'I am afraid that you may not reach your goal as quickly as you anticipated.' David Hadley did not want this, delay could affect his pay and prolong his time shepherding the prisoners.

'What delay?'

'The city fathers have heard that you are proposing to take these men through the city and they will not grant you or anyone permission to bring such a rabble through the streets of Cambridge.' Hadley looked up at the horseman with anger in his eyes,

'What am I supposed to do, fly them across on the wings of giant birds?' The rider looked down with a harsh look on his face,

Corporal, I am Captain Jenson and my duty is to carry out the orders of Parliament's Army and their orders are to comply with the wishes of the city fathers so you will do as I order.' Hadley knew he would have to comply, he was only a lowly corporal so he politely asked how he could march around the city and still achieve his goal without losing too much time.

'How well do you know the city roads?' Hadley again looked up at the captain,

'I know the city well but I am not so sure of the way to get me to Milton.' The captain turned to his sergeant,

'Our men know this area well, don't they?' The sergeant nodded and then said

'Most are from the area and know the roads well.'

'Good, good.' He turned back to Hadley. 'I will provide a guide for you, he will meet you, shall we say, a mile from the city and then lead you to the Milton Road.' He then spoke to a trooper who had arrived at his side. 'Do you know of a meeting place that could be easy to find? The trooper nodded,

'Yes sir, there is a drovers track that meets this road just a little under a mile from the city, it has been used for many years and should be clear to anyone.'

'Good, good.' He turned back to Hadley, 'This trooper will meet you where the drovers track meets this road and he will guide you from there.' The captain seemed satisfied with the outcome of their conversation, as he was about to leave, he turned back to Hadley,

'A word of warning, Corporal, this town has had many guises, it has been for the King then for Parliament. There have been nuisances performed by the locals and soldiers have been set upon and their hands injured. This was many months ago but be careful and watch which way the wind blows.'

Hadley thanked the captain in a subservient manner that some would call ill-mannered but the captain did not seem to notice. With that the captain ordered the troop to the trot and they rode off with hooves beating and bridles jangling.

*

Jamie was surprised how many people were on the road, they carried all manner of things, from poultry to wheat. There were a variety of carts and wagons some with single driver's others with families holding on for dear life. He asked a soldier as he moved alongside,

'What is this, why so many on the road?'

'It's market day in Royston, it happens every Wednesday.'

'Is this a big affair.'

'Oh yes, it is one of the biggest in the area especially for the trading of corn and malt, so I am told.'

'Do you know where we will be sleeping tonight?'

'I am told that we will be sleeping in what was a Royal Palace, or at least part of it.' Jamie asked the question that was on most men's minds,

'Will there be food?'

'You can never be sure but I hope that whatever we find will fill our bellies.' He turned back and quickened his pace checking that those he passed were not ailing.

Jamie and Tom had more trouble staying on their feet as the road had become rutted and broken. The wagons had damaged the already poor surface. Many of the men stumbled which could cause injury if they were not careful. Tom looked at the first buildings they came to in Royston. He could see good houses, although they may have seen better days, their plaster was still relatively clean. As they passed, men and women stopped and stared at the lines of men in rags with hair and beards in disarray, they recoiled as if they would catch some deadly disease from the prisoners.

It was late in the day when Hadley turned the men into a large area with buildings on each side. The market had finished for the day and the streets were crowded with those making their way back to their homes. Jamie looked up at the way some of the houses jutted out partly across the street and thought that he should look out for anything that might be thrown out of any window. Tom looked around there were various buildings, some that were very grand but all were starting to need repair. Corporal Hadley led the men into a large open space between the buildings that appeared to be a stable yard and pointed out that this was where they would be spending the night. As they entered the yard Hadley was met by a tall slim man dressed in good quality clothes, he looked at the corporal,

'Are you Hadley?' The corporal confirmed that he was. 'We did not meet when you last visited.' He was looking at Hadley, virtually inspecting him his eyes travelled down Hadley's body taking in his dress and stance.

'I am the mayor's clerk and it is my responsibility to make sure you and these men,' he looked at the lines of men waiting to enter the stable yard, make no trouble and leave this place as quickly as possible. If you have any problems, no matter how small, you are to report them to me, is that understood.' Hadley felt as if he was being spoken to like the man's servant. With that the Clerk turned and walked out of the stable yard. Hadley knew that the man could cause him trouble if things did not go well.

Hadley stood in front of the men and pointed to the building in front of them, they looked like stables to Jamie,

'Your night will be dry and there will be hay for you to bed down on.' The corporal walked along the line of men. 'You will receive food soon and the same rules apply, you will form and orderly line and once you have finished eating you will move into the stables.' There was the usual mumbling from the prisoners as they looked at their lodgings for the night. There was the aroma of something cooking and from another series of buildings men and women brought out large cooking vessels that appeared full. Behind came children carrying loaves of bread. Jamie and Tom felt their stomachs ache for food. The prisoners got into line and waited their turn.

Those in the town who had been told that the prisoners had fought for the King had sympathetic feelings others were not so kind. Jamie could see some smiles on the faces of the women who ladled the thick vegetable stew into the prisoner's bowls, as he reached the point opposite one young woman, she stared into his eyes with a compassion that he had not seen for many months. They held each other's gaze but the spell was broken when Tom pushed Jamie in the back to get him to move on, Jamie thought for a moment of what could have been with a girl like that but it was not to be. He took his bowl and collected bread then sat against the wall of the stable. He looked back trying to see the girl but her face was lost behind the hungry prisoners.

Once their bowls had been emptied and small beer had been drunk Jamie and Tom were pushed into the stables, they were huge with enough room for at least forty horses, each stall could accommodate eight men easily. There was hay enough for the men to cover the floor and give them some comfort when sleeping. Corporal Hadley was happy that there were only two main doors to the stables one at either end of the building. He would station one of his soldiers at either door and relieve them during the night, they would sleep in the hay loft between their shifts. It was after the men had been fed that he was sought out by someone from the kitchen who carried two baskets,

'This is food for you and your soldiers.' The woman said in a voice that could only have come from the local area. Hadley called to Will and Henry,

'Come you two our food is here.' On hearing this the two men walked briskly to where Hadley had pulled a table and a bench together and the woman had laid out the meal. Their eyes bulged at what they saw, there was bread but beneath a linen cloth they found cold meats, chicken, pork and beef, not a great deal but plenty for them and with it a jug of good beer. They were in a Royal place so why not eat like royalty, Hadley thought as they started to tear the bread apart.

After their prayers were finished and the men settled in the stalls the three soldiers made the best of what they could find in the hayloft. The night passed peacefully enough and as the sun rose Will shook Hadley by the shoulder until his eyes were open.

'It's time to get the men ready.' He said almost whispering. Hadley shook himself and went down into the yard. He found a pump and washed his face vigorously then after shaking the water from his hair called for the men to be brought from the stables into the yard. As they started to leave the stalls there was a commotion that made Hadley stop what he was doing. Henry came running from the stalls,

'We have a dead man.' He spluttered. Hadley took hold of Henry's arm,

'Dead man, you say. Where is this?'

'The body is in the farthest stall and is quite dead.'

'Show me.' Henry led the way, prisoners were still in the process of leaving the stalls and parted to make way for Hadley and Henry. When they reached the stall, Henry pointed to the body,

'Who is he?' Hadley asked as he got closer to the form that lay face down in the straw. A prisoner standing by the stalls entrance said,

'He is Duncan from Inverness.' Hadley grasped the body and began to turn it over. As he did Henry took a step back, the front of the man's tattered jacket was covered in blood, his hands were clasped together as if in prayer and it was clear to him that the blood had come from the man's arms or wrists. Hadley looked from the body to the man who had given the name,

'What is your name?'

'I am Andrew, also from Inverness.'

Hadley was now a worried man, how was this done and why?' This man had not been brought to his attention before and he had no reports of fights or arguments between these men. He took the man from Inverness to one side,

'Tell me about this person?' He saw a look of doubt cross the man's face.

'I knew little about him, he was within himself most of the time. It was after we departed from the horror in London that he became very quiet, very few words came from his mouth. When I last spoke to him, he told me that his god had forsaken him and his faith had left him, he was deeply troubled. After that he kept away from others, ate alone and slept as far from his fellows as he could.'

'So, this action of self-murder does not surprise you.' Hadley could see the troubled look that came over the man's face.

'I am surprised by any man taking his own life, it is against the lords wishes, he has broken the sixth commandment so in my eyes and those of others he is a sinner.'

Hadley looked closer at the body, he separated the man's hands and found that he was clutching a sharp slither of glass about six inches long, it could have come from one of the buildings many broken windows. Hadley saw the cuts on the man's wrists, they were deep and had been made with one thought in mind, this man wanted to end his life.

'Henry, tell Will to keep the men away then go and find the mayor's clerk, if he has not yet risen get him up and tell him there has been a loss of life, but no more, is that clear.' Henry nodded and ran out of the stall.

'Go and join the rest of the men.' He spoke to those who were still in and around the stall, they filed out into the yard, each of them surrounded by others wanting to know what had happened.

It was within minutes that the face of the clerk appeared around the entrance to the stall,

'What is this, is the man really dead?' He squatted next to Hadley who pointed to the still oozing cuts on the man's wrists. 'Is this self-murder?' His voice shook, if it was, it was an unholy act. Hadley shook his head again and thought why would anyone kill themselves especially after all that these men had been through. Both men stood and looked down at the lifeless form on the straw. The clerk was a man who had to make decisions about many things and knew that he would need the help of certain people, the minister for one. He was also aware that he needed to get the prisoners out of his town as quickly as possible.

'I will get bread and cheese for your men that should keep their minds from what has happened here. Stay here until I return then we will talk.' He left in a hurry pushing past those still in the door way of the stables. Outside Jamie and Tom looked on with natural curiosity, what was going on? They had seen men going in and out of the stables and there was word that a man had died but nothing more. Their attention was drawn way from the stables as several women appeared with baskets of bread and cheese, food was the one thing that could take their minds off of what was happening in the stables.

There was no commotion or disruption to the order of things to do with the prisoners, the men knew that something had happened but did not take a great deal of interest only to see that it was not a close friend who had been the centre of the incident. Hadley stayed close to the body, he looked again at the wounds on the man's wrists. They had been inflicted with the shard of glass which Hadley carefully picked up. It was long and razor sharp. He noticed that where the shard came to a point that it could have been used to stab as well as slice, he would look around for any other pieces, he did not want to provide the men with anything that could be used in anger.

The clerk returned together with the minister from St John the Baptist Church. The minister immediately crossed himself as Hadley moved away from the body.

'This is a bad death.' The minister's face took on a look of controlled horror, he knew that the townsfolk still had strong beliefs regarding the taking of one's own life. The old ways of treating the body seemed barbaric to the minister and he had no intention of letting those of his congregation carry out any such actions. He knew that they would balk at the thought of a self-murderer being buried in the churchyard, they would rather the body be taken to the crossroads and buried to confuse the spirit of the restless victim. He would, if necessary, bury the poor man in the plot set aside for criminals, as it was an offense against God and he would hope that that would placate his congregation.

Time was passing and Hadley wanted to leave Royston just as quickly as the mayor's clerk wanted to get rid of him and his charges. The clerk raised the matter of an inquest but thought that the town council together with the local magistrate would be content with a verdict of suicide without involving more people than necessary. The clerk left the scene to contact the magistrate and get his agreement. It took over an hour for him to complete what he wanted to do eventually he returned with good news. He had gained agreement from the magistrate that the death would be recorded as a self-murder and the body was to be buried as the minister directed. The clerk took Hadley to one side,

'I will take responsibility for the internment of the body which will take place as soon as possible. I have gained agreement from the town council that we will cover any cost involved although they should be of little consequence. You will be at liberty to take your charges out of the town as soon as you are able, are we in accord?' Hadley looked around at the men there seemed to be no one who was close to the dead man. He called out to the one person who said he knew the deceased, the man from Inverness stepped forward, Hadley asked,

'Do you wish to ask for anything for this man?' There was a moments silence,

'No, he was known to me but not as family, only as one who came from the same town, as long as a prayer is said for him that is all I ask as I would for any man.' Hadley nodded and then went back to the clerk.

'I am ready to leave whenever you agree, I leave the burial in the hands of the minister and trust the Lord that I have no more of this.'

'You are at liberty to leave whenever you feel ready.' The look of relief on the clerk's face was almost tangible.

Hadley would let the men finish any food they may have left and then start the next part of their journey which would be to Cambridge. As Royston fell behind them Hadley felt a sense of relief, he had visions of being held there waiting for the magistrate to conduct an inquest which could have taken days and what would he have done with the prisoners then. He would have had to send them on under the charge of Will and Henry, who he had every faith in but would have preferred to continue leading the men without the possibility of something going wrong. The column made its way through the streets of Royston and then out into the fields and a sense of freedom for the soldiers but not the men.

They passed through several villages which seemed like many others that they had encountered on their march. Jamie nearly collided with a small cart that was in a hurry to get passed them,

'You are in a hurry, is there a fire?' He asked the young boy of about thirteen who was leading a small horse.

'I need to get bye, I have things to get to my father, I am in a hurry, please get out of my way.' The men laughed, it was not a common sound, laughter was a rare commodity amongst the prisoners. 'Where are you going?' Jamie asked,

'To the village mill.'

'And what village is that, pray tell?'

'It is Harston.' The boy looked at Jamie as if he was an idiot not knowing the name of the village.

'And how far is that?'

'No more than one mile.' With that he pulled on the horse's reins and stepped forward.

They moved aside to allow the boy to pass. Jamie saw the look on the boy's face as he noticed the ragged state of the men, they must have been a very frightening sight. Jamie glanced down at his tattered breeches and boots that were almost gone, his jacket was a filthy rag draped over his shoulders and that together with matted hair and beard he knew anyone looking at them for the first time would have thought them monsters. They watched the boy disappear into the distance and Jamie together with Tom wished they had his freedom.

The column marched on until they came to a well-trodden track that crossed the road on which they were travelling. Hadley could see a horse grazing on the verge of the road, sitting close by was a dragoon eating what looked like an apple. Hadley moved a little ahead of the column and called to the dragoon,

'Are you our guide?' The dragoon got to his feet and brushed himself down.

'Yes, I am to show you the way around the City of Cambridge and set you on the road to Milton.' Hadley felt a little of the weight lifted from his shoulders, all he would have to do for the rest of the march was to follow this man. He called the column to a halt,

'Will, let the men rest for a short time we still have some distance to travel today and we will be busy when we arrive at our destination.' Will and Henry gave the order to rest and the men immediately collapsed at the side of the road. Hadley walked to the dragoon,

'How far do we have to march to get to Milton?' The dragoon cleared his throat and took a swig from his leather bottle.

'It is no more than five miles and it will be over flat ground although the path is not in the best of conditions it should not take longer than three hours, possibly only two.'

'Do you know who is waiting for us in Milton?'

'I believe it is a Captain Emery, but things change so quickly and I could be wrong.'

'Thank you, I will get the men to their feet and we can make a start.' Calling to Will and Henry, Hadley gestured for them to get the men to their feet. There was a murmur of annoyance from the men but they did as they were ordered and the march around Cambridge began.

*

As they marched to the east of the city Jamie could see the land stretching out before them. The skies became wider, there were no hills or clusters of buildings clouding their view. The ground appeared to take on a dark hue and water could be seen clearly in the distance. Cattle were grazing in some pastures and crops of green could be seen on the horizon.

'This is far from the mountains and glens of home.' It was Tom speaking as his eyes looked across the landscape. Jamie followed Tom's gaze, he had not seen such a wide expanse of land before, it seemed to go on forever. There were few hills or even trees but what Jamie did see was several rivers winding their way through the fields. He could see the dragoon leading the way, he had not mounted his horse and walked alongside Hadley. Jamie could just hear what was being said. Hadley asked the dragoon if he knew what awaited them at their next stop,

'I think there are several things waiting for you but I am not sure exactly what. Before I left there had been several wagons arrive, I could not see what they were carrying, everything was covered with stiff cloth but whatever it was there was a lot of it.' This aroused Hadley's curiosity, what could it be? It would not be for him to concern himself with as he would hand over the responsibility of the column to the officer waiting for him, the column marched on.

The daylight was beginning to fade as the tired men saw the village of Milton come into sight. There were not many buildings a few cottages and several inns which amused Hadley as it appeared that the village must house many drunkards to enable the inns to survive. The dragoon mounted his horse and rode in front of the column, Jamie could see two horsemen riding to meet them, the one on the left was a little taller in the saddle than the other and as they got closer the dragoon touched the tip of his cap,

'Captain, this is Corporal Hadley who has been leading the column since it left the capital.' Hadley stepped forward and like the dragoon touched the tip of his cap. The officer looked down from his saddle,

'Corporal Hadley, do you have the same number of men as you had when you left London?' Hadley wondered for a moment if the loss of one man might jeopardise the payment of his wage. Hadley drew a breath,

'I have one less than we started.' The officer looked at the men in the column, he thought it was a miracle that the corporal had lost only one.

'How was the man lost?' Hadley would tell the officer exactly what had happened.

'It was a self-murder, a prisoner had somehow managed to get hold of a slither of glass and he had slit his wrists. He had been one to set himself aside from his fellows and his actions where not noticed until the men were called to rise.' The officer of dragoons dismounted and asked,

'What happened to the body?'

'It was buried by the minister at Royston in a plot set aside for those who die as felons.' The captain nodded as if to agree with what Hadley had said.

'I am sure that the responsibility of the death of a man in those circumstances will not be left at your door. Follow me we have a lot more to discuss and the light is fading quickly.' The corporal thought that things were turning out well, he would now hand over the charge of the prisoners and then get away from them as quickly as he could. The captain looked Hadley up and down, his appearance was not the best.

'I realise that you are in haste to leave the column and return to your homes however, I would strongly suggest that you remain in Milton this night. There is a good inn that you might stay in and I will make sure that the innkeeper sends any bills to me. You may consider this a bonus for completing your duty. I am right in thinking that you and the two with you will now leave the army?' Hadley felt his shoulders relax even more, it was the first time that he had thought that leaving the army was reality. He had been fighting and marching for nearly three years and had not seen his family since leaving to join parliaments army in the west. The captain continued,

'Your wages will be paid to you by the paymaster in the garrison at Cambridge. I have written details of your service to parliament and when presented to the paymaster you and your men will receive what they are owed. Is that satisfactory?' Hadley now straightened his back and looked at the captain,

'That is perfectly acceptable to me and I am sure that my men would agree.' With that the officer looked at Hadley and unexpectedly bowed,

'Thank you, corporal, good luck and god speed.' With that he took the reins of his horse and led it towards the column of men. Calling to his sergeant he had the men gathered closer to him, he then remounted his horse and looked around the sea of faces staring up at him.

Jamie had followed what was going on as best he could. As they had marched through the village, he had seen a large building not far from a small church, its square tower was of light stone and glinted as the last rays of sun began to fade.

'Jamie, do you know this place?' Jamie turned to face Tom,

'No, but I think that we are in a different country, the land is very level and there is a lack of woodlands. What we are to do here I do not know.'

'I hope we are told soon and that there may be food for us before nightfall.'

'I hope so too.'

The mounted officer breathed in deeply and then started to address the prisoners,

'I am Captain Emery and I shall be in charge of this column from now on. You will be quartered in the tithe barn,' he pointed to the huge building about one hundred yards from where they were gathered. 'In that barn there is a residual of tithe given to the manor which is not to be touched by you, my men will punish any man who is seen close to any of the items that are being kept there.' He looked around and could see a look of disinterest in the faces of the prisoners. 'You will be fed and watered in the next hours, you will then be taken into the barn and shown where you are to sleep. In the morning you will form your column and wait for my orders or those of my sergeant,' he gestured to the mounted dragoon beside him. 'You will then be given new clothing and boots, you will form orderly queues and do as you are ordered. There will be no crowding or pushing every man will be dealt with in good time, any man out of order will be punished, is that understood? There was a murmur from the ranks of men in front of him, he turned to his sergeant,

'Carry on Sergeant Saunders and bring before me any man who does not follow your orders.' The sergeant touched the tip of his cap,

'Yes, sir.' The men could smell food and looked around searching for any sign of where the smell came from. Jamie and Tom, together with the others in the column made their bowls ready to receive whatever food came their way. Two of the barn doors opened and in the entrance were two huge cauldrons with steam rising from the surface of what was being held inside them. The column lunged forward, the soldiers had a little difficulty in keeping the line straight with the tips of their swords they stopped any breakdown of order. As Jamie and Tom drew closer to the point where the food was being ladled into bowls Tom said,

'It smells better than what we have had before.' Jamie had to agree there was a faint smell of what Jamie thought was beef or was that just wishful thinking. They moved forward and eventually arrived in front of two large soldiers who were slopping ladles of brown pottage into the prisoner's bowls. 'Look, I can see meat I think.' Tom lifted something out of the soup like mess in his bowl, in was meat, something they had not eaten for many days. Jamie and Tom moved away from the barn and sat against a wall, they greedily ate what they had been given. The taste was like manner from heaven, there was meat and barley together with a variety of root vegetables and they had been given a huge chunk of bread which they eagerly dipped into the broth. Following the pottage, the men were given chance to empty their bowls then they were filled with small beer which was welcome after the long days march.

*

    Hadley together with Will and Henry made their way from the barn, they watched briefly as the men lined up for their food. Hadley had no regrets about marching the men from London but was happy to see the back of them. They made their way into the village and entered the White Horse Inn that the officer had told him about. The innkeeper was welcoming but looked down his nose a little when he clearly saw the state of the soldiers clothing. They had a change of shirts and stockings in the packs that they carried but not much more. After a brief discussion with the landlord, they agreed on sharing one room between them. Hadley thanked God that they were not all in one bed. Will and Henry could share but he was not going to be kicked by the two men standing by his side and as for the smell, well if he could get as far away as possible from them that would be good. With the accommodation sorted they asked what was available from the kitchen and they were pleasantly surprised with the choice that they were given. They decided upon roast beef with vegetables for all, followed by the best beer that the innkeeper had, the three men settled down to a good meal and after prayers they fell into a peaceful night's sleep.

Hadley woke Will and Henry at first light, it was a day that he had been waiting for. His two companions struggled to caste off the deep sleep that they had fallen into.

'Today my fine lads will be one of joy and hopefully good fortune.' He smiled as he watched the two struggle out of the bed they had shared that night. After collecting their belongings and packing them into their snap sacks they made their way down the stairs and into the main room of the inn. They were met by a young woman who, they thought, would be a servant or relation of the innkeeper.

'Good morning.' Her voice was softer than Hadley expected, she gestured to a table, 'Will you be breaking your fast with us or are you leaving straight away?' Hadley looked at the two men who seemed to fill the space around him. 'We hoped to have a good meal before we set off, what do you have?'

'I will check in the kitchen, I think we have cold meats and possibly and egg or two.' She left them to seat themselves and wait for their breakfast. Henry asked how the day would go? Will looked up,

'I don't care as long as we get away from the column. I have seen enough of the prisoners to last me a lifetime, all I want is what is due to me and then a swift journey home.' The other two nodded in agreement. The girl returned,

'We have some boiled ham, eggs and bread and perhaps some cheese, will that do for you?' 'Yes,' they said almost in unison, then they sat back and waited for the food to come. They ate with gusto, the meal was accompanied by several types of pickle and preserve which added flavour to the meat. As they finished the innkeeper appeared,

'Are you ready to go?' Hadley spoke for the three of them,

'Yes, we are now full and ready to take our leave. Is there anything you need from me before we leave?' The innkeeper took a sheaf of paper from the pocket of his apron.

'I need you to sign or make your mark on the bill I will present to the officer, can you write?' He was looking at Hadley,

'Yes, I can write I have been well schooled by the church in my early years.' With that he took the pencil from the innkeeper and signed his name on the bottom of the bill, he didn't look at the cost, he just wanted to leave. The three men slung their snapsacks over their shoulders and headed for the door. The innkeeper wished them good fortune and a speedy journey home. The three waved as they made their way out of the inn.

As they made their way to the Cambridge Road, they could see the prisoners lining up in front of the barn. There were piles of clothes and shoes, several men were organising the jackets, breeches and shoes into sizes, Hadley was glad he was not involved, he could see some of the men that he had become aware of during the march, they were looking bemused as various items of clothing were being held against the prisoners. Two men in particular looked around turning from the clothing being issued and watched the three soldiers making their way back to Cambridge. Jamie nudged Tom and pointed to the three men,

'They are the lucky ones, they will not be marching with us again, their lives will return to normal, they will be with their loved ones in the coming days, I wish we were going with them.'

Jamie raised his arm and waved, unexpectedly the corporal, who was looking in his direction, waved back, then turned and the three men grew smaller as they made their way back to sanity.

CHAPTER 18

Jamie looked down at the rags he was wearing, he had not changed any of his clothing since leaving Scotland and that seemed years ago. His jacket was almost falling apart, his breeches were stained and stiff with grime and as for his shoes, they were no more than thin pieces of leather tied to his feet with strips of old clothing. As he drew nearer to the tables where the new garments and shoes were being distributed, he said to Tom that they should try to wash their feet before putting on new stockings and it would be sensible to try to get some of the layer of dirt from their bodies as well. There were three tables each having a man distributing garments and shoes, Jamie could see the face of the man behind the first table, the sweat was already trickling down his brow, he was working feverishly, he looked at the person in front of him, glanced at his size then handed a Jacket to the prisoner. Why he looked at each man's size was a mystery as the clothing was one size only.

Tom collected the course woollen jacket and moved on. He took the cloth between his fingers,

'This will not be easy to wear, it feels as if it could take your skin off.' Jamie looked at the material in his hands, it was not of the finest silk by any means and would, as Tom said 'Take your skin off.' The line slowly moved forward, stockings were given to each man, they were wool and no doubt would keep their feet warm in the coming days and weeks ahead.

The most difficult thing was shoes, getting the right size was a case of trial and error. The prisoners had little time to see if those that they were given fitted. Measurements were crude, Jamie knew that three barleycorns made an inch and that twelve inches made a foot but that didn't help those with feet that had been marching since leaving Scotland. Somehow Jamie and Tom managed to get shoes that were not too bad a fit, with their new stockings to pad them out they felt a lot better than those they currently had. Breeches were again of one size, held tight around the waist with a draw string and an undershirt would afford them some comfort against the coarse material of the jacket, again one size only. The last item was a woollen cap, not the most elegant of headwear but hopefully, Jamie thought, would keep their heads warm and dry.

As they passed the last table a voice repeated,

'Place your old rags over there.' The soldier pointed to a growing pile of filthy clothing that had a few moments ago been their only possessions apart from the bowl that they had their meals out of. It hadn't registered with Jamie that the clothing was white, not pristine white but a sort of greyish dull cloudy white. He knew that this would make it easier to identify any prisoner either when working or running. Tom and Jamie headed for the river that ran alongside the barn. They sat with their feet in the cold water trying to remove the crust of dirt that they had collected on the march. Quickly they dried their feet on the rags that they had not yet thrown on the pile, Jamie also took the cold water in his hands and attempted to wash the parts of his body that he could reach easily before being ordered to hurry.

Captain Emery stood and watched the line of men being given fresh clothing and then he paid particular attention of what they did next, some threw their old rags away as quickly as possible then don their fresh garments, others took their time trying to fold and turn the cloth for an easier fit. He did notice two men washing their feet, this was interesting to him it did show that some of the prisoners still retained some personal pride. He made a mental note of the two men's faces.

      The hours passed quickly and the one hundred and fifty-four men eventually had been given the new clothing. Tom tugged at the sleeve of Jamie's new jacket,

      'It looks like food, maybe we will get the same as last evening, possibly more meat.'

      'Anything would be good, perhaps we will find out where we are bound now that we are clothed in these wonderful garments,' he gracefully let his arm fall away in a mock bow, I think we may be presented at court.' Tom laughed, it was good to hear, they had been fed and clothed and although still suffering from the aches and pains gained from the miles of road that they had covered, life was a fragment better than it had been for some time. Tom had been right, their food was the same as the day before, probably out of the same pot with a great deal of added barley and oats, it was food and Jamie sat with Tom as they scooped the thick pottage from their bowls.

      They were to spend a second night in the tithe barn, which was a luxury for the men. They all had some difficulty in sleeping in the rough material of their new clothing but to most this was soon overcome and the snoring and farting returned with a vengeance. Captain Emery and Sergeant Saunders had stationed troopers at strategic points to prevent any attempts to escape by the prisoners.

'Make sure that our men get some sleep, we have a march tomorrow which may have some difficulty as we approach the workings.' Saunders looked at the man he had followed over many months,

'I don't think they will prove any problem, sir. They have new clothes and full bellies which they probably have not had for some time.'

'We will see tomorrow.' With that he mounted his horse and headed towards the inn where he would spend the night.

*

Captain Emery was surprised to be met by his sergeant at the door of the White Hart Inn,

'Good morning, Sir, I believe we may have some discontent in the ranks of the prisoners.' Emery shook his head trying to get some sense of reality back into his mind after a decent night's sleep,

'What seems to be the problem?' He sat at a table in the main room of the inn where he hoped he would get something to start the day with.

'There are ill feelings about their new clothing, some are saying that they are dressed liked common criminals.' Emery looked up from the plate of cold meats and bread that had been placed before him,

'What in heavens name have they got to complain about, they are criminals, they have killed soldiers of the parliament and tried to place another Charles on the throne of England.' Sergeant Saunders looked longingly at the plate of food before his Captain, he had only eaten a bowl of pottage and still yearned for a little more.

'There are one or two trouble makers, the main body seem to be content with what they have been given.' Emery crammed a piece of ham and bread into his mouth and stood up from the table, he spoke as he chewed,

'Lead the way sergeant let us tackle this problem straight away so that I can get back to my breakfast.' They left the inn and walked back to the barn.

'You will get the troopers mounted and have them draw their swords, they will then rest easy and await my command.' Saunders touched the tip of his helmet in acknowledgement.

When they reached the place where the men had gathered, Emery collected his horse's reins from a trooper and led the animal to a position where he could see the lines of prisoners clearly. The ranks of white garbed men standing in the first rays of sun looked as if a they had all risen from the nearby graveyard. He heard Saunders give the command for the men to mount and then draw swords, he turned towards them and felt a sense of pride as the well-trained men carried out well-rehearsed moves. The blades of their swords rested on their right shoulders with the light glinting on the steel blades, he turned back to the prisoners. There were three men standing a few paces in front of the main body, those he presumed would be the ring leaders,

'I understand you have a grievance that you wish to take up with me, is that correct?' The man in the middle of the three spoke,

'We are soldiers, not criminals. This clothing is for those who have murdered, stolen or injured not for those who have fought in battle.' Emery did not say anything, he held the gaze of the man before him then slowly looked up to the sky as if seeking divine inspiration,

'Are you saying the you will not wear the clothes given to you?' The man opposite Emery was not as sure as he was when he had first approached the captain.

'We cannot be treated like criminals we have our faith and our pride.' Emery scanned the faces of the men before him. He thought that there were probably few who agreed with their spokesman,

'I hear what you say, but you must realise in the eyes of parliament you have committed a crime, that of taking up arms against the elected members of the house of commons, you have killed many and destroyed much. I understand that you carried out your actions in the name of your king, but he is your king not ours.' There was a ripple of comment which ran around the prisoners. Emery continued, 'If you do not wish to wear what you have been provided with then I must ask you all to remove the garments, shoes and caps.' The spokesman looked at Emery in disbelief,

'But we have nothing else, you have taken what we had, we would be naked without these.' He tugged at the white jacket he was wearing.

'It is your decision you either wear what has been provided or go without.' The look on Emery's face told the men in front of him that this was no idle threat. The prisoners could not press their needs by force as the company of dragoons were far too many and even if they tried to use force they would be cut down within minutes. Emery studied the face of the leader, it showed frustration and supressed anger which slowly changed into one of submission, he knew he had little choice but to continue to wear the clothing they had been given. The men fell into line and the column stood ready to depart. Emery told his sergeant that he would return to the inn to finish his breakfast and that he, the sergeant, should set the men on their way. The troopers were to remain mounted and control the column from the saddle and he would catch them up on the road to Earith.

CHAPTER 19

As the lines of prisoners headed out of Milton they were met with wide open fields and a sky that seemed never-ending.

'Where are we headed for now?' Tom was his usual curious self. He looked at the countryside on either side of the road, all he could see was flat green land with perhaps the occasional copse breaking up the horizon, he also noticed how the laying water had increased, there were waterways but not rivers that cut across the land which he hadn't seen before. Jamie followed Tom's gaze and was fascinated by the lack of high ground, there was livestock grazing in some of the fields, both cattle and sheep, the one thing that stood out was the colour of the earth, it was rich and dark, to Jamie it looked as if anything could be grown here.

The column of grey clad men wormed its way along a road that had seen many feet both human and animal. Dragoons kept their distance, horses whinnied and shied, the men talked little and low. Jamie turned from looking at the great expanse of land,

'It may be that we will be put to work, I have heard from the soldiers that many have been used to alter the rivers in this country so do not be surprised if you are given another spade and told to dig.' Tom lifted his hands and inspected the rough callous skin that had formed across his palms.

'We are used to the spade and digging so we may be useful.' Jamie turned over his own hands, they had the marks of those that had dug many graves. He did not want to think about those that he had covered with earth all he wanted was to think of a better future if that were possible. Tom wiped the sweat from his eyes the sun was not as strong now but there remained warmth in the middle of the day.

A horseman rode swiftly by the column heading in the direction of the Captain, Jamie watched as he pulled on his reins bringing the animal to a halt alongside Emery. Jamie could just make out what passed between them.

'Captain Emery?' The rider's voice was short of breath it appeared that he had been riding hard and for some distance. Emery looked round,

'Yes.' The rider caught his breath,

'Sir, I have a message for you from the Garrison at Cambridge.' This gained Emery's total attention,

'What is it man, and who is it from?' The rider reached into the inside of his jacket and produced a sealed letter, he handed it to the captain.

'It is from the Colonel who wishes you to return to the garrison once you have delivered those in your charge.' Emery took the letter and broke the seal. Jamie could see the captain study the paper in his hands, as he read Jamie noticed his face taking on a deep shade of red, the news cannot be good, Jamie thought. Emery finished reading the letter and looked at the rider who had delivered it,

'Are you to return with a reply?' Emery asked.

'Yes sir, I have been told it is of great urgency that your response gets back to the Colonel as quickly as possible.'

'Tell the Colonel that I received his orders and will comply with them, also tell him that I hope to reach Cambridge no later than nightfall this day.' The rider tugged his horse round and set off back to Cambridge, he was soon a speck in the distance. Emery called for his sergeant to join him. Emery and the sergeant left the road and dismounted, they found a dry piece of ground and sat.

'There is news from the colonel.' The sergeant did not hear a great deal of joy in his captain's voice. 'I have to return to the garrison with all haste as soon as we have settled the column for the night. I shall be returning to Cambridge with the majority of the men, I will leave four troopers with you and there will be some foot soldiers joining us at Earith so in total you will have about a dozen men. You are to wake the men at first light and take them west along the road and join those that are digging a new river. You are to seek out the clerk of works who will give you instructions of where the prisoners are to be taken, once that has been completed you will be directed by the clerk of works to where you and our men can spend the night.'

'And you sir, what will become of you?' The sergeant was not happy with what he had been ordered to do.

'I shall meet you the following day and by that time I hope to have clarified what is contained in this.' He waved the letter with a look of concern. 'Whatever you hear from those in Earith regarding the situation with the excavations pay no heed too, I shall be in a position to explain all when I next see you.'

'How far do you think it is to Earith?'

'We are almost in sight of the town so it will be three miles at the most. Now back to the column and sergeant, select four men to continue with you after Earith, make sure they are good, sound men.' The sergeant nodded and mounted his steed. Emery read the letter again, it had news which did not please him. Part of the message was that the officer in charge of the troops at the excavation had been taken ill and that he would be taking charge of the area, this was not what he wanted, he was a soldier not a prison guard even though he had been shepherding these ghostly figures since they left Milton.

He would put his case to the colonel, his life in the army had been one of action not looking after prisoners. Emery was not a man who enjoyed watching over individuals who did not want to be in the depths of a strange country. He had proved himself on many occasions in battle, he had killed and he had saved lives what he could not relish was the thought of caring for these men and others like them. He got up and brushed himself down, mounted his horse and took his position at the head of the column.

As soon as they reached Earith Emery handed over the responsibility of the prisoners to his sergeant, gave the order to form ranks to his dragoons then turned his horse back towards the Cambridge Road and started his horse into a trot. Sergeant Saunders sat in the saddle and watched the troopers grow smaller as they headed south.

Jamie knew that things were about to change, life presented him and his fellow prisoners with a variety of challenges each day that they marched across this fearful land. Beneath the empty skies Jamie could feel that there were things that would not auger well for him or the rest of the prisoners.

Jamie and Tom fell in with the rest of the column and marched towards Earith. The road was reasonable, not too much damage from wagons so they made good time. On reaching the outskirts of the town Jamie could see some sort of earth works,

'What is that.' He asked nobody in particular. The men around him looked at what he was pointing to. One of those who had retained a modicum of humour said that it was probably where they would be spending the night, little did he know how close to the truth he was. Jamie studied what appeared to be some sort of defensive structure,

'What is this place?' He asked one of the foot soldiers who had recently joined Sergeant Saunders,

'That is the Bulwark, it is there to help protect the river crossing although it may not be needed now that the fighting is over.' Jamie stopped for a moment, 'Now the fighting is over' it was something that he had not really contemplated, no more battles, no more killing but he and the men around him were still victims of the war with parliament and the war was not over for them, not by a long way. Sergeant Saunders brought the column to a halt by the side of the bulwark, the men sat and rested. Saunders was not in the best of moods, he had been confident in his duties when riding with a company of dragoons but being left in charge of these men in a place that he did not know did not put him in the best frame of mind. It was with some relief when he saw four men riding towards him. The men were well dressed and had good horse flesh beneath them, they came to a stop in front of him,

'Are you in charge of these men?' His voice was clipped and full of its own self-importance. The Sergeant had met his like before and just hoped he would not prove difficult.

'Yes, I am.' He looked round at the men sitting on the raised earthworks of the Bulwark. 'And who may I ask are you?'

'I am the Clerk of Works and have been asked to arrange to quarter these men for the night.' The look on his face was one of controlled annoyance as he took stock of what he had to deal with.

'My captain had told me to seek you out, but you have saved me that trouble, do you have a place for the men to sleep tonight?'

'Where is your captain, should he not be here?'

'He has been called back to Cambridge by the colonel but he will be returning tomorrow once he has concluded his business. Now where do I take the men?' The clerk mumbled something under his breath,

'This man,' he pointed to the rider next to him, 'will guide you to the barn in which you will rest for the night, he will then take you to the place where you will be employed. Food will be brought to you in the next hour or so after that I will see you and your captain tomorrow, do you have any questions?'

'How far is it to our destination?'

'No more than five miles so your journey tomorrow will be a short one.'

'Will there be any more food for the men in the morning?'

'There may be some bread and cheese but no more and that's if the gods smile kindly upon you.' With that he turned his horses head and left the Bulwark. Jamie had heard the conversation, he hoped that the barn would have plenty of straw and that the food would be sufficient to quell their hunger. Their guide drew his horse alongside the sergeant,

'If you follow me, I will show you the way to the Old Mill barn where you are to sleep.'

It took no time at all to reach the large wooden structure that was known as Old Mill Barn, it looked as if it could easily accommodate all the men and more if necessary. As the prisoners entered through the large doors, they could tell that they were not the first occupants. There were signs that livestock had been kept in the stalls, there were the remains of fodder and its resultant cow pats.

'Find your selves a place to bed for the night, you will be called when food arrives.' Sergeant Saunders climbed the rickety stairs to the upper level of the barn, he found a good area where his men could sleep and keep watch. The march had been no more than twelve miles, however, the men were tired and hungry so hopefully, he thought, they would settle down peacefully after having eaten.

The food came, it was the same as they had been given before, large cooking vessels containing pottage with bread and no more. The men ate with gusto, licking every morsal from their bowls before filling them with weak beer. Saunders arranged the times for the guards and then led the way to the place where they would sleep. As the men joined him, he knelt and prayed. His prayers were for a peaceful night and that the days ahead would not prove difficult for him or the captain, and then he slept.

The morning arrived with birdsong but the clear sky of the day before was gone. The air was full of mist that hung across the land and there was a dampness that the month of October sometimes brought to the fens. Jamie and Tom followed the line of their fellow prisoners to where the bread and cheese was being handed out,

'What will today hold for us?' Jamie watched the men in front of him eagerly grab the bread that was offered.

'Another march, we always march, when will we rest from marching?' The tone of Tom's voice told Jamie that the lad was reaching a low ebb.

'We have food to eat and the clouds have not showered us so far.' He tried to sound optimistic but there was no energy in the way he spoke. The column formed up, lines of men in the grey-white uniforms slowly placed one foot in front of the other. Jamie was impressed by the cottages they passed, their pink walls and thatched roofs gave a sense of orderliness although he could see that the small plots of land that went with them held little to sustain the occupants. There were poppies growing close to the doors and other herbs that Jamie recognised, he suddenly felt a yearning for his own home, his brother and uncle and to see his friends if they were still living. He thought of Alec and how they had made their way back home after Dunbar, was Alec still alive, probably not. He was jolted back to the present when the sergeant called for them to turn to the west, the line altered course and they began to leave the town of Earith behind. It was the waterways that took their attention. There were channels on either side of the road which led to greater earth works, Jamie could not really understand why they had been dug but no doubt he would soon find out.

They had been marching about a mile when Sergeant Saunders brought the column to a halt. Jamie could see he was talking to what appeared to be a farmer who was in the process of chopping wood, beside him stood a woman, probably his wife, who had a small child standing unsteadily by her side. Jamie could not hear the conversation that passed between them however shortly after the men in the column were told to take a drink from the troughs situated by the path that led to the cottage. The men did not have time to take out their bowls, they used cupped hands to gather as much water as they could and eagerly sucked every drop from their fingers. Although they had a guide, Jamie heard the sergeant ask how far it was to the place where prisoners were employed, the farmer said that it was a further mile or so along the road that they were on. The sergeant thanked him and the column moved on. As he passed the family group, Jamie could see that the woman holding the child had features that some would call pretty and others possibly call them striking, he held the vision of the woman in his mind as they marched to their destination.

Tom asked Jamie what he thought the noise was that seemed to grow louder as they marched along the road.

'It sounds like men's voices together with the scraping of earth.' Tom then saw a scene that he could not understand. There appeared before them a stretch of land that was swarming with ant like creatures. They were at different levels shovelling earth from one stage to another, baskets of earth were being hauled to the tops of huge banks and wheelbarrows full of earth were being pushed and pulled along planks. It was madness to Tom's eyes, he could not understand what was happening, he heard voices but could not understand the language being spoken, he turned to Jamie,

'Is this another hell that we are to enter?' His voice was one of a man who was nearing the end of his tether. Jamie grabbed his shoulder,

'Stay calm, we have seen many things on our march, many horrible things and this is just one more that we have to make the best of. Let us wait and see what this place has for us, we can either let it rule us or we can rule it, be strong Tom, stand firm.' With that he released his grip on Tom and together they stood waiting to be told what to do and where to go. As they stood on the muddy soil Jamie saw the Clerk of Works ride up to the sergeant, their conversation was easy for Jamie to hear,

'Sergeant you are to take the men further down the side of the works, they will be given tools and made into small parties. They will then be told where to dig and where to place the earth. Their first task will be to repair some of the damage to the south river from which they will learn how to make good any faults, after that they may be moved to another part of the excavation.' Before the sergeant could give any orders the clerk also asked when the sergeants captain would be returning as there were matters of some urgency that required his attention.

'The captain should be here shortly and I have no doubt that he will be able to answer your questions on his arrival.' Sergeant Saunders was curious, why so many questions for Captain Emery to answer when there should be an officer in the area who was responsible for all that occurred here. He would wait for his captain who should be with them well before noon. The column was divided up into work parties, each party was to be equipped with spades, wheelbarrows and a number of planks which they picked up and carried to the earthworks where they would be carrying out repairs. Sergeant Saunders was relieved when he saw Captain Emery approach,

'Sergeant what is the position as regards the men?' Saunders explained how they had been broken into groups and issued with tools and that they would be working on the south bank. 'What of their accommodation and rations?' Saunders shrugged his shoulders,

'I have not been told of either, things moved quicker than I expected but I will visit the Clerk of Works and get as much information as I can.' The captain looked a little disappointed he had thought that his sergeant would have gained more information than he had.

'It's something that I can take up with the clerk, I have to speak to him next but before I do, I have some news that you may not find to your benefit.' The sergeant was now even more interested to find out what the captain had been told when he visited Cambridge. 'My talk with the colonel was disturbing, have you been told anything of the officer who commanded here?'

'No sir, nothing, I assumed he would be here waiting for our column to arrive but I have seen nothing of him.'

'Nor will you see anything of him because he died three days ago and nobody thought it wise to inform me.' The sergeant looked across at his captain,

'How did he die?'

'Like you I wanted to know, at first, I thought he must have had some accident or other but it transpires that he was a victim of something more deadly, he contracted the sweating sickness. His demise left a gap in the chain of command covering the excavations and I have been selected to fill that gap and take command of the area, not only the prisoners working on the drains but also the supply of everything from shovels to bread.' The sergeant's immediate thoughts were what would become of him, would he be kept in this god forsaken place or would he be allowed to return to the garrison at Cambridge.

'And what of me, will I be needed here or can I have leave to go back to normal duties?'

'As I said, the news I have may not seem to be of benefit to you.' Emery looked at his sergeant with a certain amount of sympathy, he knew that being stationed in this area was not something that soldiers dreamt of, it was more of a nightmare. 'You are to remain here with me and assist in the running of this affair. An Ensign will be joining us together with a new Quartermaster, I doubt very much if the ensign will be of much use until he becomes wise to what is required of him and I will need to speak to the quartermaster to review what has been organised by way of supplies.'

'How long before they arrive?'

'They should be with us in no more than seven days but we will have to set things in motion immediately so be prepared for some hectic but interesting hours ahead.' Saunders did not like what he had heard and the look on his face was clear for all to see but he had very little option so he gulped a lung full of air and asked,

'Were do we begin?' Emery noted the look on his sergeant's face which was understandable in the circumstances.

'Our first port of call is to seek out the clerk of works and try to get an up-to-date picture of what we have here. I will try to find out where the man is hiding and bring him here, so please see what you can discover about our new place of employment and meet me here in one hour, and before I forget there should be a lieutenant of dragoons here have you come across him?'

'No sir, I have only spoken to the Clerk of Works and that was the briefest of conversations.' Emery shook his head, he had a great deal of organising to do.

Jamie and Tom picked up the spades they had been given and followed the rest of the men like lost sheep. He could not see where the sergeant had gone and was mystified as to what he and the rest of the prisoners were required to do. The whole place seemed chaotic, he could see some men working on the bottom of a huge trench and others pushing wheelbarrows along planks and tipping their contents on the next level up. They had been left in the charge of two foot soldiers who did not seem all that interested in what was happening. The two men carried on a conversation, what about Jamie could not quite understand. It was only when the sergeant returned that they found out what they should be doing.

'You will go with this man,' he pushed forward a not too healthy-looking man in clothes that had seen better days, he will explain what you are to do, I will give you further instructions when I have them myself.'

Jamie followed with the others in his party which numbered about fifty men, some began to dig where they were told and others took full wheelbarrows of earth along planks and deposited their contents on the banks of the trenches which were then flattened out by others. The sergeant went across to see how other teams of men were doing, they were all carrying out similar tasks and as they shifted the earth the banks slowly grew higher.

'What is this that we have now become, are we to dig the earth like moles or are we to drown in these feted waters like rats.' Jamie's voice had taken on an air of defeat, they had marched many miles for what? To dig the earth so that waters could be controlled, he looked at his hands, they were used to digging but how long could his mind remain clear? He looked across at Tom and could see that he was thinking along the same lines.

They continued to dig and move the earth, it was some hours before the captain returned. Minutes later two men rode up to him, one was an officer and the other not in uniform but in dark clothes with a white collar of linen. They came to a standstill close to where Jamie was digging. Emery looked at the young officer,

'And who may you be?' The young officer cleared his throat,

'I am Lieutenant Dixon.'

'Well Lieutenant Dixon, I am Emery, Captain Emery and I have been given command of the men here and I hope you are in a position to tell me all that goes on in this place.' Emery looked at the young man who was older than he first appeared, he must be mid-twenties, Emery thought.

'I will do my best.' His voice was not that of a high borne member of society more of a merchant's son. Emery hit Dixon with a torrent of questions some of which were answered not buy the lieutenant but by the Clerk of Works. It transpired that the numbers of soldiers and dragoons at the excavations exceeded one hundred. There were ninety men, fifteen of which were dragoons, there were two sergeants and five corporals included in the number. Emery tugged at his chin,

'I know that there is a replacement Quartermaster arriving shortly together with an Ensign, but you have made no mention of the provost?' The Lieutenant rubbed his eyes wearily,

'The provost is a law unto himself, or so it seems. He is a Captain by the name of Hancock. Although he is of the same rank as you the only authority he has is to control any runaways, not only here but in the larger area. He has been known to ask for assistance in the pursuit of those who have tried to leave not only these diggings but also those in other parts of the Great Fen.'

'Are there many that run?' Emery wondered if the provost would prove difficult to handle.

'Fortunately, not many, fenland is not the easiest of terrains to cross or hide in and the population are not friends of the diggers.'

'What happens to those he captures?'

'All men working here know that the penalty for desertion of the diggings is the most severe there can be, any man caught can be struck down by Hancock and his men, or they can be brought back and hung. That is another reason why we have few runaways.' The conversation continued. They covered many things and the Clerk of Works gave Emery a good idea of what was planned. Emery caste his eye over the work that was being carried out noting that the men would have to be escorted at the end of each working day,

'You have explained where the men would be eating and sleeping but now, I need to know where they will be working, when they begin each day and for how long will they be employed?' The captain turned to his left and watched Sergeant Saunders approach.

'Lieutenant, this is my Sergeant, Saunders by name, he will be my main means of communication, whenever he gives you an instruction it will be from me and any questions you may have are to be relayed through him back to me. We will meet at the start of each day whenever possible and,' he turned to the Clerk of Works, 'If we could meet at the start of every week to go over what you have in mind, I would be grateful.'

The four men sat on their horses and discussed how the men were to be used and so the labour of the Scottish prisoners began. The following day Emery asked both Lieutenant Dixon and Sergeant Saunders of what they knew of the local people, the response he received was not the most informative.

'It is my intention to visit as many of the local villages and farms as I can. It seems as if the previous quartermaster has arranged good supply lines but there may be areas that he has not explored. Do either of you know of any of the farms close by?' The Lieutenant said that although he had been in post for some months he had not been in contact with the local population as his time was spent mainly controlling those working on the embankments.

'What about you sergeant?' Saunders rubbed his chin,

'We did stop for water on the way here and the farmer seemed to be of good nature and very obliging. He had a young family and worked both livestock and crops.'

'Excellent, he may be my first call, did you get the name of the farm?'

'I think it was Brooks farm and that naturally was the name of the farmer.'

'That will be my first call and sergeant as you have met the farmer you will accompany me.' Saunders nodded,

'When shall we make this visit?'

'We will strike while the iron is hot and make a visit tomorrow.' The sergeant thought he had enough on his plate but reluctantly agreed with his captain.

Their visit to Brook farm was short but informative, Emery decided that the farmer would be a good source for provisions and he would recommend the farmer to the new quartermaster when he arrived.

To Jamie and Tom, it was bedlam, hundreds of men, some digging others trying to manoeuvre wheelbarrows, some levelling out the sides and tops of steep embankments. Jamie thought that even though this seemed like total confusion, when they looked a little more closely there was some organisation in the madness that surrounded them. They began to settle into a routine, they would sleep the best they could, there were barns and other buildings that had been requisitioned as quarters for the men, there were also temporary huts that were full of holes and did not give much cover from the weather. Jamie and Tom were fortunate that they had managed to get into a large barn and laid claim to a small area where they slept.

The October weather remained dry however, those who knew the land also knew that storms could erupt any time during the month. Jamie noticed the change in the temperature and the darkening of the skies,

'We are going to get wet, very wet.' He looked towards the heavens. Tom followed his gaze and he too felt the chill. Their clothing would not help them stay dry, their shoes would sink into the mud and life would not be good. The rain started the following day, lightly at first then it took on power and became heavy. The excavation slowed as the men found it more difficult to move the earth to the top of the embankments. All those concerned with the diggings took on a sombre face as they tried to carry out their daily tasks in the wet October weather. Emery could see the young lieutenant struggling towards him.

'Sir, I have to report that two men have foolishly tried to leave the workings without permission. Their absence was discovered this morning, they have taken some food that they had been secreting and from what I can gather headed to the north. What they hope to achieve I do not know as the only path north leads through the worse fenland you could imagine.' A look of sheer anger spread across Emery's face, how dare they try to leave his command.

'Shall I send word for Captain Hancock?' Emery thought for a moment, he could not send a search party to look for the escapees, it was probably best left in the hands of the provost.

'Yes, send word and when he arrives, he is to report to me.'

'Very well sir.' Lieutenant Dixon called to a dragoon and sent him off to locate the provost who he thought was currently in the Black Horse Inn in Earith.

Within the hour a flushed faced officer arrived at the diggings. Emery had erected two huts where he could control things out of the rain, but low and behold no sooner had he set himself in the huts the rain stopped. The man who presented himself to Emery was not what he had expected, he was a little older than Emery but not the stern-faced fanatic that Emery had imagined. Hancock had the character of a father who was more used to balancing children on his knee than hunting down escapees. Emery could see an almost friendly countenance as Hancock presented himself.

'I am Hancock, provost of this area, and I understand you have runners.' His voice went with the rest of his appearance, it was not exactly gentle but definitely not harsh.

'You will have been told that I am Emery, in command of the excavations.' Emery could see that the provost was taking the measure of him. It was their first meeting and neither man had yet to fully decide on the nature of the person sitting opposite. Emery continued,

'Two men left during the night, I do not think they would have travelled far, not in this weather.' Hancock knew the lay of the land, he was aware of the conditions and that the locals seemed to have no time for Scottish prisoners on the run.

'I shall need several of your dragoons to assist me, is that possible?' He looked at Emery questioningly.

'That will be of no difficulty.' He called out to Saunders who was standing within earshot.

'Sir?' Sergeant Saunders had an idea of what his next task would be and, in his mind, had already selected six dragoons for the job.

'Sergeant this is Captain Hancock.' They nodded in acknowledgement of each other. He is in need of six dragoons can you please arrange for them to report to the captain as soon as possible.' It was not a request but an order. The sergeant touched the tip of his hat and with a 'yes sir' departed to get the selected men together and get them ready to move.

'How long do you think you will need to recover the prisoners?' Emery was fully aware that when caught the escapees would not be treated with kindness.

'It may take longer than usual if this weather does not clear but I would say that I should have them within three days at the most, normally I would be able to deal with the problem within twenty-four hours. The runners are on foot and do not know the area as well as me. I have brought with me three of my own men who will take the lead in tracking these men.' Emery did not want to ask what would happen to the men but thought he had to.

'When they are caught what will happen to them?' Hancock looked a little surprised at this question.

'If they are not killed in pursuit then they will be brought back and hung.' Sergeant Saunders arrived back in the hut to tell the captain that the men were ready. Hancock raised himself and made to leave.

'It has been a pleasure meeting you and I hope we have a lasting relationship but not only in respect of escaping prisoners.' Emery stood and held out his hand, the firm grip of Hancock again surprised him, the man in front of him was indeed a man of many surprises.

'God speed and I hope your work is quickly concluded.'

Emery looked out from the hut and watched as Hancock and the dragoons rode off towards the north. He wondered if the men would escape or finish their lives at the end of a rope. His thoughts then turned back to the farm he had visited earlier. He was convinced that an agreement could be reached with David Brook and he looked forward to a mutually beneficial understanding between the army and the farmer. He would make it his business that all those involved gave the Brooks every assistance.

*

David Brook had finished his early morning tasks, making sure his animals were in good order and that the cows had been brought in for milking. He dashed back to the farm house trying to avoid as much of the rain as possible. As he entered the kitchen his wife looked up from feeding their son and had to supress a laugh, the sight of David standing with his hat drooping over his face with raindrops running down his chin made him seem more attractive to her than ever. He removed the sodden hat and flicked it at her, water flew across the room and speckled her face, he smiled,

'I have discovered some discrepancies in the accounts, nothing major but they need resolving as quickly as possible.' Sarah knew that he would not be able to rest until he was satisfied that all was in order.

'Are you going to see the quartermaster in this weather?'

'It's easing off now and by the time I get myself ready I hope we will see a break in this awful wetness. I need to get the figures sorted in my mind so that I can be as quick as possible.'

'Will you see only the quartermaster or will you try to contact the captain as well?'

He thought for a moment, there were one or two things he could talk to the captain about especially the activity of some of the soldiers and how they supplemented their rations with items from his farm.

'Yes, if he is available, I will sit down with him and talk over a few things but that should not take much time.'

David gathered his ledgers and put them into his large leather satchel. His wife placed their son on the floor and went towards him, she reached up and took the wet hat from his head,

'You cannot wear that, I am sure you have another.' David looked down at her, she was all he wanted in life, a beautiful woman and a healthy son. He kissed her tenderly then turning took hold of a dry hat, picked up his satchel and made his way to the door.

'How long will you be.' She asked.

'I hope to be back before midday but all depends on the weather and how long the quartermaster will need to agree with me.' She smiled again, she knew her husband would badger the poor quartermaster until he agreed with his figures. David went to the stables, saddled his horse and headed off to the excavations.

*

The story that Thomas Dower's mother, Sarah, had told him had now come full circle. He had been at this stage of the story many times and no doubt he would visit it again in the years to come. Thomas had told the tale to his own children and his daughter, Rebecca, had safely kept all the family records and would let all see what had passed between the cousins whether in England or abroad. The children must be told of their family history, where they came from and what dangers those who had gone before had suffered to bring them to the place where they now dwelt.

CHAPTER 20

The year of 1714 held many changes, Queen Anne had passed away and George of Hanover had ascended to the throne. Life continued on Brooks farm, cows were milked and the land held crops of wheat, barley and a variety of vegetables. Thomas Dower was woken from his dream of things long ago, it was the voice of his grandson, Peter. As he tried to straighten his tired body he smiled at the young boy with a sense of pride. What would those who he had been dreaming of think of this boy and the life he had. His mother, Sarah, her husband Jamie who had seen such things as many would never even contemplate had laid a path for those that followed in their wake.

*

The Dower family had grown, Jamie and Sarah had four children and with William it made a houseful. Their eldest son Thomas had three children of his own, Rebecca, Andrew and Mark. Rebecca in turn had given him four healthy grandchildren Peter, Sarah, Robert and John. Rebecca and her husband had taken over the running of Brooks Farm after Thomas had become ill and unable to cope with the stress of managing a large farm. Thomas still enjoyed life with Rebecca and her family following the untimely death of Mary his wife, his grandchildren were his pride and joy. Thomas looked again at the bright face of his grandson.

'What is it Peter?' The boy walked up to the side of his grandfather's chair and took his hand.

'I have spoken to mother of the story you told us, she knows everything about the family.' Thomas squeezed his grandson's hand as he did, he knew that his daughter, Rebecca, would tell the story in such a way that anyone listening would be captivated.

'Has your mother told you of her favourite story, the one she treasures most?' A puzzled look spread across the boy's face.

'No, I don't think she has. Do you know which story it is grandfather?'

'Yes, I do it is of your Great Uncle William, but maybe it would be better if she were to tell you herself.'

'But she is always too busy to tell me of anything, could you not tell the tale?'

Thomas was weary, his night had been broken by thoughts of the past and sleep seemed to evade him.

'I will tell you some of the story the rest you must hear from your mother who I am sure will make time to relate it to you.'

'Please grandfather, please tell me and should I get the others?' Another smile spread across the lined face of Thomas Dower.

'No, this time I think it will be better if it were just the two of us.'

Peter drew up a foot stool and perched himself in front of the man who was about to tell him a story. Thomas closed his eyes for a moment and gathered his thoughts, he began with the day when the Dower family were returning from church some sixteen years after Jamie Dower had married Sarah.

Both Sarah and Jamie were surprised to see two strange horses tethered to the rail outside their farmhouse. The horses were fine and looked expensive, the saddles were well cut with bags to match. They walked a little faster towards their front door, as they were about to open it a head appeared, it was the young girl who they had employed as a maid,

'You have visitors ma'am.' She did a little curtsey although it was unnecessary in Sarah's eyes the young girl thought it proper.

'Who are they Mary and where are they.' The girl blushed a little.

'I asked them to wait for you in the big room.' It was what she called the main room of the house where most family gatherings took place.

'Did they give you their names?'

'No ma'am, they said that they were friends of the master and he would know them when he set eyes on them.' At this Jamie shook his head, he had not asked anyone to visit and he had no idea of any 'friends' who would call after church. Jamie led the way into the main room. He saw the backs of two men who had taken seats in front of the fire. They stood as Jamie and Sarah entered the room. Jamie looked at both men but did not recognise either. The visitors looked back at Jamie both smiling, they approached him with outstretched arms but stopped as they saw the blank look on Jamie's face. They dropped their arms the taller of the two stepped forward,

'Mister Dower, it appears that your memory is lacking, do you not recognised those who have spent days, if not months, in your company?' The second of the two then spoke,

'And those who shared both toil and hunger alongside you?'

Both men had accents that Jamie could not immediately place, there was a trace of Scotland in their voices but it was hidden amongst a lilt that he had not heard before. Jamie looked carefully at both men, it started to dawn on him that these men could be from his past but then how could they, those that he had known many years ago had been killed or died after being taken away. He looked again at the taller man, there was something in his features that reminded Jamie of someone he had last seen at Worcester when they both fought for the king. He shook his head,

'Alec is that you, but you were killed at Worcester, I was sure that you had been struck down.' Then turning to the second man he strained his eyes and tried to picture the man in a different place in a different time, slowly a face that was a lot younger and very much thinner entered his mind,

'Robert, it cannot be you and you cannot be together. Is this some trick you men are playing on me?'

It took some time for Jamie to come to terms with the fact that his two friends were still alive. They took hold of each other's hands firmly then embraced in a way that only men can do.

'Come, sit and tell me of what has happened to you since we last met.' Sarah ushered the youngest children away leaving William, their eldest son, with his father and their guests. Jamie took a glass and placed it in front of each man then proceeded to fill it with a good amount of strong wine. It was Alec who spoke first. His tale of how, when he had been separated from Jamie at Worcester, was one that intrigued not only Jamie but William was almost mesmerised by the story Alec told.

After the fighting and when they had been herded together, Alec had looked around for Jamie and could not see him, then he had been pushed and cajoled into a group of men that had been assigned to a company that dealt with the Americas. Robert listened on while Alec continued. He had been taken to Bristol and there had been placed aboard a vessel which he discovered was bound for the New World. It took six weeks to cross the ocean, six weeks of hell, he had thought that his time spent marching and fighting was bad but the fear and the unknown surpassed any dread he had previously held. It was when he had arrived in Virginia that his troubles really started. He had been sold as an indentured servant, no more than a slave, to a plantation owner. His life was not his own, he had no choice but to work on the tobacco crops. The work was hard and life did not seem to matter to the owners of the plantation. It was here that he met Robert and they discovered they had plenty in common, particularly the knowledge of a certain Jamie Dower. They became friends and tried to help each other any way they could.

Robert then joined the conversation, he told of how after meeting Alec that life appeared a little better. The work was hard and the days long, however, after about two years something happened that changed their lives. As they walked back from the fields, they smelt smoke and as they got closer to the house, they saw flames licking at the wooden veranda. It was almost a matter of instinct that they ran to try to quench the flames. Robert had seen Alec rush into the burning building and emerge carrying a child, he called out that there were others and placing the child he was carrying on the grass he turned and ran back into the flames. Robert could see that there was more than enough for Alec to cope with and he dashed into the burning building. Through the smoke he could see two more children, one laying on the floor the other gasping and clutching its throat. He picked up the child from the floor and grabbed the others hand and made his way out of the building. As Robert was rescuing the children, Alec had fought his way through the flames and up a flight of stairs, he kicked in the first door he came to but the room was empty, he heard a faint scream and tackled the second door and as he entered the room, he could just see the figure of a woman, as he took hold of her, she gasped,

'My daughter, Elizabeth, find my daughter.' She pointed in the direction of the next room, Alec dragged her out as far as he could then smashed through the door of the adjacent room. His eyes stung and his throat was screaming out for air, there was the body of a young woman on the bed, he grabbed her arm and pulled, she seemed as light as a feather and he managed to get her out of the room, then together with the other woman he somehow descended the stairs and broke out into the air and sunlight.

Robert then drew breath and took a sip from his glass. Jamie had been listening to every word with great interest as was William who imagined the scene, the flames the heroics and the horror. William asked 'What happened then?' Robert continued to tell of how the rescue of the women and children resulted in them being raised from indentured slaves to positions of some importance. The plantation owner could not do enough for them, they were treated well and became almost a part of the family, in fact it was two years later that Alec married Elizabeth, the girl he had rescued. Alec told of how he and Robert had become a vital part of the management of the plantation. They were responsible not only for the labour used but also for the bargaining of prices for the crops, although the final say was always with the plantation owner.

*

Time had passed quickly as their stories were told, Jamie looked at the darkening sky outside.

'Have you a place to sleep, I am sure we could arrange for beds to be set up in such a way that you could spend a reasonable night with us.' Alec smiled and looked from Jamie to William, he knew that it would mean disruption to Jamie's family if they took him up on the offer.

'It is no problem, we have rooms and stabling at the White Hart in Earith but we would like to return to hear of your life since we last shared a bowl of pottage.'

'Yes, you must return tomorrow, what are your plans, how long are you here for and are you returning to the Americas?' Alec took a last sip of the wine from his glass,

'We are here for four more days, we have concluded our business in Bristol and London but must be back in Bristol soon, as our ship sails for Virginia in ten days' time.'

They stood and again embraced each other then they thanked Sarah for sparing her husband to talk to them.

'You have much to discuss and I am sure that you have much more to tell over the coming days. I will prepare a meal for us tomorrow and you shall eat with our family.' Alec and Robert thanked her and made their way to their horses. As they rode off Jamie watched the expression on William's face, the boy had been transfixed by the stories that had been told and heaven forbid what he would make of what Alec and Robert would tell in the days ahead.

'Can life be any more exciting than what they speak off.' William's voice was full of wonder as he thought of America and new beginnings.

Over the following days Alec and Robert visited Jamie and Sarah each afternoon. They told of how the New World had strange people and very strange animals. How life was just beginning and fortunes made. Each time they spoke William became more captured by the thought of adventure and fortune. On the third evening after Alec and Robert had departed William sat opposite his father and mother, although he did not carry the Dower name, he was still considered to be Jamie's son although he still went by his real father's name of Brook. He looked from his mother to his father,

'Am I to remain on the farm for the rest of my life?' Jamie had seen the way William had looked when his two friends were telling their tales, he knew that William was yearning for adventure and that what he had heard from the two men had set his head spinning and his mind racing. Jamie looked at his wife, she then looked at her son, he was close to his seventeenth birthday and so far, had not been far from the farm. She did not want to see him leave but knew that one day he would go, she had not thought of him travelling to the other side of the ocean, possibly to another county or even London, not America.

'Your life is your own, if you want to make your fortune elsewhere then so be it. My only concern is that you lead a happy and honest life.' In her heart she did not want him to go, he was her only link with David her first husband, the man she had loved first and the man who had always had a place in her heart. She turned and looked at William.

'It is a long and perilous journey if you wish to follow Alec and Robert, think carefully, how would you survive without your family, could you cope with the fears and troubles of not having the security of your family.' Jamie saw that William could only see what he wanted, the thrill of travelling the seas, other lands other people.

'If it is my decision, I would welcome your advice but I feel I need to let go of the strings that tie me to this place and seek a life of my own.' Jamie watched his wife's face change and take on a look of deep concern, she would be the one who would miss the boy the most.

'You are and always will be in our hearts, you are a good son and have been a great help to me in running the farm, however if you want to fly the nest then I will not stand in your way.' Sarah felt a tightness in her throat,

'If it is your wish to leave then you must, if you do not you will always wonder what would have happened with your life if you had.'

That night mother, father and son did not sleep well. Thoughts of their lives and what would become of them went round and round in their heads and as day broke, they still had a feeling of uncertainty about William's future.

After Jamie had given instructions to the farm workers and checked the milk yield for the day he sat with his wife, they knew what they had to discuss but it seemed to be difficult for the first word to be spoken. It was Sarah who started,

'William is so young, how would he survive so far away from home in a land that holds so many dangers.' Jamie looked at his wife, she cared for her first born more than anything else. His features reminded of her of her first husband, David, and she did not want to lose that. Jamie said,

'You must remember I was only a year older than William is now when I went to fight the English at Dunbar. The likelihood of me being killed was high and it was only my own stupidity that saved me. Let's wait and see what Alec and Robert have to say on the matter.' They left it at that and continued with their daily workload.

It was after two o'clock when Alec and Robert arrived back at the farm. They were warmly welcomed by Jamie and Sarah. After the usual greetings they sat around the main table,

'We have some important, life changing questions for you.' It was Sarah who when she spoke had a quiver in her voice. 'William has listened to your tales and stories of the New

World. He has become fascinated by what you have said and he has asked if it would be possible for him to return with you to America.' There, she thought, the question has been asked, and now what sort of answer would they give. Alec and Robert where taken aback, they had seen that William was very interested in what they had to say but they did not expect this. It was Robert who answered first,

 'Any move of that sort takes a great deal of courage, the journey alone has hazards that are not seen anywhere else on this earth.' Alec then felt the intensity of Sarah's eyes almost pleading with them to say it was not possible, he told the truth,

 'As Robert has said the dangers are many, the life is hard but the rewards are there and they can be reached if a man devotes himself to his own cause.' Jamie cleared his throat,

 'We have been through many horrors on our life's journey, we have seen starvation, death and sickness that would dissuade anybody from taking the path that we trod. If William was set on following you, could you take responsibility for his health and wellbeing?' The two men looked at each other their eyebrows raised a little and then Alec said something that Sarah did not really relish,

 'We have many responsibilities on the plantation, we have many workers that need a firm hand and good organisation. Our lives are full without much time for pleasure but if William was to decide that was what he wanted then I know we would be able to give you our word that we would take care of his needs and see him employed well.' Sarah took Jamie's hand for comfort, her grip was tight and Jamie could feel her tension.

'It will be his decision and whatever that may be we will give him our blessing.' Jamie saw the pain in his wife's eyes, she knew that William would not be with them forever but this was unexpected, why did these men have to come and disrupt their lives so, they said that they should let William sleep on it and if he was still of a mind then a decision would be made tomorrow. She turned towards Alec,

'If William still wishes to go, could you secure him passage on your ship?' Robert replied that it would be easy to accommodate William not as an emigrant but as a merchant and that he would travel in better conditions than most. Again, this was not the answer Sarah wanted, she racked her brain for more questions that might stop William from leaving but she could not think clearly and the points she raised were easily answered by Alec and Robert. Jamie had listened to the conversation, he had not said a lot because he had seen William grow and become a man. He was at a stage where he needed to go his own way. Jamie had thought that would be with a relative or neighbour where he would continue to gain experience in farming and then be in a position to take over from him when the time came. They had two other sons, a third being lost at the age of two years and a daughter, any one of who could eventually step into Jamie's shoes so the farm was not at risk of being lost. His thoughts centred on his wife, she was the one person who, if she felt strongly enough, could possibly stop William from leaving.

'We shall leave the decision until the morning and then prepare for whatever is decided.' Jamie sighed, it had been a draining conversation and they all could do with something to relax them. He took out a flagon of wine which was not of the best quality but would do. Sarah brought her expensive glasses to the table and the wine was poured, as they took the first sip William appeared, Jamie held out a glass for him which he took carefully, he asked his mother,

'Have you talked of my wishes?' His eager face searched those sat at the table. Sarah softly told him that he was to consider the proposition overnight and if he was still of the same mind then they would not stand in his way,

'But think carefully my son, there is a great deal at stake and as Alec has said it has been fifteen years since they were last in England and it may be another fifteen until they return if at all. So, think long and hard, do you want to sacrifice what you have for the unknown?' William held his mother's gaze and felt the love that she had for him. For the first time since he had started to think about leaving did his heart almost burst, he reached out and laid his hand on his mother's shoulder.

'I promise I will think of all that has been said.' With that they sat around the table in an uncomfortable silence all had their own challenges to consider. Alec and Robert left to get back to the White Hart for their evening meal. As they ate, they talked of what had been said that day in Brooks farm. Although the responsibility for looking after William would be initially fraught with dangers once they had returned to the plantation things could be set in motion for William to become part of the management of the land and those who worked on it. It would be a decision needed the following day as they had to leave for Bristol to enable them to sort out some last-minute items, then board the ship in time to sail.

Sarah woke Jamie, she had not slept well but by the grunting that Jamie made she thought that he had spent a peaceful night.

'We need to get on with our work and then speak to William. Alec and Robert will be expecting our decision as will William. The morning had just begun when William entered the kitchen, he had already been working for several hours which had given him time to rehearse how he would give his final decision to his mother. Sarah looked up, she really did not want to hear what William was about to tell her. He walked towards her and took her hands in his, Jamie had also entered the room,

'Mother I have come to a decision and that is that I not only want to start a new life but I also need to prove to myself that I am able to face the new and strange life that awaits me in the New World. I would like your blessing before I go and father if you can give me any advice, I would be more than grateful.' It was the decision that Sarah had expected, not what she wanted but expected. She could feel her eyes start to fill and no matter how hard she tried could not hold the tears back. William kissed her cheek and placed his arms around her shoulders. Sarah drew away from William's embrace and wiping her eyes turned to her husband. Jamie watched how difficult it was for Sarah to come to terms with the thought of losing her son, he took her hand as she released it from William, the decision had been made and now things had to be arranged with haste.

Alec and Robert were not totally surprised at Williams decision, they had talked about the arrangements needed to ensure William had an easy journey. He would need a horse, his luggage would go with theirs on the pack wagon, a cabin would need to be organised on the ship which would probably mean William sharing with others, that should not come as a great surprise to him and many more things would need to be taken care of. After their initial discussion Sarah asked Alec when they would need to depart for Bristol, his reply knocked the wind from her lungs, Alec wanted to leave the following morning.

'But so soon, are we only to have a son for just one more night?' Alec had sympathy written across his face.

'I am sorry but if we are to conclude our business and be in time to sail, we will need to leave early tomorrow.' Sarah looked at Jamie, he could see that she had been close to tears.

'They have things to do in Bristol and time and tide wait for no man.' He held his wife close he could feel her heart racing in her chest. He gently moved so that she could be close to William. 'Alec, will you tell William what he will need for the journey and William you will have to gather all you can and place them into the trunk in our room. Looking at Robert, Jamie asked how much room would William have on the ship.

'Space is limited, so I would suggest that he take only what he would need for the voyage, we can arrange to get him clothes and other items when we arrive in Virginia.' It was the first time Robert had mentioned the name of the place where they were headed, it brought a sense of reality to what was happening.

The rest of the day proved to be one of searching and packing. Alec and Robert remained at the farm until late guiding William on what he would need and items that he should leave. As they were about to return to the White Hart Sarah caught Alec by the sleeve,

'How long does it take for letters to get from America to England?' Alec had to think carefully he knew that he could not give Sarah any false hope.

'Ships travel on a regular basis between American and English ports, if all was to go well correspondence could take no more than six or seven weeks to arrive here. We have regular orders and bills sent from the plantation to the merchants in England so it is possible to use the same route for letters to you from William.' This pleased Sarah to a degree then she demanded that Alec or Robert would ensure that William would write and despatch a letter no less than every fortnight. Alec took hold of William,

'Did you hear that? You are to write to your mother each fortnight or we will be at you with a big stick.' Although Alec spoke of the matter lightly, he knew that Sarah was very serious and if she did not receive regular correspondence then there would be hell to pay. The activity that took place was as if they were in a dream or from Sarah's point of view a nightmare, things were placed in the trunk and then removed as they were deemed unnecessary. At the end of the day the night gave them some peace, although William's excitement gave him little chance for sleep, Sarah with Jamie spent a restless emotional night.

The sun rose on Williams final day at his parent's farm. All was done that could be done, Alec and Robert appeared early they had brought the small cart that they used for luggage and various things that they had acquired for those on the plantation. Jamie had saddled William's horse and stood with Sarah to watch them leave. William embraced his mother then his father, how long before they would be able to touch each other again was for the gods to decide. William mounted his horse and together with Alec and Robert slowly made their way from the farm. Sarah could not take her eyes from her son's back and when he turned in his saddle and waved farewell, she could not hold back the tears anymore, she lifted her arm to wave and as she did her heart sank. She felt Jamie's arm pull her to him and she thanked the lord that she still had him, her other two sons and their daughter.

*

Thomas Dower had not slept, his mind was still full of the story of his family. He had continued to think and dream of everything he had been told by his mother. He had taken a walk in their garden to try to clear his head. As he walked through the sweet-smelling blooms he heard the voice of his grandson,

'Grandfather wait for me.' Peter ran to his side. 'Grandfather I spoke to mother about the story you told.'

'And what pray tell did she say?'

'She said that there was much more and that we should ask you to tell us of the others in our family.'

'Well, your mother is the best person to tell you of how wide the family has grown over the years. She has a box of secrets and those secrets are the letters that came from your Great Uncle William. He is your mother's favourite relation, as I have told you before, although she has never met him or his family. William travelled to America and gained wealth and authority in Virginia. His letters to his mother have been kept within the family and correspondence has been maintained between family members after your Great Grandmother passed away.' Peter asked,

    'So, who can tell me more of our family not in England but in America.' His grandfather ruffled Peter's hair and smiled,

    'That is a story perhaps your mother can tell, but that will be for another time.

The End

Milton Keynes UK
Ingram Content Group UK Ltd.
UKHW020941090923
428316UK00010B/179